THE LOCKET
AND THE LIE

ROBIN T. POPP

LARKSPUR LANE PUBLISHING, L.L.C.

Also by Robin T. Popp

TEXAS AFTER DARK SERIES
Death at the Double R
The Ghost Whisperer's Gambit
The Locket and the Lie

OUTER FRINGE SERIES
Phoenix Rising
Echoes of the Fallen

NIGHT SLAYER SERIES
Out of the Night
Seduced by the Night
Tempted in the Night
Lord of the Night

THE IMMORTALS SERIES
Immortals: The Darkening
Immortals: The Haunting
Immortals: The Reckoning
Beyond the Mist

SUN SERIES
Too Close to the Sun

Contents

Chapter One

It was after dark, and John Morris stared through the front windshield of his car at the road stretching out before him, barren and seemingly never-ending. Symbolic of his life, he thought dismally. Not that he'd been headed anywhere particularly great before he ended up in prison, but a fulfilling future looked even less likely now.

John hadn't started the fight that fateful day nearly three years ago, but neither had he walked away, and that had been the problem. If only he had, then Steve Lopez would still be alive.

Involuntary manslaughter had been the charge.

A ten thousand dollar fine and two years in a Texas prison had been his sentence, thanks to a lenient judge.

Not a day went by that John didn't feel guilty for taking the life of another person. Unfortunately, regret and guilt don't bring back the dead, and so he had to move on with his life as best he could.

Unfortunately, that was easier said than done. It didn't take long to learn that most people didn't care what circumstances led him to prison. That he was an ex-convict was enough for them to want nothing to do with him. It was a disappointing but not unexpected reaction from people meeting him for the first time. He could almost forgive them for their caution. What had hurt, though, had been the same reaction from his family and friends. He'd hoped they would be more understanding.

He was getting used to disappointment.

At least he wasn't without money. Prior to his incarceration, his grandparents had left money for him in a trust when they passed. So, fifty thousand dollars had been waiting for him when he got out.

He'd spent twenty of that buying a used car, new clothes and a few essentials, like a cell phone, duffel bag and clothes. Then he'd hit the road in search of a place to call home.

Sadly, he had yet to find such a place, and the delay meant he was slowly burning through his money.

The job interview in Brownsville, Texas, had made for a long, depressing day. There was no way in hell that company was going to offer him a job. He'd known it the moment he'd sat down at the interview table at 9:00 that morning. Instead of walking out there and then, he'd stuck around. For the experience.

More fool me, he thought, purposely misquoting Shakespeare.

Now he was headed to El Paso. A friend from college, one of the few who'd stuck by him, ran a construction company in El Paso. He was looking for workers who knew how to use a hammer. All he had to do was show up, and the job was his. It wasn't the type of job John had in mind when he'd attended college. His degree was in finance, but no one wanted an ex-con handling their finances, so he was having to fall back on the only other skill he had—construction.

He flexed his shoulders, which had grown stiff after hours of driving, and debated driving through the night, but the long day of interviewing had been more exhausting than he'd expected.

Checking his phone, Google Maps showed few cities in this area, and he was thinking he might have to spend the night in his car when he spotted a sign for the next small town.

Las Palomas.

Fifteen miles ahead.

He'd never heard of it but hoped it was big enough to have a decent hotel. If not, well, tonight wouldn't be the first night he'd spent sleeping in his car.

He drove another five or six miles. The night was thick with shadows, the beam of his headlights carving only a narrow path through the dark. He almost didn't see her. Then, just past the bend, there she was—a woman standing on the side of the road, one arm raised as if she'd been waiting just for him.

He slowed, rolling down the window.

"You all right, ma'am? Need a ride somewhere?"

She leaned down, her face pale in the glow of the dash lights. "If it's not too much trouble."

"Hop in," he said, reaching over to unlock the door.

She slid into the seat, smoothing her jeans, and gave him a small, grateful smile. "Thank you. It's been such a long wait, but I knew you'd come."

"Not many cars on this road at night," he said. "Glad to be of service."

"I'm Marie."

He gave her a quick smile. "I'm John."

She tilted her head, her dark eyes catching the light in a way that made John glance twice. "It's nice to meet you, John. Do you believe we meet people for a reason?"

He gave a little laugh, shaking his head. "Not sure about that. Life's more about chance, I figure. Right place, right time. That kind of thing."

"Oh, no," she said softly, her smile faint and knowing. "Some people are sent to us. To fix what's broken. To bring light where it's been dark too long. You were brought here for a purpose."

John felt a prickle at the back of his neck. Odd thing to say to a stranger, but the way she said it wasn't flirtatious or desperate—it was calm, almost reverent.

"Well," he said after a pause, keeping his tone light, "guess I should be glad I showed up when I did."

Her smile lingered, unreadable. "Yes. You should."

John tightened his grip on the steering wheel and focused back on the road. She was probably just a woman with a knack for saying things sideways. Still, he couldn't quite shake the echo of her words.

She fell silent, and John didn't try again to engage her in conversation. One thing you learned in prison was to respect a person's right to their own thoughts.

They drove in relative silence with the only sound coming from Marie's necklace as she ran the heart-shaped locket back and forth along the chain.

Having reached the outskirts of town, John slowed the car as they approached the first stop sign.

"Take a left at the next stop sign," she instructed, "and then another left at the stop sign after that."

Following her instructions, John realized they were entering a more residential area. There were a couple of newer style, small homes that soon gave way to older homes.

"That one." She pointed to a large, older Victorian home at the end of the street on the right side. The lights were off inside the home, and it looked deserted.

He pulled his car over to the curb and put it in park.

"Will you be okay?" He peered through the window at the darkened home.

"Yes. I'll be fine," she assured him, opening the door. "Thank you for the ride. It was kind of you."

"You're welcome," he told her. "I'm glad I could help." He hesitated, then added, "Say, you wouldn't happen to know if there's a place in town I can stay the night, would you?"

Her smile warmed, as though she'd been waiting for him to ask. "Ruby Mae's Bed-and-Breakfast. Go back out to the main road and continue into two until you reach Third Street. Turn right. It'll be the only yellow house on the block. You can't miss it."

John nodded, relieved. "Thanks. That'll save me some time hunting around."

She stepped out of the car, her long hair catching in the breeze. "Good night, John," she said softly.

Before he realized it, she was walking up the front walkway. At the door, she paused long enough to glance back and lift her hand in a faint wave. John blinked, and in that instant, she was gone. No creak of hinges, no sound of a door closing—just gone.

He rubbed at his eyes, thinking he must be more tired than he realized.

Still, he remained at the curb a few moments longer before pulling out his phone. A quick search brought up the number for Ruby Mae's B&B. When Ruby Mae answered and told him she had a single vacancy left, he felt a flicker of gratitude—and a faint chill.

Casting a last glance at the big Victorian house, John pulled away from the curb and headed back the way he'd come. By the time he reached the main street, he'd forgotten all about the woman. His full attention was focused on locating the B&B. Ruby Mae had promised him a decent bed and a home-cooked breakfast in the morning. Maybe his luck was changing for the better.

—◆○◆—

The next morning, John left the B&B well-rested and full of the first home-cooked breakfast he'd had in a long while. Ruby Mae had been the quintessential grandmother type, doting over him, making sure he was comfortable and well-fed. He wondered how differently she'd treat him if she knew he was an ex-con? He tried to push the worry aside.

Over breakfast, he'd asked her about potential job opportunities in town, and she'd urged him to check out the bulletin board sitting at one end of the town's park. That was where the locals posted notices about everything from upcoming social events, rideshares from Las Palomas to one of the bigger Texas cities, and job opportunities.

He would check it on his way through town, and if he found something promising, he'd call Ruby Mae and ask her to hold his room one more night.

With that goal in mind, he left the B&B, almost absently noting as he climbed into his car that the house's color was green, not yellow. It was when he turned in his seat, to back his car out of its parking space, that he noticed a flash of silver on the front passenger-side floorboard. Putting the car in park, he leaned over to take a closer look.

Lying there was the silver heart-shaped locket and chain Marie had been wearing the night before. He had no clue how it had ended up in his car when the last time he'd seen it, Marie had still been wearing it.

Retrieving it from the floor, he held it up to examine the chain, quickly seeing the problem. The clasp had broken. Mystery solved.

Remembering the way the woman had played with the necklace, he knew it must have sentimental value. Curious, he pried the heart-shaped locket open. Inside were two pictures. The one on the right was Marie, and the one on the left was of a young girl, probably five or six years old, if he had to guess.

Yes, Marie would want her locket back. He considered going inside to ask Ruby Mae if she could mail it to the woman but then realized he knew neither Marie's last name nor her address. Last night, he hadn't paid attention to the name of the street or the house number, but despite not knowing the address, he knew he could find it again.

Dropping the chain and locket into one of the empty front seat cup holders, he left the B&B parking lot and retraced his route to Marie's house.

It amazed him how different everything looked in the light of day, and more than once, he questioned whether he was on the right street.

When he finally reached the house, he pulled to the curb and studied it. Last night, under the cover of darkness, the house had been impressive. In the light of day, however, he saw that time had taken its toll. The pale blue paint was chipped in places and had peeled away altogether in others. Several of the siding boards looked like they needed to be replaced, as did many of the shutters.

The frame appeared level and straight. With time and money, he thought this house could be restored to its former glory, and there was a part of him that longed to work on such a project.

Every summer throughout junior and senior high school, he'd worked alongside his dad, restoring old homes. Those were some of the happiest days of his life.

He sighed. Now, his father wouldn't even talk to him.

Shrugging off the dismal thoughts, John took the locket from the cup holder and got out of the car. As he headed up the front walkway, he heard the whine of a rotary saw coming from inside. It gave him a warm feeling to think someone was working on saving this old home.

Climbing the porch steps, John waited for a break in the hammering and sawing inside, then knocked hard.

Footsteps approached, and the door opened.

Marie answered the door, but instead of greeting him, she frowned at him, confused.

"Um—hello. Do I know you?"

"Yeah, I'm John," he said. "We met last night. I gave you a ride home."

Her eyes narrowed. "No. That wasn't me. You've got the wrong person." She started to close the door.

He blocked it with his hand. "Wait, Marie—"

"What did you call me?" Her voice sharpened.

"Marie," John repeated, exasperated. "That's the name you gave me."

"M-my name is Teresa."

He sighed. "Fine. Teresa, then. You want to pretend I didn't pick you up, that's your business. I just thought you'd want this back." He opened his palm, showing her the locket.

She froze. Her work gloves slipped from her hands, falling to the floor. Color drained from her face as she stared at the necklace, trembling. "Where did you get that?"

"It was in my car," he replied. "The clasp's broken. Must've fallen off last night before I dropped you off."

She reached for the locket as if it might bite her and then opened it with shaking hands.

"My God," she whispered. "This is my mother's. It disappeared the night she did."

John blinked. "Your mother?"

She looked up, her face pale and stricken. "She vanished fifteen years ago. No one's seen her since. And this"—she held the locket tightly, voice breaking—"was the only thing she never took off. How do you have it?"

"I told you"—he began, but she cut him off, panic and suspicion rising.

"Did you … did you hurt her? Did you steal this from her?"

"What? No! I didn't hurt anyone."

Her eyes darted toward the kitchen. She backed up, fumbling a hand into a toolbox on the table by the front door until her fingers closed around a hammer. She raised it, trying to keep her voice steady. "Then explain to me how my mother's necklace ended up in your car."

John lifted both hands, instinctively taking a step back. "Easy. I don't know how else to say it. I picked up a woman last night who looked exactly like you. She said her name was Marie. I dropped her off here. This morning, I found that locket on the floorboard of my car."

"That's impossible," Teresa shot back, clutching the hammer. "My mother's been gone for years."

John's gaze flicked past her, taking in the room beyond. Boxes were stacked against the walls, a rotary saw was set up in the front parlor, crown molding leaned against the wall, and a lone air mattress lay in the corner. The place looked more like a construction site than a home.

"You … live here?" he asked, unable to hide his surprise.

Her chin lifted a fraction. "It was my grandmother's house. When she passed, she left it to me. I'm turning it back into the bed-and-breakfast it used to be." She swallowed, still gripping the hammer tight. "Not that that's any of your business."

"Whatever," he muttered, and turned to leave.

Suddenly, she was in front of him, hammer still gripped in one hand and a cell phone in the other.

"You're not leaving," she said, her voice low but fierce. "Not until you tell me—and the police—exactly what happened last night."

John froze, disbelief flickering across his face as he watched her thumb frantically tap the screen.

Chapter Two

Teresa Thacker's eyes darted between the broad-shouldered stranger before her and the glowing keypad of her phone. Her thumb hovered over the call button, her hand trembling so badly the device threatened to slip through her grasp. Seeing her mother's locket in a stranger's palm after fifteen years drove adrenaline spiking through her veins. Finally, she pressed 9-1-1 and held the phone to her ear, heart pounding in her throat.

"Bev, it's Teresa," she said urgently into the receiver. "I need someone at my grandmother's house—now."

The dispatcher's calm voice came softly but steadily over the line. "Okay, Teresa. I'm sending a unit. Is anyone injured? Are you in danger?"

"No—well, I don't know." She exhaled in a choked laugh that ended with a sob. "There's a man here with my mother's locket."

"Chad's on his way. Can you stay on the line until he arrives?"

"Yeah."

An awkward silence fell until she heard the distant wail of sirens growing louder as they wound through the neighborhood streets.

The man before her, John, shifted his weight. "I'm not here to hurt you," he said again, voice low and careful, palms raised before him.

"Save it," she snapped, voice brittle as glass. "You can explain to the police how you came by my mother's locket."

He said nothing, keeping his hands in view. The patrol truck eased to a stop, tires crunching on the gravel driveway. Lights flickered overhead—red, then blue—casting lurching shadows across the front porch.

"Chad's here," Teresa told Bev, ending the call and slipping her phone into her pocket.

Moments later, Officer Chad Lucero stepped from the truck. His uniform was crisp, and he walked toward them with his right hand hovering near his holstered service pistol resting low at his hip. He climbed the front porch steps and stopped, scanning Teresa, who was feeling flushed and still held the hammer in a trembling fist. John, the stranger, on the other hand, appeared unnervingly calm.

"Just the two of you here?" Chad's voice was level, professional. "Anyone else in the house?"

"Bubba's supposed to be upstairs working," Teresa said, jaw tight. "But it's been quiet for a while, so I'm guessing he ducked out the back." She caught Chad's raised eyebrow and blurted, "That man's hardly ever around, and when he is, it feels like he's doing more damage than repairs."

Across from her, John lifted one dark brow but didn't speak.

Chad's jaw clenched. He stepped forward, but kept a respectful distance. "Sir, I need you to turn around."

John complied, placing his palms flat against the wall. Chad patted him down—one practiced hand brushing the man's pockets, the other hovering near his own holstered weapon—then withdrew a wallet. He stepped back. "All right. You can turn around." He unfolded the wallet, extracted a driver's license, and read aloud, "John Morris. Amarillo. What brings you to Las Palomas, Mr. Morris?"

"Just passing through."

"He had my mother's locket," Teresa interjected, voice sharp as a snap of cold air.

Chad frowned. "Say that again?"

Teresa reached into her front pocket, where she'd stashed the locket when she'd reached for her phone. Pulling it out, she held it up. The sunlight caught the locket's engraved initials. M.T. "This belonged to my mother. She never took it off—she was wearing it the morning she disappeared, fifteen years ago. If he's got it, he has to know something about what happened to her."

Chad turned back to John. "How did you come by it, Mr. Morris?"

John cleared his throat and spoke in a quiet, measured tone. "I was east of town yesterday evening. It was late. I saw a woman walking along the shoulder of the road and offered her a ride. She ... she fidgeted with the locket as we drove. I dropped her off at this address, spent the night here in town, at Ruby Mae's, and this morning I found the locket on my passenger-side floorboard."

Chad nodded. "Can you describe the woman?"

John gestured toward Teresa. "She looked like her. Exactly like her."

"It wasn't me," Teresa snapped, hurt and disbelief warring in her voice.

Chad raised a hand to quiet them both. "Did this woman give you a name?"

John hesitated. "Marie. She said her name was Marie."

Teresa's face went slack. "That's my mother's name," she whispered, voice cracking. Her knees weakened and both Chad and John moved to steady her.

"Let's sit down," Chad said gently. He herded them through the doorway, into the narrow kitchen, where the smell of morning coffee lingered in the air. He grabbed three bottles of water from a case on the counter and handed them out. John twisted off the cap of his and drank. Teresa ignored her water, clutching the locket as if it were her only tether to the past.

"I understand why you called, Teresa," Chad said, settling at the wooden table scarred by years of use. "Showing up with your mother's locket is ... perplexing." He looked at John. "But I don't think Mr. Morris had anything to do with her disappearance."

Teresa's eyes flashed. "How can you be sure?"

Chad flipped John's license between his fingers. "According to this, Mr. Morris would have been twelve when your mother vanished."

Teresa exhaled slowly, the air escaping her like a punctured balloon. "Oh." Color returned to her cheeks, but tension still coiled in her shoulders. "Then how did he get it?"

Chad spoke carefully. "Maybe exactly the way he said he did." When she didn't seem to agree, Chad continued. "Teresa, it's been fifteen years. It's more likely your mother is dead than that she's been hiding all this time."

Her fist tightened around the chain. "She can't be dead," she said, voice small, then fierce. "If she were, she would have come to me, not some stranger."

"Maybe she couldn't," Chad said with gentle sympathy. He turned back to John. "You dropped the woman here last night?"

John rubbed his temples, trying to keep up with the conversation. "Yeah."

Chad paused, then offered, "We could call Zelda." Then, to John, he explained. "She reads auras, sees the energy both the living and dead leave behind. Whoever was in your car last night, she'll at least be able to tell us if that person was alive, or a ghost. She might even recognize whose aura it is."

John scoffed, a humorless bark. "You can't be serious."

Chad shrugged. "I know it sounds absurd, but it's legit. She's helped solve more than one case by reading the energy patterns people leave behind—call it witchcraft or intuition." He pulled out his phone.

Teresa watched him punch in a number, then turned to John, her voice sounding shaky. "I'm sorry I accused you of ... of taking my mother. It's just—" She swallowed hard.

John ran a hand over his face, trying to ignore Chad's mumbled conversation into the phone. "Officer Lucero, I don't believe in ghosts. This is crazy." His gaze flicked to the curtained window, half expecting a phantom silhouette to appear.

Chad looked over at John and smiled as he slipped his phone back into his pocket and held out his hand. "Call me Chad." They shook hands. "Welcome to Las Palomas. Weird is normal here."

"What does that mean?" John asked.

"According to the local coven—yeah, we have witches, too—Las Palomas sits on a convergence of ley lines which is why ghosts are attracted to it. Ghosts haunting houses is about as unique here as brown grass in the summer—as in, not at all." Then, to them both, he said, "Zelda's on her way—ten minutes."

John stared from Teresa to Officer Lucero, waiting for them to start laughing at the joke. They didn't. Instead, they were somberly waiting for a woman to come over, look into his car and tell him if he gave a ghost a ride home last night. John sighed, running a hand through his hair. It seemed he'd driven into looney-town and now had a front-row seat to the Twilight Zone, Texas edition.

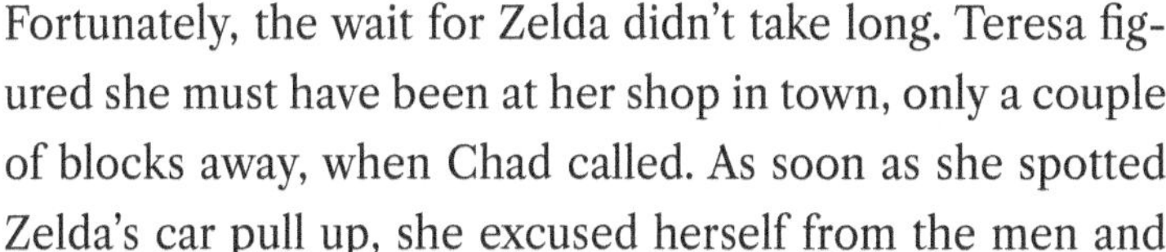

Fortunately, the wait for Zelda didn't take long. Teresa figured she must have been at her shop in town, only a couple of blocks away, when Chad called. As soon as she spotted Zelda's car pull up, she excused herself from the men and opened the front door.

Zelda's appearance rarely changed. She had long dark curls, a riot of bracelets around each wrist, and wore a peasant blouse and skirt that swirled around her legs as she mounted the front porch steps.

"You doing okay?" she asked, coming forward to give Teresa a hug.

Teresa nodded. "Just buried in house renovations."

Zelda's smile softened. "Understandable."

Chad and John emerged from the kitchen. "Thanks for coming," Chad said. "This is John Morris."

John extended a hand. "Nice to meet you."

"Zelda Zahn. It's nice to meet you." She clasped his hand, her bracelets jangling. Teresa caught the way Zelda studied him—whether out of interest or assessment, it was hard to tell—and felt an unexpected pang of irritation. She pushed it aside.

After a beat, Zelda released John's hand and glanced between them. "So. What's going on?"

Chad gave the short version. John had picked up a woman last night who looked like Teresa, dropped her here, and found a locket in his car this morning. Teresa held it up.

Zelda's expression sobered. "So, you want to know who was in his car."

"Exactly," Chad said.

"Then let me look." She turned to John. "Mind if I check your passenger seat?"

John dug his keys from his pocket, then held them a moment longer. "Mind if I come along?"

"I'd prefer it," Zelda said, plucking the keys from his hand with a grin. "I'm guessing you don't believe in aura reading."

"You'd be right," he said. "No offense."

"None taken." Zelda flicked a teasing glance at Chad. "He didn't believe either. Until recently."

Teresa's eyes widened at this revelation, and she glanced at Chad, who gave a sheepish smile, his face tinged with a hint of red. She shot him a questioning look.

Chad shrugged, a small smirk playing on his lips. "That's a tale for another time," he said, waving it off. "For now, let's just say Zelda convinced me she knows her way around auras."

Zelda turned to Chad with a teasing glint in her eye. "Speaking of, how is Bambi?"

"Her name was Cammie, and thanks to you, my mother's heirloom jewelry is back where it belongs, and Cammie is doing community service work in Austin these days," he replied.

Zelda gave Teresa a knowing wink, her expression smug. "I'll be right back, with John in tow," she said, heading toward the front door, John close behind.

John followed Zelda across the porch, down the steps and into the late-morning sunlight. The humidity clung to his skin, amplifying the sensation of being watched. He glanced back. Sure enough, Teresa and Chad stood at the front window, Teresa half-shrouded in lace curtains that looked like they hadn't been washed since the Carter administration. Chad's face was impassive, cop-serious, arms crossed and ready to spring. John gave them a bland nod and kept walking.

Zelda walked straight to the passenger side of his car and, without hesitation, unlocked and opened the door. For a moment, she just stood there, not moving, letting the air settle. She turned to John and raised one brow, as if to say, You coming or what? He joined her at the curb, close enough to see her nostrils flare as she took a slow, deliberate breath.

"You mind?" she asked, tossing him the keys.

He caught them, and stood by the open door, unsure what to do. Zelda leaned through the open passenger door and stared at the seat as if it might confess something.

She didn't chant or wave her hands, just breathed in, slow and shallow, and looked around. At first, John thought she was playing to the audience—maybe Chad and Teresa needed a show—but then she reached out, palm hovering an inch above the seat, her hand held steady.

"There's a trace," she said softly, her voice sounding different, less performative, more clinical. "Not just one, either. Three, maybe four people, but one is stronger than the others."

John stepped around her, scanning the interior through the front windshield for evidence—hair, fabric, blood, something physical to anchor this in reality. He saw nothing but the stubborn grit of West Texas dust and a crumpled receipt for gas station beef jerky. "You can tell all that just by sitting there?"

Zelda ignored him, muttering, "Residual energy, fresh. It's so strong it drowns out the rest. Someone really wanted to be noticed."

John stared at her, half expecting her head to spin 360 degrees. Instead, Zelda turned, looking straight at him. "What did she look like?"

"Like Teresa."

"Interesting," Zelda said, that cool, documentary tone still in her voice. She blinked hard, the effect snapping her back to herself, then looked away as if embarrassed. "We're done here." She stepped back and waited for John to close up the door and lock the car.

Then he followed her back to the house and up the steps. She knocked twice on the door before letting herself in.

Inside, the house felt different. Lighter, maybe, or just less tense—which was weird, because Chad and Teresa were standing where he'd left them, both looking like they hadn't moved except to breathe. Chad had his hands on his hips, posture open and cop-casual, but Teresa's arms were crossed, fingers digging into her own biceps. Her face was tight, as if bracing for a punchline.

"Well?" Chad asked.

Zelda paused in the entry and looked directly at Chad. "Your guy's legit," she said, jerking a thumb back in John's direction. "He had a passenger in his car. A woman, from what I can tell. You didn't mention she was dead."

Chad grunted, as if he'd been expecting this. "I thought it best not to give you too much information."

Zelda shrugged, as if she'd expected it.

"Was it my mother's ghost?" Teresa asked, sounding hesitant, like she wasn't sure she wanted to know the answer.

"I'm sorry, but I never met your mother, so I don't have a pattern I can match, but the energy signature is ... let's say, familiar. The similarity between the ghost's aura and yours is strong, like it would be between relatives, so it might be your mother's." She reached out and laid a comforting hand on Teresa's arm. "I'm sorry."

"Thank you." Teresa drew in a shaky breath. "It's strange. While I thought she was alive, even if I believed she'd abandoned me, there was still hope. Now ... if she's dead, that hope is gone. But at least it means she didn't choose to leave me."

Silence settled over them. John shifted uncomfortably, feeling like a pawn in someone else's chess game, which, given the supernatural undertones, was deeply ironic or just plain sad.

Zelda's eyes scanned the room, pausing on Teresa longer than necessary. "Did your mother ever live here?"

The question seemed to drag Teresa out of her thoughts. "Yeah, she grew up here."

Zelda nodded, as if this confirmed some theory of hers. "Would you mind if I looked around?" She didn't wait for permission, just started walking, trailing her hand lightly along the wall as if the paint might whisper secrets.

John watched her but didn't follow. He felt the urge to bolt out the door, into his car, away from this town and its motley parade of the living and the dead; instead he stayed rooted in the foyer, the old house creaking around them.

They watched as Zelda walked through the rooms on the lower level and then headed up the stairs. John heard her walking through the upstairs rooms, stopping and opening first one window, then another, before closing them. A short while later, he heard her climb the stairs to a third floor. Ten minutes later, she came back downstairs and joined them.

"Interesting." She walked over to Teresa. "I knew your grandparents, of course, and I see traces of their auras all over this house. And that of Mrs. Petrie next door. She and your grandmother were friends, I believe. And there are others. Some of them strong."

Teresa nodded. "The house used to be a Bed & Breakfast."

"That accounts for some of the fainter auras," Zelda said. "Have you had a lot of folks here working on renovations?"

"Just me and Bubba." Teresa sounded worried.

"Really?" Now it was Zelda who sounded confused. "I recognized Bubba's aura, but there are four auras I don't recognize."

"I wonder who they belong to?" Teresa sounded worried enough to make John curious. Not that he should care, but he found he did.

"Thanks for coming out, Zelda," Chad said, seemingly unconcerned with the unexplained auras.

"Of course, but before I go," she turned to John. "Can you tell me where you picked up the ghost? I'd like to take a look around." She turned to Chad. "You might want to take a look as well." When he looked confused, she cast a quick glance at Teresa before turning back to him. "Ghosts linger in places that hold significance for them. Like maybe where their bodies are resting."

Chad sucked in a breath. "I guess we'd better go look."

"I'm going with you," Teresa announced.

Chad shook his head. "I really don't think that's a good idea—"

"If you don't let me ride along, I'll just follow you," she told him.

"Fine," he capitulated. He turned to Zelda. "Do you mind driving? My truck might feel cramped."

"Not at all."

He turned to John. "What about it? Would you mind showing us where you picked her up?"

"Sure." John still didn't believe in ghosts, but damned if he wasn't starting to sip the Kool-Aid.

CHAPTER THREE

IF PRISON HAD TAUGHT John anything, it was to go with the flow until he could find an exit. So, with that guiding thought, he slid into the front passenger seat of Zelda's car, giving her clipped directions toward the road he'd taken into town.

The daylight changed everything. What had been shadow and suggestion last night was now a flat, endless stretch of scrubland. He worried the place would look too ordinary for him to recognize, but he timed the distance from where he remembered picking Marie up to the first stop sign on the edge of town.

"Here," he said finally. "Stop here."

Zelda eased the car to the side of the road. When John climbed out, the heat hit him like a wall, the air humming with cicadas. The land around them was barren—hard-packed earth, brittle grass, no houses, no reason for anyone to be walking here. It was the kind of place where something—or someone—could vanish without a trace.

Chad and Teresa joined him, both quiet, while Zelda started her slow walk along the shoulder. She moved deliberately, eyes half-lidded, crossing back and forth, pausing, then drifting on. To John, it looked like she was chasing ghosts in circles. But ten minutes later, about a hundred yards down, she cut abruptly left, leaving the road.

"Watch out for snakes!" Chad called, though his voice carried more unease than warning.

John, Teresa, and Chad followed, their footsteps crunching on dry ground. Zelda's movements grew tighter, almost spiraling, until she stopped near a stunted mesquite bush.

Teresa's voice cracked as she called, "Well?"

Zelda didn't answer at first. She just stood there, head tilted, listening to something none of them could hear. Finally, she came back toward them. "She was here," she said simply. "Her aura is strongest in this spot."

Teresa's breath hitched. "You think her body's buried here?"

Zelda glanced at Chad before answering. "All I can say for certain is that her energy lingers. Strongly."

The words dropped like stones. Teresa's shoulders sagged, her face pale. "Isn't there anything we can do?"

Zelda looked to Chad. "McAllen has a cadaver dog team. They could confirm if there are human remains buried out here."

Chad exhaled, rubbing the back of his neck. "I'll have to see if I can swing that—authority, budget, the works. But ..." He met Teresa's eyes. "You deserve answers. I'll try."

She managed a small, wavering smile. "Thank you."

"Zelda," Chad said gently, "do you have anything in your car to mark the spot?"

She tossed him her keys with a shrug. "You're welcome to look."

In the end, he improvised—tying one of Zelda's spare hand towels to a mesquite branch, the white fabric stark against the scorched landscape. It drooped like a surrender flag, or maybe a warning.

Nobody spoke much on the drive back. The silence hung heavy, as if they'd left more behind than they'd found.

A short while later, Teresa stood in the driveway with John, watching as Chad's truck and Zelda's car disappeared down the road.

"I'm sorry about your mother," John said, breaking the silence.

"Thank you." Teresa shifted awkwardly. "And I'm sorry I accused you of—whatever I thought. It was stupid."

"It's okay." His mouth tipped in a wry smile. "Seeing that locket would shake anyone up."

She gave a half-laugh. "Yeah, even around here, ghosts take getting used to."

"I should get going. I hope you find the answers you're looking for."

"Thank you." He turned toward his car, and on impulse she called after him. "John? You want a bottle of water for the road?"

"No, but thanks," he said, lifting a hand in farewell. He paused as a battered pickup rattled by, waiting for it to pass before opening his car door.

Instead of continuing down the road, the truck pulled over to the curb and stopped. Two men climbed out.

Watching them approach, Teresa's stomach sank.

They were rough-looking with stained shirts, jeans streaked with oil, and faces shadowed with several days' neglect. One was bald, the other with lank, greasy hair hanging to his collar. Both moved with a kind of casual arrogance that made her skin prickle.

"Can I help you?" she called, trying to sound firm.

"Heard you were hiring," the greasy-haired man said, both eyes blinking together. "Me and my buddy, we've both done construction. We're looking for work."

Relief flickered—an excuse to refuse them. "Thank you, but I've already got someone."

Instead of leaving, they kept coming, boots crunching up the walkway.

"Bet this house was something back in the day," Baldy said, his thin smile revealing brown uneven teeth. "Lot of work to get it back in shape. More than one person can handle. We'd work cheap."

They were close enough now that she caught the reek of stale beer on their clothes. Her throat tightened. "I'm not looking for more help."

The long-haired man tilted his head, eyes sliding toward the house. "Old place like this? History in every board. How about you give us a quick tour?" He turned back to look at her, both eyes blinking at once, making Teresa wonder if he had a condition like Blepharospasm.

Her heart thudded. "No."

He stepped closer, his buddy looming behind him. "That's not very neighborly. We just want a look inside."

The word "inside" dripped with something that made her pulse spike. For the first time, she wondered how far they'd be willing to push.

"The lady said no."

The voice came from behind them, and Teresa's breath caught as both men turned. John Morris stood a few yards away, broad-shouldered and steady, a crowbar hanging loose at his side. His stance made it clear he knew how to use it.

"Get back in your truck," he said, his voice low and sharp. "Now."

The men stared at him, weighing their odds.

"Now!" John barked, lifting the crowbar so the steel glinted in the sunlight.

"Yeah," Baldy muttered. "We were just leaving." He tugged on his buddy's sleeve.

But the other man lingered a beat too long, menace simmering beneath his forced grin. He blinked, both eyes. Then blinked again. "No reason to get excited. We were just looking for work."

"There's no work for you here," John said evenly.

Finally, the man's grin collapsed into a scowl. The two backed away across the yard, slow and deliberate, before turning and heading for their truck.

The engine roared to life, tires spitting gravel as they pulled away.

Only when the truck's rumble faded did Teresa realize her hands were shaking. She turned toward John. He was still standing firm, crowbar in hand, the very picture of some-one who would fight to protect what mattered.

For the first time in a long while, something inside her flickered—something that felt dangerously close to attraction.

John continued to stand in the yard and stare after the two men as they drove away. Only once they'd disap-peared around the corner at the far end of the block did he turn to Teresa.

"Are you okay?"

"Yes, thank you. Those guys were a little intimidating."

"Yeah." They were also ex-cons, but he kept that infor-mation to himself. When he'd approached the men from behind, he'd recognized the prison tats each man had on the back of his neck. "They seemed unusually interested in seeing your house. Any reason why?"

"Maybe they wanted to see if I had any antiques worth stealing in there. I don't. Not really. The furniture is old but probably not valuable to anyone but me."

He'd had the same thought. That they were casing the place to see if it was worth coming back later to steal something. If they came back during the day, he didn't think Teresa's handyman would be much help. And it would only be worse if they came back at night when she was there alone.

"Look, it's none of my business, but maybe you should get a room in town and stay there for a couple of nights," he suggested.

"Thanks, but that won't be necessary. I'm sure I'll be fine."

"I just think that it might be safer for you to stay someplace else. At least until you get your locks fixed."

"What do you mean? My locks are fine."

"I noticed the deadbolt on your front door is barely catching. It wouldn't take much for someone to get that door open." He stared at her as his thoughts raced. He should get in his car and leave. That was the smart play here. And yet, he found he couldn't. "I could fix it for you."

She looked worried, biting her lower lip, but then shook her head. "No, but thanks."

Why he couldn't let it go and be on his way, he didn't know. "Tell you what. Go inside and lock the door. If I can't get the door open with minimum effort, then we'll both know you're right and I'll leave."

She thought about it for a moment, then finally nodded. "Okay." They both went up the front porch steps. He waited outside while she went in and closed the door. He listened for the sound of the deadbolt, not liking the way it stopped short of being fully engaged.

The door was a left-side opening door, so taking hold of the handle, he tugged the door to the right and then shoved against it with his shoulder until the door opened.

He stepped inside to find Teresa staring at him in shock.

"Like I said, the deadbolt isn't catching properly. See here?" He pointed to the doorjamb. "This hole in the jamb needs to be drilled out more so the deadbolt can go all the way in. And it would be better if you had a strike plate mounted on the jamb rather than leave it bare wood like it is." He looked at her. "Any chance you have a drill and extra strike plate lying around?"

"Actually, I do," she admitted. "I intended to replace all the locks on the doors and windows. It's on the list of many things that Bubba hasn't gotten around to."

"If you have the replacement lock for the front door, I'm happy to install it for you."

"Are you sure? I hate to impose."

He shook his head. "It's no imposition," he assured her.

She smiled. "Follow me. I've got the replacement locks and tools in the kitchen. I really appreciate this."

"No problem. I might take you up on that bottle of water, though."

"I have soda and beer in the fridge as well, if you'd rather either of those."

"Just the water, thanks."

Teresa showed him the locks and tools, and while he studied them, she took a cold bottle of water out of the fridge.

"Is there something I can do to help?" Teresa offered, following him to the front door, still holding his bottle of water.

"No. I think I've got this. If you have something else you need to do, feel free to do it. I'll holler if I need help."

Shrugging, she set the bottle of water on the table by the door and ran upstairs to see if Bubba had returned while she was gone.

Chapter Four

Chad was feeling a little overwhelmed. What a time to be "acting" chief of police.

Until a week ago, Dane Wolfe, had been filling in for Police Chief Samantha "Sam" Hunter while she was recuperating from a gunshot wound. Then, last month, one of the town's favorite ghosts, La Llorona, had started scaring off visitors. The town had hired a very attractive ghost whisperer to deal with the problem. Gina Castillo had not only tamed Llorona, but she'd won Dane's heart. Last week, they'd gotten married and now were away on their honeymoon.

Chad was appointed acting police chief only until Sam passed her physical and mental evaluations. So far, he'd left her alone, not wanting to bother her. Now, though, maybe it was time to bring her into the loop. After all, they might be on the verge of solving a fifteen-year-old cold case!

Sam's house was located just outside of town. When Chad knocked on the door, Sam answered wearing old shorts and a "Las Palomas High School, Home of the Phantoms"

T-shirt. She was red-faced, sweaty and had a towel draped around her neck.

"Hey, Chad. Come on in." She led him into the kitchen, where she gestured to the kitchen table. "Have a seat. You want a drink?"

"Sure, water's fine." He took a chair and waited for her to take two bottled waters from the fridge and hand him one. Then she took a seat at the table and used a corner of the towel to wipe her face.

"Sorry, you caught me working out. My physical is coming up. I want to make sure I pass."

"You look good," he told her, not wanting to point out the dark circles under her eyes.

"Liar." She snorted, then shrugged. "I have trouble sleeping, but otherwise, I'm doing okay."

"Give yourself a break. You got shot, for Christ's sake. You almost died. That would give anyone nightmares."

"Not almost, Chad. I died."

He wasn't sure he'd heard her correctly. "What?"

"In the helicopter while they were transporting me to the hospital. I coded, and they worked on me for four and a half minutes. They were about to announce time-of-death when, suddenly, my heart started up again."

"Oh, shit!" Chad felt shell-shocked. He hadn't realized they'd come so close to losing her. "I'm so sorry."

"You'd think that would be what's keeping me up at night, wouldn't you?"

"It's not?"

She shook her head. "Flatlining like that for several minutes left me, um, I guess 'changed' is the best word for it."

"Changed? In what way?"

"Let's just say that Gina is no longer the only one in town who can see and talk to ghosts. And I don't mean I see *Llorona* or *El Muerto* or any of the other ghosts that make themselves visible to everyone. I'm talking about the less powerful ghosts—the ones most," she used her fingers to make air quotes, "'normal' people can't see."

Chad was too stunned to say anything. Fortunately, Sam saved him from a prolonged awkward silence. "I know. It's crazy, right? I thought I'd lost my mind the first time I saw a ghost."

"When was that?"

"I was still in the hospital. A patient down the hall who'd just passed away walked into my room, looking confused. When he realized I could see and hear him, he didn't want to leave. Of course, I didn't know he was dead; but there I was, talking to him like I'm talking to you. I couldn't understand why the nurses were being so rude and ignoring him. I was giving them some pretty nasty looks, which they were starting to return."

"How'd you figure out the patient was dead?"

"Zelda." She said it as if it should have been obvious. "She came to visit me and realized what was going on. At least she waited until the nurses left before breaking the news to me. Otherwise, we both might have ended up in the Behavioral Health Unit."

"Wow!"

"I know, right? I was totally freaked out. Zelda, on the other hand, was ecstatic because now it gives us something in common, more or less."

"Gives you, Zelda and Gina something in common," he corrected. "Which now explains something about Gina." Sam gave him a confused look. "It's not common knowledge, but Dane told me that Gina couldn't see ghosts when she first came to town. It wasn't until she nearly drowned. Now that I think about it, Dane said when he pulled her out of the river, she wasn't breathing." He sighed. "If it takes nearly dying in order to see ghosts, I'm happy to pass."

"Right?" She gave a soft laugh. "Enough about me. What brings you over?"

Reminded of the case, he smiled. "I have some big news."

"Is this about Marie Thacker?"

He felt some of his excitement leech away. How had she known? "Did you talk to Marie?"

She smiled. "No. Zelda called when she left the Thacker house."

He should have guessed. "I'd like to bring in cadaver dogs to search the area where John first picked up Marie's ghost. Is that okay with you?"

"You don't need my permission to request a team, Acting Chief of Police Lucero." She leaned over and playfully punched him in the arm.

He made a face. "Maybe not, but I'd feel better having your approval."

"You have it then. And maybe I'll go over there with Zelda to look around. I want to see if this new ability of mine can be useful."

That sounded promising. "If you can't get Zelda to drive you, let me know. I'd be happy to drive you over."

"Thanks, Chad." She studied him closely. "How's everything else going?"

"So far, so good," he told her.

They chatted for a few minutes more, until he thought she started looking tired, then he made up an excuse to leave so she could rest.

"Take care of yourself, Sam," he told her, getting to his feet. "We miss you back at the station."

"Thanks." She got up to walk him to the door. "And thanks for stopping by. I appreciate it."

"You bet." He was at the door when she stopped him.

"Chad?"

"Yeah?" Hand on the doorknob, he turned around to face her.

"I haven't told many people that I can see ghosts," she told him. "Just you, Zelda, Mom and Nanna, so far. I'm still trying to come to terms with it."

"I understand. Your secret is safe with me."

"Thanks."

He gave her a last nod and then left, heading back to the station. He wanted to get the request for the cadaver dogs submitted today. The sooner he put in the request, the sooner they'd have some answers.

"I really wish you'd let me pay you," Teresa offered several hours later. Not only had John replaced the locks on the front and back doors, but he'd checked the locks on all the windows—especially the ones on the ground floor.

"No worries," he told her. "I was happy to do it."

They were standing in the kitchen, and at that moment, the front doorbell rang. She excused herself to go answer it, leaving John in the kitchen. She returned a few minutes later with a large pizza and a six-pack of cold Diet Coke, which she set on the kitchen table.

She knew she shouldn't be inviting a perfect stranger to join her for dinner, but there was something about him that made her feel like she could trust him. "At least let me feed you." She flipped up the pizza box lid, releasing the aroma of freshly baked crust, cheese, pepperoni and sausage to fill the air. "I've got a large supreme here, and there's no way I'm going to eat all of this myself."

He looked over at the pizza, and she heard his stomach growl. It occurred to her they'd both missed lunch.

"Well, I am a little hungry," he admitted. "But only if you're sure you don't mind sharing."

"Great!" She hurried over to the sink to wash her hands and then went to the pantry to grab a couple of paper plates. She stopped on her way back to the table to tear two paper towel sheets off the roll. She pulled out a chair for herself and gestured to John to take the other.

"Don't stand on ceremony with me," she told him, reaching into the box to grab a slice of pizza, which she put on her plate. "Help yourself."

He followed her lead, grabbing a couple of slices. "When did you order this?"

"It was while you were checking the upstairs windows. I had a feeling you wouldn't let me pay you and," she shrugged, "I was hungry." She picked up her pizza and took a bite, using her free hand to break the string of melted cheese hanging from her mouth to the slice of pizza in her hand.

"Oh, wow," she said, giving a moan of appreciation. "I love pizza and The Leaning Tower of Pizza makes some of the best."

He gave a grunt of laughter. "The Leaning Tower of Pizza?"

"Yeah, catchy, right?"

He took another bite. "It _is_ pretty tasty," he admitted after swallowing.

For several minutes, they ate in silence. After Teresa's hunger was no longer top-of-mind, her curiosity surged to the forefront.

"What brings you to Las Palomas? It obviously wasn't the ghost sightings, since you didn't realize we have such a thing."

"Just passing through," he said. "On my way to El Paso."

He wasn't exactly forth-coming on information about himself, so she tried a new tactic. "Where'd you learn how to replace door and window locks?"

"My father runs a construction business. Growing up, I used to help him out after school and during the summers. I might have picked up a thing or two along the way."

"Any chance you know how to hang and patch drywall? Maybe refinish wood floors?" Her questions weren't subtle, but she wasn't trying to be subtle.

He lowered his half-raised slice of pizza back to his plate as he looked at her. "Yes, I know how to do those things."

Her thoughts raced. "Would you be interested in a job? The pay's not great, but I could occasionally include meals."

He shook his head. "Thanks, but I don't think that would be a good idea."

"Oh, okay." She was more disappointed than she wanted to admit. "I understand." Not really, but she didn't want to make an issue out of it.

They continued eating, and Teresa let the conversation turn to safer topics, like the weather and descriptions of neighboring towns.

When they finished eating and the pizza box sat empty on the table, the tang of tomato sauce still hanging in the air, Teresa leaned back with a sigh, surprised by how easy the evening had felt. For the first time in weeks, she hadn't thought about how much damage Bubba had done earlier that day or the growing number of unpaid bills. It had been a good evening, with good food and, surprisingly, good company.

When John stood to go, she walked him to the front door. He paused a moment, hand resting on the new brass knob, giving it a testing jiggle. "Solid," he said with quiet satisfaction. "No one's getting past this lock without a fight."

Something unspoken passed between them. His reassurance followed by her gratitude.

"Thanks again for dinner," he added, then disappeared into the night, his boots crunching down the walkway until the sound faded.

Teresa closed the door, turned the deadbolt with a firm click, and rested her palm against the cool wood, studying her reflection in the new brass lock. For the first time since moving back into the house, she felt safe. Safer than she had in years.

CHAPTER FIVE

Feeling unsettled, Sarah Novak stood on the front porch of the Meyers Bed and Breakfast, her reflection ghosting faintly in the polished brass lock. The door itself was freshly painted, the wood smooth beneath her fingertips, the kind of solid craftsmanship that whispered of security and permanence. It was the sort of detail she never would have noticed before—before Donny, before Bobby, before the impromptu decision that had landed her here.

She adjusted her grip on her suitcase and glanced up and down the quiet street. Two days on buses had carried her across backwater towns and dusty crossroads, each mile giving her too much time to think. Donny had called this a vacation, a stop on their way to Mexico where money—and freedom—waited. But even as she smoothed her skirt and prepared to enter, she couldn't shake the gnawing suspicion that Las Palomas was less a getaway to a better life and more of a detour along an already disappointing path.

It had been Donny's idea from the start. Flashy, fast-talking Donny, who lit up every room and left her breathless with promises. He'd said they'd meet here, that his brother Bobby would join them. He had the same dark hair and sculpted cheekbones, but where Donny's energy vibrated like a live wire, Bobby's felt grounded. Solid. He was the kind of man who made you feel safe without even trying. She couldn't help but wonder how different her life might be now if she'd met him first.

But she hadn't, and Donny had dazzled her from the start. Flashy and fast-talking, with a grin that turned heads and a laugh that made you feel you were in on something big. He was all sharp edges and dangerous heat, like a sparkler burning down to the wire. And she'd fallen fast—too fast.

He hadn't cared about her job. Classy escort, she reminded herself, though even that line had worn thin. He'd told her she was smart, beautiful, talented—that her fashion designs were good enough to make it big. He said he believed in her and had promised big things, bigger than she'd ever dared to dream. A future with enough money to start her own clothing line; enough money to provide a life where she could finally stop scraping by.

All she had to do was trust him.

And she wanted to. God help her, she wanted to. She reached up and touched her cheek—the left side. The bruise had faded, barely visible now beneath the light make-up she always wore. But she remembered the heat. The shock.

A misunderstanding, he'd said when he apologized and promised never to do it again.

She had believed him.

Mostly.

Bobby would be here, she reminded herself.

Still, her hand trembled as she finally reached for the door handle and pushed the door open. The scent of fresh varnish and plaster dust mingled in the air, the smell of a house mid-renewal. Her nerves fluttered, but the moment she stepped inside, they were drowned out by the booming voice that greeted her.

"There she is!" Donny strode across the foyer like he owned the place, grinning wide, arms out as though he might scoop her up in a bear hug. "You made it, Baby Doll. Knew you would."

Before Sarah could answer, Bobby appeared from the hall. He wasn't as loud as his brother, but his presence steadied her. He offered a smile that was smaller, gentler. "How was the trip down?" he asked, his voice low enough to belong only to her.

Sarah smiled, grateful for the kindness in his tone. "Long, but I'm glad to be here."

Donny clapped Bobby on the shoulder as though that were thanks enough. "She's fine, she's fine. Don't go fussing. We just got here a short while ago ourselves. Let's go out and see what this town offers."

Bobby shot him a look. "Give the girl a chance to settle in first."

"I'd appreciate that," Sarah admitted softly, though Donny waved it off with a laugh.

Before the brothers could spar further, a new voice chimed in from the stairwell. "I see our new guest has arrived." The woman descended with careful grace, her floral dress brushing against the banisters. She smelled faintly of lavender, her gray-streaked hair pulled into a bun that had once been tighter than it was now. "Welcome, dear. I'm Mrs. Meyers. Come, let me show you to your room. Please excuse the smell of paint and sawdust—we've been busy with renovations."

Sarah's gaze darted to the hall where a ladder leaned against the wall, a fresh coat of pale yellow brightening the plaster. "Thank you, ma'am," she said, offering a polite smile.

Mrs. Meyers patted her arm, then led her toward the staircase.

Donny called after her, his grin still broad. "Don't get too comfortable, Baby Doll. We're taking you out tonight!"

CHAPTER SIX

LAS PALOMAS, TEXAS
PRESENT Day

John stopped at the gas station on the edge of town to fill up with gas and grab a coffee for the road. Then he set off. He'd only gone about fifteen miles when a figure walking along the side of the road caused him to slow down.

"What the hell?" It couldn't be. But as he got closer to her, he recognized the woman as none other than Marie Thacker. As he drew even with her, she turned her head toward him and smiled.

To say he was freaked out was an understatement. He stepped on the accelerator to hurry past her.

Unable to resist, he glanced in the rearview mirror, only to find she wasn't there. He was both confused and relieved. He drove a little further, most of his attention focused on the view in the rearview mirror. The road behind him remained empty.

Turning his attention to the road in front of him, his heart skipped a beat at the sight of the woman standing in front of him. Even knowing it was a ghost, he slammed his foot on the brakes and jerked the steering wheel.

The sound of the impact never came. Instead, Marie Thacker vanished as his car plowed through the space where she'd just been standing, and John was left fighting for control as his car skidded across the asphalt.

For a long moment after the car came to a stop, John sat there trying to catch his breath and calm his nerves. What the hell had just happened?

He shook his head, trying to clear his thoughts. Then he put the car in park and got out, looking all around. The street was quiet, and from all appearances, deserted.

"You have to turn back."

At the sound of the woman's voice, he ducked his head back into his car to see Marie Thacker sitting in the passenger seat.

"Who-who are you?"

"You know who I am, John," she replied, calmly, sympathetically.

"You can't be here," he told her. "You're dead."

If he'd hoped logic would work, he was mistaken. Marie stayed where she was.

"You need to go back," she repeated, this time more urgently. "Please!"

"Back where? Why?" It was all he could think to say.

"Back to Las Palomas. My daughter is in danger."

Immediately, images of the two ex-cons he'd confronted earlier sprang to mind, and he didn't question the wisdom or logic of taking orders from a ghost. He got back into the car, put it in gear and started back for Las Palomas, his foot growing heavier on the pedal the more worried he became.

Reaching her house, he parked his car in front and got out. At first, all he heard was the silence of the night.

Then he heard breaking glass.

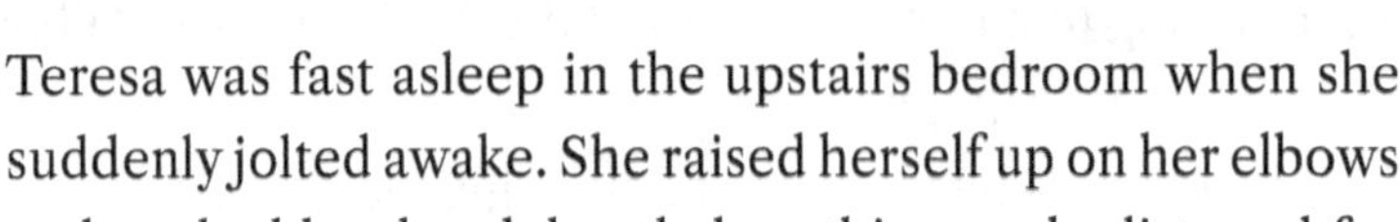

Teresa was fast asleep in the upstairs bedroom when she suddenly jolted awake. She raised herself up on her elbows and cocked her head, barely breathing as she listened for a repeat of the noise that had awakened her.

It was difficult to hear anything above the sound of her racing heart.

Afraid to move but knowing she had to look around, she shoved the bedcovers aside and swung her legs over the side of the bed. She grabbed her phone off the bedside table and then tiptoed to the bedroom door. She wanted to put on her shoes but knew she would move more quietly barefoot.

Hoping the noise that had awakened her was simply from the house settling, she instinctively knew it wasn't. Someone was trying to break into her house. But why? There was nothing to steal except for a few old pieces of furniture, a rather average set of tools and an empty pizza box. Still, she couldn't silence Zelda's voice in her head talking about all the strange auras she'd seen along the side of the house.

After several long minutes, when she still had heard nothing, she relaxed a little, which was why the sound of shattering glass a moment later startled her so badly.

Terror shot through her, and she froze, unsure what to do.

Call the police.

She dialed 9-1-1 and they answered on the second ring.

"This is Teresa Thacker," she whispered loudly, giving them her address. "Someone's trying to break into my house. I heard a window break."

"I'm dispatching an officer to your address. Is there someplace you can hide?"

"Maybe," she whispered, still frozen in place.

"Go hide. An officer is two minutes out," dispatch assured her.

"Okay." She headed for her closet but stopped when she heard shouting coming from the front lawn. There was no way an officer had gotten there that fast.

She debated for a second on what to do, but then the sound of fighting had her rushing to the window to look out. Beneath the streetlight's glow, she could make out three men fighting on her front lawn. It was hard to see their faces, but one of them looked like John.

But who was he fighting?

Pulling on a robe, she ran downstairs, pulled open the front door and stepped out onto the front porch.

"I called the police!" She shouted. "They're on their way."

Not a moment later, a police truck turned onto her street, siren wailing and lights flashing.

The two men fighting with John broke away and ran down the street. She soon heard an engine start. She ran to the street curb, and when the police truck stopped in front of her house, she pointed in the direction the two men had run.

"Two men. They went that way," she shouted through the open truck window, noting the officer who'd responded to her call was Chad.

When he looked past her, she realized John had joined them.

"You hurt?" Chad asked.

John shook his head. "I'm fine. Be careful; I don't know if they're armed."

Chad nodded and took off.

Teresa turned to John. One of his eyes was already swelling shut, and he was holding his jaw like he'd taken a punch to it.

"Can you walk? Or do you need help?"

"I can manage."

"Then come inside. Let's get some ice on that eye."

She was grateful when he followed. She flipped on the overhead lights as she led the way to the kitchen.

"Sit at the table," she ordered, grabbing a dishtowel off the side counter and carrying it to the refrigerator. Opening the freezer, she was grateful she'd recently thought to purchase a bag of ice. Grabbing a couple of handfuls, she wrapped them in the dishtowel and carried it over to John. She held it out to him and, barely glancing up at her, he took it and touched it to his swollen eye. At the contact, he winced but didn't remove the ice.

"Thanks."

"I don't know what you're doing here, but it's lucky for me you were."

She thought she saw him grimace. "Luck had nothing to do with it. Your mother told me to come back."

It took Teresa a moment to process his words. "My mother?"

He nodded. "I was on my way out of town when she appeared in the middle of the road. Scared the shit out of me if you want to know the truth. When she told me you were in danger, though, I took her seriously."

"Hmmm. I wonder why she didn't warn me of the danger?" She was more than a little upset that her mother would choose to appear before a stranger rather than her own daughter, but it wasn't John's fault. "Well, thank you for coming back and dealing with those men."

He lowered the pack so he could meet her gaze and gave her a small smile. "You're welcome. You should be safe now. I'm sure I scared them off, and if I didn't, having the police chase after them will make them think twice about coming back." He stood and carried the pack to the sink. "I should probably get going."

"Now? Don't be silly," she heard herself saying. "I have an extra bed upstairs. I aired it out earlier today when I did mine. Sleeping on that air mattress was getting old. Anyway, you can sleep in the extra bedroom and leave in the morning. I know you must be exhausted."

"Well," he hesitated, then admitted, "I am tired."

"Then it's settled. You'll stay here."

Just then, there was a knock at the door. Teresa's heart jumped at the sound, and for a moment, she was afraid the men who'd tried to break in had come back. Then she realized how silly that was.

"It's probably the police," John told her, already walking toward the door. She followed him and was relieved when he opened the door and Chad was standing there. He looked from John to her, a speculative glint in his gaze.

"Mr. Morris, I'm surprised to find you're still here," he said. "I thought you'd left town."

"I tried," John replied ruefully as he stepped back to allow Chad to enter.

"My mother's ghost appeared to him again and told him I was in danger," Teresa said. "So, he drove back to check on me."

"When I arrived, I heard breaking glass so I went to investigate. When I saw the two men, I confronted them. Did you catch them?"

"They got away," Chad admitted. "Did you get a look at them?"

John shook his head. "It was too dark to see them clearly."

"I'll have a patrol car drive by a couple of times tonight, just to be safe."

"Thanks, Chad," Teresa said.

"You want me to call Marshall to come out and fix that window tonight?"

Marshall Smith owned the local glass shop, and she didn't want to think about how much he'd charge her to come out in the middle of the night. "That's okay," she said. "I'll call him tomorrow."

"Okay, well, if you have some extra lumber lying around, I could tack a board up over the window."

"That's okay," John answered before she could. "I'll take care of it."

Chad raised an eyebrow and looked at her for confirmation.

"I offered to let John stay in the extra bedroom upstairs tonight. It seemed the least I could do after Mom made him come back." She quickly relayed the story John told her.

"I wonder why she keeps appearing to you?" he asked, echoing her own thoughts. Then, to Teresa, he said, "Are you sure you want Mr. Morris staying here?" He turned back to John. "No offense, but we don't really know you."

"None taken," John replied.

"I'm sure," she said, giving Chad what she hoped was a reassuring smile. His concern was perfectly reasonable but, though she couldn't explain it, something about John's presence made her feel safe.

"All right," Chad said, breaking into her thoughts. "Call 911 if there's any more trouble. I'll swing by tomorrow to check on... things." This last was directed at her, but they all knew it was meant for John.

"Thanks," she said, meaning it. If she was suffering from a complete loss of judgment, then it would be nice to know someone was looking out for her.

John and Teresa saw Chad to the door. After he left, John turned to Teresa. "Mind if I use some of that wood over there?" He pointed to a pile of wood neatly stacked against the wall in the front room. "And maybe some of that plastic sheeting? I can patch the window until you get someone out here to replace it."

Glad not to have an open window letting all the A/C out of the house, Teresa held the plastic in place over the window while John methodically hammered boards into place, the rhythmic sound echoing through the air. Once their task was complete, he carefully returned the hammer to its designated spot and headed out to his car parked in the driveway to retrieve his suitcase.

Inside the house, Teresa led John to a room on the second floor. Her room was further down the hallway. She explained that while the rooms on this level were all relatively well-maintained, these two were in the best condition and were the only two still furnished.

The hallway had a single bathroom, which they would need to share. John expressed his gratitude, offering Teresa the chance to use the bathroom first. They exchanged warm goodnights before parting ways.

Back in her bedroom, Teresa gently closed the door and headed toward her bed, the soft glow of the lamp casting a warm light on the room's cozy decor. At the last moment, she turned back and secured the lock on the door. It wasn't that she distrusted John, but she acknowledged the reality that he was still largely a stranger to her.

With a sigh, she removed her robe and then slipped into bed, pulling the soft, inviting covers over her, welcoming the fabric's comforting embrace. "Uncle Bill?" she hailed the resident ghost, speaking softly so John wouldn't hear her. "Can you keep an eye on him for me?" As if in response, a gentle breeze rustled the curtains, despite the window being tightly shut. Feeling reassured, Teresa closed her eyes, confident that Uncle Bill's protective presence was watching over her.

Chapter Seven

JOHN WAS JOLTED AWAKE by the harsh, jarring sound of drywall being smashed to pieces. He reluctantly climbed out of bed, curiosity piqued despite being tired, and followed the noise to a bedroom at the far end of the hall. There, he discovered a grungy, slightly overweight man wielding a hefty sledgehammer, relentlessly pounding at the wall. His lips moved in a constant murmur, words tumbling out as if he were having an animated conversation with himself. His large hands swatted at the empty air in front of his face, as if an invisible swarm of insects pestered him, though John saw nothing but dust motes dancing in the sunlight.

"What are you doing?" John inquired, raising his voice to be heard over the chaos.

The man spun around, his expression twisted with irritation. "Who the hell are you?" he demanded, eyes narrowing suspiciously.

"I'm John. A friend of Teresa's." A slight exaggeration. "Who the hell are you?"

"Bubba. Teresa hired me to do some work around the house?"

John felt his eyebrow arch. "Demolition work?"

The man eyed John, his expression dour. "I don't see how that's any of your business."

John let it go. "Teresa had some trouble here last night. I don't suppose you'd know anything about that?" He kept his tone steady yet probing.

"I don't know what the hell you're talking about. What sort of trouble?" Bubba shot back, his voice gruff.

"Doesn't matter," John said dismissively, glancing around the room. It was mostly intact, save for the gaping hole in the wall that marred its otherwise pristine condition. "Why are you tearing down that wall?"

"Looking for a leaking pipe, not that it's any of your business," Bubba grumbled, his focus returning to the wall.

"Aren't there less destructive ways of finding the leak?" John questioned, knowing damn well there were.

Bubba scrutinized him closely, eyes narrowing further. "Who'd you say you were?"

"John," he replied, catching the sound of a door swinging open downstairs. He turned on his heel and left the room, leaving Bubba to his demolition. Descending the stairs, he entered the kitchen where Teresa stood, her hands full with a drink carrier bearing two large cups and a cheerful pink pastry box. She turned, her face lighting up with a smile upon seeing him.

"Good morning. I ran out and bought coffee," she raised the drink carrier slightly, "and donuts." She raised the pink pastry box. "In all the excitement yesterday, I forgot to go to the grocery store, or I would have made you eggs and bacon. Sorry."

She set the cups and box on the kitchen table before crossing over to one of the kitchen cupboards. There, she found the sweetener and powdered creamer and carried them over to the table.

"Have a seat," she invited him as she went to the pantry to get out two paper plates. She set one in front of him as she took the seat across from him at the table. "I hope the bed wasn't too uncomfortable?" she asked, stirring creamer into her coffee.

"No, not uncomfortable at all, in fact."

"Good." She took a drink of her coffee and pretended she could feel the caffeine spreading throughout her body, waking her up. While the quality of her sleep last night had been good, she hadn't slept nearly long enough to feel refreshed today.

"Are you fixing up this house in order to sell it?" John asked.

"No. Several decades back, this place used to be a bed and breakfast. When my grandmother passed, I thought it might be fun to turn it back into a B&B." She grimaced. "I'm learning that the idea of it is more fun than the reality.

Another crash came from upstairs, and Teresa's head jerked at the noise.

"What the hell?"

"Your handyman is demo'ing the wall in the last bedroom upstairs," John told her.

"He's what?!" Shouting, she jumped up from the table.

John followed her as she hurried up the stairs and down the hallway.

"What the hell are you doing?" She yelled, running into the room and grabbing the sledgehammer away from Bubba just as he was about to take another swing at the wall.

He turned on her. John, not liking the surly expression on the man's face, stepped into the room, taking a stand next to Teresa.

"Looking for a leak," Bubba snarled.

"There's no leak behind this wall," Teresa bit out. "You had no right to destroy this wall." She took a deep breath, trying to control her temper, knowing what needed to be done. "You're fired. I want you to get your stuff and get the hell off my property. Don't come back. Ever."

"No problem," Bubba growled. "Just give me my money and I'm outta here."

"I'm not giving you a dime. Any money you might have earned I'll be using to pay for the damage you did. Now get out of here before I decide to press charges and call the police."

When Bubba didn't move, John stepped forward. "You heard her. Get your shit and go."

After a second of glaring at John, maybe sizing him up to see how tough an adversary he might be in a physical fight, Bubba finally capitulated. "Fine. I'm leaving. Good luck finding anyone else to help you."

Teresa and John stood in the room and listened to Bubba stomp down the stairs.

"I'm going to follow him, make sure he doesn't damage anything else before he leaves," John told her.

The confrontation had taken a toll on her, and Teresa barely held back tears as she turned to him. "Thank you."

He nodded and walked out, leaving her alone in the room. Her gaze went over to the destroyed wall. How could anyone be as inept as Bubba? Thanks to his renovation help, she was more behind than before she'd started. And she worried he might be right when he said she wouldn't find anyone else to help her. Then again, working alone had to be better than working with Bubba. Firing him was long overdue, and she didn't regret doing it.

She made her way downstairs and found John standing by the front window.

"He's gone," he told her. "I wasn't sure what tools were yours and which were his, so I hope he didn't steal anything."

She grimaced. "Most of the tools were his." She mentally added the purchase of more tools to her growing expense list. She was starting to think it would take a miracle to finish these renovations.

"Maybe you should call Chad and let him know you fired Bubba. It wouldn't hurt to have a police presence in the neighborhood, just in case Bubba feels vindictive.

Teresa blew out a breath, fighting her growing depression. "Yeah, that's a good idea."

"I'm sorry," he said.

"Thanks." She wasn't sure what he was apologizing for. Maybe he was apologizing for her rotten luck. He looked around the room, and she knew he was about to tell her it was time for him to go. There was nothing she could say or do to stop him, unless— "That job offer is still open." She smiled. "In addition to the not-so-great pay, I can offer you free room and board." He started to shake his head. "And home-cooked meals—well, on the good days at least."

"I'm sorry," he told her. "I have a job waiting for me in El Paso. I'm sure you'll find someone who can help you."

"Yeah, I'm sure. Like those guys who tried to break into my house last night," she muttered. Then she caught him looking at her, concern in his expression, and she waved her hand. "No, stop worrying. I'm not that stupid. I'll find someone. Or maybe I'll just do the work myself. It'll take longer, but at least I won't have to worry about someone else destroying my property under the guise of helping."

"I'm really sorry."

She tried to smile and lighten her tone when she spoke. "Don't be. None of this is your fault. I really appreciate all your help."

He stared at her a moment longer and then, after giving her a quick nod to acknowledge her words, he left to go upstairs.

Teresa remained where she was, standing by the front window, gazing out, her attention on the sounds upstairs of John packing his belongings. She turned when she heard him coming down the stairs.

"Thanks for letting me crash here last night," he said.

"It was the least I could do."

"I guess this is goodbye then."

"I guess so." She walked toward him, holding out her hand to shake his. "It was very nice meeting you, John."

His hand felt warm wrapped around hers.

"You, too, Teresa. Good luck with everything."

Reluctantly, she withdrew her hand and let it fall to her side. "Thanks. Safe travels."

After he left, Teresa returned to the front window and watched until he'd driven away. Then she turned around to face the unfinished front room. This room wasn't too bad. Crown molding was mounted at the top of half the walls. She knew how to use the rotary saw and while it would be tricky mounting the rest of the molding without someone holding it in place, she could do it. Then all that remained to finish the room was to paint the walls, then sand and refinish the hardwood floors.

I can do this!

She sighed. Who was she kidding?

As her stress ratcheted up another notch, she headed into her kitchen. Baking was her number one stress release, and if ever there was a time to bake, it was now. Without making the conscious decision to do so, she started working on the kitchen, cleaning it until the sink and countertops practically sparkled. Next, she dug through the cabinets, locating her grandmother's cookie sheets and baking tins. It appeared that her grandmother had replaced many of them recently as they looked barely used. That was a relief. At least she wouldn't have to spend money replacing them. She had enough expenses with the renovations.

Finally, she looked in the pantry. She'd thrown away all the food the first week she was in the house and replaced it with the basics, but there were still a few things she needed before she could start baking.

Once she'd put together a list of items, remembering to add much needed coffee pods, she headed off to the grocery store. The sooner she got back, the sooner she could start baking. She needed a fresh outlook on her situation, and she knew from experience that everything looked better over a cup of freshly brewed coffee and still-warm-from-the-oven raspberry crumble muffins.

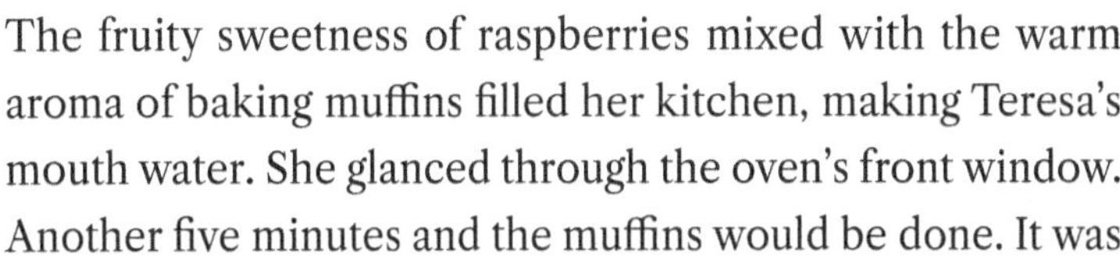

The fruity sweetness of raspberries mixed with the warm aroma of baking muffins filled her kitchen, making Teresa's mouth water. She glanced through the oven's front window. Another five minutes and the muffins would be done. It was time to start brewing the coffee.

A knock sounded at her front door just as she was about to press the button on her Keurig to brew a cup of coffee. She dropped her hand without pressing the button, took a quick peek at the muffins and then went to answer the front door.

Peeking through the peephole, she was surprised to see John standing there. She opened the door.

"Did you forget something?" She asked.

"No," he replied, looking awkward.

"Oh, no. My mother didn't force you back again, did she?"

He shook his head just as the timer on the oven went off. "No, nothing like that. I—"

"Hold that thought," she interrupted him. "Come on in," she invited, leaving the door open as she hurried back into the kitchen. Grabbing the oven mitts off the counter, she turned off the oven, opened the door and pulled out two trays of freshly baked muffins. She carried them over to the kitchen island where she'd set the cooling racks. By then, John had followed her into the kitchen.

"Sorry," she said to him as she transferred each muffin from the baking tin to the rack. "I didn't want these to burn."

"Wow. They smell great, but I'm kind of surprised to find you baking. I thought you'd be hard at work on the house."

"Yeah, well, I should be, but when I'm stressed, I bake." She finished transferring the second tray of muffins to the cooling rack and then slipped the tray into the sink to clean later before turning to John. "I was about to make myself a cup of coffee. Can I interest you in a cup? And possibly a muffin? While we eat, you can tell me why you came back."

"I'd like that. Thanks."

She plated four muffins and handed them to him. "Would you mind taking this to the table? I'll start the coffee."

She brewed two cups of coffee and carried them to the table along with a couple of paper towels.

After checking that the sweetener and creamer were still on the table, she placed his coffee and a paper towel in front of him and then took the seat across from him.

"Help yourself," she said, gesturing to the muffins before plucking one from the plate for herself.

She carefully peeled the paper cup from the bottom of her muffin while studying John from beneath her lashes. She'd been unaccountably depressed when he'd left earlier, sure she'd never see him again. It had been difficult to mask her excitement at seeing him standing on her front doorstep.

Still studying him, she took a bite of her muffin and briefly allowed herself to savor the buttery goodness of the muffin and the way the sour tang of the raspberries was offset by the sweetness of the crumble topping. When John took his first bite of muffin, she nearly laughed to see his surprised expression.

"This is fantastic," he told her.

"Thanks. It's my own recipe. I experimented with it until I got it just so."

"I don't mean to sound so surprised, but wow."

She smiled and continued to nibble at her muffin as he finished his first muffin and then looked longingly at the two remaining on the plate.

"Please, have another," she urged, taking great satisfaction from the way he devoured the muffins.

He'd finished a second muffin and half his coffee before the silence between them grew awkward.

"I guess I should explain why I came back," he began.

"Okay."

"First, I want you to know I have no hidden agenda and I'm not a threat to you."

"Okaaaayyyy." Where was this going? She finished the last of her muffin and took a drink of coffee, her gaze never leaving his face. It was clear from his frown and drawn eyebrows he was struggling, but she didn't know why. "I can't promise not to react to whatever it is you're going to tell me, but I'm guessing this isn't something that gets better with anticipation."

He met her gaze, and his features relaxed into a smile. "You're right. So, here's the thing." He took a deep breath. "Not quite three years ago, I was at a bar with a couple of friends. We went there to celebrate; I don't remember what.

Partway through the evening, a couple of guys started messing with us. I should have walked away," he heaved a sigh. "But I didn't. I ended up outside in the back parking lot with Steve Lopez. I'd never met him before, but I'll never forget his name. We'd both had too much to drink and started fighting. Steve got in a couple of good punches before I hit him back. Unfortunately, I knocked him off-balance. He fell and hit his head against a concrete wheel stop. It broke his neck, and he died instantly."

"Oh, my God," Teresa gasped, trying to absorb the horror of his story. "That's—that's—" She struggled for the right description. "Horrible," was the only thing that came to mind.

"It was," he agreed solemnly. "Not a day goes by that I don't regret getting into that fight. I took a man's life. It's a hard truth to live with."

"But it sounds like it was an accident. A horrible accident, but still an accident."

"It was, but I was still responsible because I could have walked away from the fight. I was charged with involuntary manslaughter and sentenced to two years in prison. I did my time and got out a couple of months ago."

"Okay." She still wasn't sure why he was telling her this. "Thanks for sharing?" It came out sounding like a question.

"That's why I refused your offer of work. I didn't think you'd appreciate it if you hired me and then found out I was an ex-con."

She studied him closely. "Is that the only reason you turned me down?"

"Yes."

"Now that I know, does that mean you'll take the job?"

He gave a half shrug. "There is one other thing." She waited for him to continue. "I need to be in El Paso by the end of the month, but that gives me three weeks to work for you. If the job is still available?"

She smiled. "When can you start?"

"As soon as I finish that last muffin."

Chapter Eight

Later that morning, Teresa was prepping the banister with a tack cloth when Chad showed up. She opened the door to find him standing on the front porch wearing the same pressed uniform as always, but he had dark circles under his eyes like a kid who'd binge-watched horror movies and then tried to sleep in the tool shed.

"Good morning," she greeted him. "You look like shit."

He gave a wry smile. "Yeah, between working double shifts and looking for your intruders, I'm not surprised. I didn't have any luck finding them. I hope that means they left town. I thought before I go home and grab some sleep, I'd come by and check on you. I don't like you being alone out here."

"Thanks. I'm fine." She opened the door wider to invite him inside. "And I'm not exactly alone."

He stepped up to the open doorway but then stopped, his gaze going past her to where John stood, painting the spindles on the staircase.

"Mr. Morris. I'm surprised to see you."

"Officer Lucero," John greeted Chad. "Nice to see you again."

Chad turned to Teresa with eyebrows raised so high in question she thought he might leave permanent wrinkles in his forehead.

"John stayed here last night," she told him. "In the extra bedroom. And he's agreed to help me with the house renovations for the next couple of weeks."

"Could we talk?"

She blinked. Isn't that what they were doing? Between the intruders last night, Bubba's destruction this morning and splinters in her right palm from a mishap with the sander, she absolutely did not have the bandwidth for any more surprises. "Sure. You want some coffee or maybe a Coke? We can talk in the kitchen." She stared at him expectantly.

He coughed and shot a furtive glance at the far end of the foyer where John was working. "Maybe we could talk on the porch?"

Teresa saw John's shoulders twitch, but he never lifted his gaze from his brushwork. Teresa got the distinct impression that he was counting—slow, even strokes, like a metronome for his temper.

She set down her tack cloth and led Chad onto the porch, pulling the door nearly closed, creating a bit of privacy. The humidity was intense, and combined with the rising heat, it wouldn't be long before she felt like a hot dog left too long on the 7-Eleven rollers. "Is this about the break-in?" she asked. "Or is Bubba pressing charges for emotional distress after I fired him?"

"What's he still doing here?" He gestured toward the door.

"John? I told you, he's helping me renovate the house. I fired Bubba yesterday after he destroyed another wall and John has carpentry skills."

"Do you think hiring a perfect stranger is a smart move?"

"Well, it wasn't when I hired Bubba. That man was a walking disaster. But John's different."

Chad didn't answer right away. He fiddled with the buttons on his shirt, then stared at the porch swing like it had offended him. "Look, I ran a background check on him."

"On John?"

"We don't know him, yet he keeps showing up. I wanted to learn more about him."

"Okay, I guess that makes sense."

He gave a quick glance through the front window, as if expecting John to be eavesdropping. As far as Teresa could tell, John was very pointedly not looking their way, but his brush strokes had slowed to the speed of a funeral dirge.

"The thing is, he's—"

"An ex-con. I know."

That obviously threw Chad off. "What?"

"John told me yesterday, and I'm fine with it. So, you don't have to worry about me."

"Did he tell you why he was in prison?"

She nodded. "He did. Involuntary manslaughter. He told me all about it. He wanted to make sure I knew the kind of man I was hiring, but the thing is, I already knew what kind of man I was hiring. He's a man who offers rides to women stranded on the side of the road at night. One who returns lost jewelry instead of keeping it. Who fixes the door and window locks on a house for a woman he barely knows so she'll feel safe in her own home. Who confronts intruders breaking into a stranger's home. Who's not only handy with a hammer and paintbrush but might actually know what he's doing when it comes to renovating an old home." The more she talked, the madder she got, so she paused to get her temper under control because she knew Chad was only looking out for her. "He's a man who made a terrible mistake a couple of years ago and now is doing everything he can to make amends and get on with his life."

Chad flinched, like he'd stepped barefoot on a scorpion, and held his hands up in surrender. "Okay, Teresa. Point made. Just ... be careful, okay?"

She nodded. "I'll be careful."

Chad didn't look convinced, but after a minute, he left. Teresa remained on the porch until he'd driven away.

When she went back inside, John was studying the banister. The sun outside made a sharp pattern through the window, catching every splatter of paint on his arms. He looked up, and met her gaze.

"You want me to leave?" There was no edge to his tone. Just a question.

She shook her head. "Not unless you need to run to the store."

His smile was small, but genuine. "Okay, then."

She headed to the kitchen, her hands shaking only a little as she took down mugs and loaded a pod into the Keurig.

She brewed two mugs, doctored the way she had before and brought one back to John, who'd gone right back to painting. He set down his brush and took the mug.

"Thanks," he said.

They drank coffee in companionable silence, enjoying the quiet of the morning. Teresa glanced around the room, admiring the work they'd done on the banister. In just a few hours, they'd made more progress than Bubba had made in a few weeks. For the first time in a long while, she thought restoring the old B&B might actually be possible.

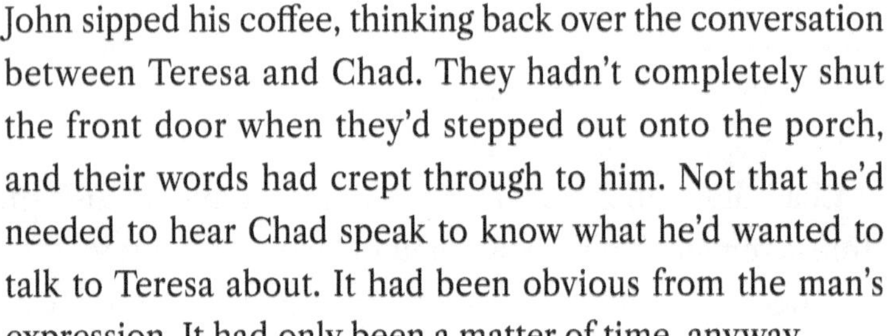

John sipped his coffee, thinking back over the conversation between Teresa and Chad. They hadn't completely shut the front door when they'd stepped out onto the porch, and their words had crept through to him. Not that he'd needed to hear Chad speak to know what he'd wanted to talk to Teresa about. It had been obvious from the man's expression. It had only been a matter of time, anyway.

What he hadn't figured on was how Teresa would go to bat for him. She could have taken the out Chad provided, thanked Chad for the warning and then quietly told John she'd changed her mind, asking him to pack up and find another town. That would have been the safe move and one he'd seen play out every time someone learned about his past.

Instead, she'd stood her ground and defended him without an ounce of hesitation. Teresa made him feel a little less like a house built on a bad foundation and a little more like someone worth something. It was a weird feeling, gratitude. It started in John's chest and spread out slowly, like it was testing to see if it would be allowed to settle in. He kept waiting for the other shoe to drop, then the rest of the wardrobe to come down after it.

"You didn't have to do that," he finally said.

"Do what?"

"Stick up for me."

She looked at him, her expression flat. "Maybe I'm just a sucker for people who don't run away when things get hard."

He shrugged, not wanting to show how much that mattered.

"You ever get tired of people treating you like a bomb about to go off?" she asked, a slight smile lifting the corners of her mouth.

John surprised himself by laughing. "Less tired. More used to it. Kind of like living next to a train crossing. After a while, the noise just blends in."

She nodded and a quiet understanding blossomed between them. With a shared glance and no need for words, they finished their coffee and got back to work.

They made it through three upstairs rooms that day before the floor sander gave up and started sounding like a wood chipper chewing on a pack of angry squirrels. Teresa let John handle the repair while she followed behind with the shop-vac, sweeping up a mountain of sawdust. They'd opened the windows and turned off the A/C while they worked, and by the time they'd finished, the afternoon sun was high in the sky, turning the house into an oven.

Teresa had just moved into the third room and turned on the shop-vac when it suddenly went dead. She flipped the switch a few times, but nothing happened. Had it overheated? Of all the luck.

Checking the plug, she found it had come loose. Huffing out a breath, she plugged it back in and flipped the switch. The shop-vac rumbled to life—then died again.

Turning back, she saw the cord had come unplugged once more.

"What the ..." She looked around. No one else upstairs. No breeze. No vibration. No reason for the cord to come loose—unless—

Her heart gave a hard thump.

Uncle Bill.

"Okay," she said aloud, warily amused. "You've got my attention."

That's when she caught the faintest whiff of smoke.

Chapter Nine

AT FIRST, SHE THOUGHT it was dust from the sander, but the scent sharpened—chemical and oily. Alarmed, she followed the smell out of the room, down the hall, and stopped at the landing.

"John?" she called.

He appeared almost instantly in the doorway of the fourth room. "Problem?"

"I think something's burning."

"I'll check it out—stay here." He rushed past her.

"Like hell," she muttered, already following him down the stairs.

They reached the utility room just as a low whoosh bloomed into a crawling tongue of flame. The fire climbed the bottom of the wall, turning faded green paint into bubbling black tar.

John didn't hesitate. He grabbed several dish cloths from the kitchen, soaked them in water, and used them to smother the fire. Teresa staggered back into the kitchen, coughing, and punched 911 into her phone with shaking fingers.

"It's out," John called, voice muffled.

The dispatcher answered just as Teresa pressed the phone to her ear.

"9-1-1. What's your emergency?"

"There was a fire, but it's out now. Still, someone should come check it." She quickly gave her address.

"We'll send a unit now. Stay outside if you can."

She hung up and turned toward John, who stood, panting slightly, studying the charred remains of the room.

"You think a wire shorted out in there?" Teresa asked. The house was old and she didn't know when or even if the wiring had ever been replaced.

"That wasn't electrical," he said. "It started low and burned fast. Smells like solvent was used."

Teresa stepped over to the doorway and peered inside. "I don't see any cans lying about," she said, frowning. "Where would the solvent have come from?"

He shook his head. Just then, sirens wailed outside. A moment later, the front door opened and several Las Palomas Fire Department volunteers poured in like the bulls of Pamplona were after them. At the helm was Fire Chief Dave Reynolds, a sturdy man in his late forties, followed by two fresh-faced firemen whose jackets still creaked with newness.

"Where's the fire?" Dave barked.

"Back here," Teresa called, summoning them to the utility room.

Dave moved past them into the room and squatted beside the blackened wall, his nose wrinkling. He touched the melted linoleum with a gloved hand. "Did you spill something and accidentally drop a match?"

"No, of course not," Teresa said, exasperated.

"We were upstairs when it started," John added. "But you can see where it started—along the base. Climbed fast. Smells like paint thinner. I'm thinking arson."

Dave's eyebrows lifted. He studied the damage again. "Yeah ... you might be right." He rose, turning to Teresa. "If they wanted to harm you, the person who started this fire would have done so at night, while you were asleep. So the house was the target. Anyone benefit from this house burning down?"

The question hit hard. *You mean besides me?* She kept that thought to herself. "No."

"Then is there anyone who might be holding a grudge against you?"

Bubba came to mind, but would he go so far as burning down her house because she fired him? She shook her head.

"We'll check the rest of the house—make sure no sparks spread up through the walls to the next level."

The firefighters fanned out. A few minutes later, one called, "Clear! No hot spots."

"I'll need to report this," Dave told Teresa.

She nodded. "I understand."

He hesitated, then nodded and signaled his team to leave. Moments later, the fire engine rumbled down the street.

Though the windows were open, the humid breeze did little to move the acrid stench of burned plastic and scorched paint. Teresa and John worked in silence, wiping down surfaces, sweeping up ash.

After a while, John glanced up. "You okay?"

She grimaced. "Not really. Faulty wiring's one thing. But arson? If we hadn't smelled the smoke—"

"Hey." John stepped closer. He didn't touch her, but his voice softened. "Whoever did this, they didn't win. You noticed the smell and acted fast."

She looked up at him, surprised by the gentleness in his tone. She wanted to tell him that it had been Uncle Bill, her resident ghost, who had alerted her to the fire, but she wasn't sure if he was ready for that ghostly revelation.

"You're not alone in this," he added when she remained quiet. "I'll help fix what I can."

She nodded, blinking away the unexpected tears. She'd felt alone for so long, she couldn't remember when she hadn't. "Thanks."

He gave a small, reassuring smile. "We'll need to get some things from the hardware store. Drywall, sealer. Maybe extra caulk for the windows."

"My brain's still stuck in panic mode. I'll never remember all of that. Can you make a list for me?"

John started to turn when a soft scratching sound stopped him. They both looked around, searching for the source of the noise.

Then, on the wall above the scorched baseboard, they saw something being etched by invisible fingers into the soot. Letter by letter, the message emerged.

B

U

B

B

A

Teresa cast a quick glance at John to see him staring wide-eyed at the message.

"Teresa—" His voice caught. "You're seeing that too, right?"

"Yeah." She stood calmly beside him, like she saw names scratched into soot every day.

"You're not freaking out."

"Nope."

"There's ... writing. In soot."

"Yup."

"From no one."

She gave him a sideways glance. "Well, not exactly no one. John, meet Uncle Bill."

He blinked. "Come again?"

"My great-great-great-uncle. He fell off the roof when he was a teenager. Never really left."

"Are you telling me there's a ghost haunting this house? And you named him Uncle Bill."

"I didn't name him. His parents did, when he was born. And I wouldn't really say he haunts the place—" He gave her a dour look. "Okay, yes, technically, I guess you could say he haunts my house."

John drew in a deep breath and let it out slowly, coughing a little, probably due to the smokey stench lingering in the air.

She watched him closely. "You okay? You look like you saw a—well, you know."

He ran a hand through his hair. "I mean … yeah. A little freaked out. But after two encounters with your mother's ghost? I guess I can roll with it."

She smiled faintly. "Good to hear."

They both looked back at the wall.

"You think he's telling us who started the fire?" John asked.

"I don't know. Bubba's completely inept, leaving a trail of destruction in his wake, but arson?" She shook her head. "I wouldn't have thought he was capable—"

"Teresa!" Chad's shout from the front of the house startled them both.

"Back here," she shouted, going out to meet him. "What are you doing here?"

"I asked dispatch to let me know if any calls come in from you or John so I could respond. They just let me know about the fire." He looked around. "Where was it?"

"Bubba set the fire," she said, leading him through the kitchen to the utility room. "Probably to get back at me for firing him."

Chad arched a brow. "You saw him do it?"

"Well, no, but I have proof." They stepped into the scorched room, and she pointed at the blackened wall where the name had been etched. "See?"

He leaned in, squinting at the rough letters. Then he straightened and gave a skeptical laugh. "How do I know you didn't scratch that yourself?"

Teresa bristled. "I didn't! Uncle Bill did it."

Chad frowned. "I didn't know you had an uncle in town. I'd like to talk to him."

She sighed, rubbing her temple. "He's … a ghost."

"Huh. I didn't know your house was haunted. Okay—"

"Wait a minute," John interrupted. "You believe a ghost actually wrote that?"

Chad turned to him. "Weird is normal here, remember? So yeah, I'm willing to consider it. However, while Judge Adams might accept that a ghost wrote that name, he still has to abide by the law and ghostly handwriting isn't exactly evidence we can use to get an arrest warrant."

"But—"

He lifted a hand. "I'll talk to Bubba. He's a Las Palomas jail frequent flyer, so it wouldn't surprise me one bit that he did it, but I need either a confession or solid evidence."

"Then what about the paint thinner can?" she asked quickly. "It was half-full as of yesterday. If it's still in the garage, and empty, you could check it for prints." Before she finished, both John and Chad were already shaking their heads. "What? Why not?"

John's voice was steady. "Didn't Bubba use that paint thinner while he was working here?"

She grimaced. "Yes, but—"

"Then his prints would already be on it," Chad said. "Not proof of anything."

Her shoulders sagged.

"I'll talk to him," Chad repeated. "In the meantime, maybe keep the doors locked. Even when you're inside."

And with that, he left, leaving the house feeling too quiet. Teresa took a deep breath, the smell of smoke still thick in the air, and looked over at John, whose reassuring smile warmed her. She pressed her palms to her face and blew out a shaky breath. "I need a beer."

"I'll get it." They moved into the kitchen, where he crossed to the fridge, pulled out a cold bottle for her, and then grabbed a water for himself.

She accepted the beer gratefully, but frowned when she noticed his bottle. "No beer for you?"

He shook his head with a faint smile. "Only on rare occasions, and even then, just a little. I'm not much of a drinker these days."

"Oh ... right." She twisted the cap off and took a long swallow, letting the cool bitterness soothe the knot in her chest.

They sat in the quiet that followed, the tick of the kitchen clock and the faint crackle of the settling house filling the air. Finally, John said softly, "Most of the damage is superficial. I'll have it repaired in no time."

Her throat tightened at the promise. "Thank you." Fire. Ghosts. Threats. And yet, standing in the ruin of her utility room, she felt something surprising—hope.

Maybe she wasn't in this alone after all.

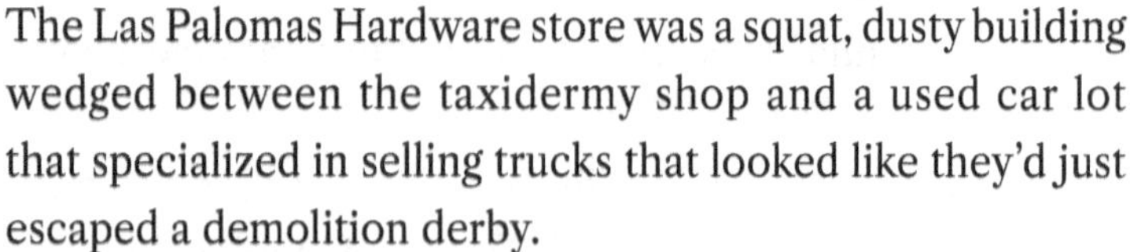

The Las Palomas Hardware store was a squat, dusty building wedged between the taxidermy shop and a used car lot that specialized in selling trucks that looked like they'd just escaped a demolition derby.

John had offered to run to the store while Teresa stayed at home to shower and change into clothes that didn't reek of the recent fire. She'd accepted his offer, but had insisted he take her truck to buy the supplies. Now, as he pulled her truck into the lot, out of habit born from his time spent in prison, he scanned the other vehicles before choosing a spot slightly apart from them. Too many close neighbors meant too many blind spots. He killed the engine, took another slow look around—windows, doorways, people passing by—then got out.

As he crossed the lot, he felt eyes on him. In the plate-glass window of the taxidermy shop, a pair of men stood watching. One smirked, elbowed the other, and both laughed. Whether at him or not, he didn't know; he just forced himself not to react, adjusted his stride and kept moving.

Inside, the place smelled of oil, fertilizer, and that peculiar old-lady-perfume scent of evaporated cleaning fluids. Hardware stores, even the bad ones, were familiar territory. In theory, anyway.

In practice, this one was different. As soon as he stepped through the door, every head in the place—there were four, counting the girl at the register—turned to look at him. The old guy with the hearing aids behind the counter gave him a long once-over before returning to his work.

"Hey," John said, keeping his tone casual. "I need drywall, joint compound, and some paintable caulk. And a few disposable drop cloths."

The girl at the register—seventeen, maybe, with a phone half-buried under the counter—pretended to study the linoleum. The old man kept ringing up a customer buying nothing more than a box of .22 shells and a pack of Big Red gum.

John shifted his weight, eyes automatically flicking over the layout of the store. Aisles narrow, shelves half-stocked. One exit behind him. Emergency door near the back. He logged them all without thinking.

"I can load the drywall myself," he added when the silence dragged. "Just tell me where to find it."

Only when the other customer left did the old man grunt, "Drywall's in the back. Watch the floors, we just mopped. Caulk's aisle three."

"Thanks," John said.

He moved down the aisles, keeping his pace steady, his basket filling with supplies. His mind kept tracking exits, shadows, people's hands. Just one of the many habits developed over the past three years. He hated how hard they were to shake.

He was checking labels on joint compound when he heard footsteps right behind him.

He spun around before he even thought to do so, his hand snapping to the wrench on the shelf. It came up with the wrench clenched tightly in his hand.

Pulse thudding in his ears, for one raw second, he wasn't standing in the aisle of a hardware store. He was back in the cellblock corridor with footsteps coming up too fast, too close.

The clerk—a skinny kid in a red vest—stumbled back a step, wide-eyed. He swallowed hard, before asking in a shaky voice, "Need help finding anything?"

Not inside. Not trapped. Just a kid. Just a store.

John forced a grin and lowered the wrench into his basket like he'd meant to grab it all along. "Got it covered. Thanks."

The kid hesitated, then nodded and quickly retreated.

John blew out a slow breath, unclenching his jaw. *You're not in prison*, he reminded himself. *Try to act normal.* But the survival instincts were deeply ingrained.

At the register, the girl—Samm, with two m's according to her name badge—took his money without meeting his eyes. He tried a polite, "Have a good one." She said nothing.

He carried the drywall outside, where the heat made the air ripple above the hoods of the cars and trucks. Across the lot, the men in the taxidermy shop window were still watching.

John wiped the sweat from his brow. This wasn't new. Every town had its stares, its whispers. This time, though, the weight of it seemed to press heavier. Maybe because Teresa believed in him. Maybe because, against his better judgment, he'd started to believe in himself.

He loaded the supplies into the truck, climbed in, and cranked down the window. As the hot wind blasted through, he let it take some of the dust—and some of the tension—with it, carrying both down the road back to the house.

Inside, he found Teresa in the kitchen, hands buried in a bowl of bread dough. She glanced up and smiled. "You survived the hardware store, I see."

"Barely," he said. "I think I'm on their Most Wanted list."

She wiped her hands on a towel and then helped him unload the supplies. Together, they carried the drywall through the house, side by side, ignoring the smell of smoke that still haunted the hallways.

As he patched the wall that evening, he heard Teresa humming in the next room. It was a simple tune, the kind his mother used to sing when she was folding laundry. For a second, he let himself pretend this was what "normal" looked like. Two people fixing up a house, sharing a meal, making things better instead of worse.

He finished the last seam and stood back to admire his work. It wasn't perfect, but it was close. That was enough.

After washing up, he found Teresa on the porch, staring out at the sunset. He stood next to her, hands shoved in his pockets.

"Thanks for the help today," she said, voice low.

He nodded. "Thanks for not firing me."

She laughed, a real one this time, and for a moment he let himself smile, too.

He'd leave, eventually. That was always the plan. But not until he'd done right by her. Not until the job was finished, and maybe, just maybe, she'd remember him as more than an ex-con.

The breeze shifted, carrying the scent of fresh bread and the faintest trace of paint. The odor of charred drywall was barely noticeable. John closed his eyes and breathed it in, letting it settle.

Tomorrow, he'd finish the wall. Maybe even start on the next room. He had time.

For now, that was enough.

CHAPTER TEN

LAS PALOMAS, TEXAS
AUGUST 1, 1945

The acrid scent of wood-smoke drifted through the open car window, mingling with the sharper scents of fresh paint and sawdust from the B&B's renovations. Sarah was sitting in the front seat of the car between Donny and Bobby, the cracked vinyl warm from the day's sun.

Donny tapped the dash and grinned at Bobby. "Let's show her how we spend a Saturday night." His voice carried the same cocky swagger as his stride, as if the whole town were his stage.

Bobby didn't answer right away, only started the engine and pulled them onto the street. The sun had slipped behind the low buildings, leaving the town draped in blue shadow. They passed shuttered storefronts and dim restaurants until Donny ordered Bobby to pull over. Sarah gazed over to the neon glow flickering in the dusty window of a bar that looked less like "visitors welcome" and more like "enter at your own risk."

She had to suppress a shiver. It not only wasn't the fancy restaurant she'd been hoping for, it wasn't a place she'd ever consider walking into alone. Nevertheless, they all tumbled out of the car and headed for the entrance.

Donny pushed open the door, and the noise rolled out like smoke—raucous music, laughter edged with menace, the clatter of glass and cue balls. He led them to a table in the back, half-hidden in shadow. Before she could take a seat, Bobby reached past Donny and pulled out a chair for her.

"Thank you," she murmured, surprised. Their eyes met—just for a second—and something unspoken passed between them.

"Of course," he said simply, then sat beside her.

Across the table, Donny let out a dry, jagged laugh. "Well, look at that," he sneered. "Ain't you the charmer." He turned his gaze to Sarah, eyes sharp. "Don't get used to it, Baby Doll."

Before she could respond, he flagged down a waitress with a snap of his fingers. She breezed past without so much as a glance.

Donny's mouth twisted. "What's a guy gotta do to get a beer in this dump?" He turned to Sarah. "Go to the bar. Get me a beer. Bobby, you want one?"

"I'll get them," Bobby offered, already rising.

But Donny's hand shot out and grabbed his arm, hard. "She can do it," he snapped. "Can't you, Baby Doll?"

Sarah nodded quickly, throat tight. She didn't look at Bobby. Didn't want him to say anything that would make things worse. She stood and wove through the crowd, trying not to let her hands shake as she reached the bar.

Behind her, Donny's voice carried.

"You keep pampering her like that, and I'll start thinking you've got a thing for my girl."

If Bobby responded, she didn't hear it over the din.

She returned a few minutes later, holding two full mugs. Her arms ached from the weight, but she forced a smile as she set them on the table.

Donny narrowed his eyes. "Where's yours?"

She hesitated. One wrong word could light a fuse. "I thought I'd bring these first. I didn't want to spill. I'll get mine in a second."

Donny grunted and reached for his beer.

Bobby said nothing, but his gaze flicked to her, watchful. Unable to meet his gaze, she hurried back to the bar for her drink.

By the time she returned, Donny had downed his drink and was waving the empty mug. "Another." This time, Bobby rose without waiting for permission.

Donny launched into a story—something about a poker game gone wrong and a guy who'd ended up in the ER after Donny got through with him. He laughed like it was the best punchline he'd ever told. Sarah sipped her drink, lips pressed tight around the rim. Bobby returned with the next round, and the cycle repeated—beer, stories, sharp glances.

Whatever they were here to celebrate had long since vanished. Sarah kept waiting for Donny to say something meaningful, something kind, something that would explain why he'd invited her here.

But as the night dragged on, the air thickened with smoke and sweat.

Hours later, her head heavy and her limbs stiff from the long travel, she leaned toward Bobby and said quietly, "I think I need to lie down."

Bobby gave a subtle nod, then stood.

"Where you going?" Donny demanded, half through his tenth beer.

"Bathroom," Bobby said easily. "You want anything while I'm up?"

"Yeah. Beer tastes like dishwater. Get me a whiskey."

Bobby looked at Sarah. She shook her head. No more.

He returned a few minutes later and set a shot glass in front of Donny. "Bartender said there's a card game in the back," he said. "Hundred-dollar buy-in. Told him you might be interested."

Donny perked up. "They got room?"

"One seat."

Donny downed the whiskey and stood, swaying slightly. "Come on, Baby Doll. You're my lucky charm."

"She can't go," Bobby said. "No women allowed. House rules."

Donny scowled. "You sure about that?"

"I'm sure."

Sarah saw the tension creep into Donny's jaw. For a heartbeat, she thought he'd lash out, but then he grinned.

"Fine. Take her back to the B&B. Make sure she gets there safe."

"I will," Bobby said evenly.

Donny turned to her and pulled her into his arms. His kiss was sudden and deep, the kind that once thrilled her—but now felt like possession. Like a brand.

When he pulled away, he smiled at her like nothing had changed.

Then he was gone, disappearing into the back of the bar without another word.

Sarah stood beside Bobby, still feeling the pressure of Donny's lips on hers.

"You okay?" Bobby asked softly.

She nodded.

But the truth was, she didn't know.

CHAPTER ELEVEN

LAS PALOMAS, TEXAS
PRESENT DAY

Teresa awakened to the aroma of coffee and scorched toast. When she went downstairs, she found John standing at the stove, jaw set in concentration, as if breakfast were a matter of life and death. She leaned against the kitchen island, arms crossed, watching him attempt to crack an egg.

The shell shattered in his grip with more force than finesse, half the yolk sliding into the skillet, the other half clinging stubbornly to his fingers.

She laughed, unable to hold it back. "I've never seen anyone crack an egg that enthusiastically."

He gave her a sheepish look.

"Don't worry," she added with a grin. "I'll give you points for effort."

A reluctant smile tugged at his mouth. "Guess I should've stuck with toast."

"Are you kidding? I can't remember the last time someone made me breakfast."

When he finally slid the eggs onto her plate, Teresa took it from him, their fingers brushing. It wasn't the neatest breakfast she'd ever seen, but it meant something—that he'd tried, for her. He put as much effort into making her breakfast as he did into fixing her house.

Thankfully, he was far better with construction than cooking.

Still, the simple gesture warmed her, more than she cared to admit.

After breakfast, they fell into a rhythm. John tackled the bigger projects—drywall repair, framing, anything that required muscle and precision—while Teresa stuck to smaller jobs like patching holes, scrubbing years of grime from woodwork, and painting trim. Around noon, they paused for sandwiches at the kitchen counter before heading back to work.

That afternoon, the rumble of an engine drew her to the front window. A battered pickup had pulled into the drive. Two men climbed out—the same intimidating pair who'd shown up days earlier, the ones who had left her unsettled long after they'd gone.

Her stomach tightened.

The knock came sharp and insistent. Teresa opened the door a crack, and there they were, grinning like wolves, the two men from before.

"Remember us?" Baldy drawled. "We heard you lost your help, so thought maybe you might be in the market to hire new help."

"I already told you, I'm not interested," Teresa managed, her voice steady despite the pulse pounding in her ears.

"Shame," the other said, stepping closer. "Place like this takes more than one pair of hands. Be a real pity if you fell behind."

"Step back," came John's voice, rougher than she'd ever heard it.

She turned. He was striding up the hall, a hammer clenched white-knuckled in his fist. His eyes had gone flat, distant—the look of a man staring down ghosts. Without hesitation, he moved in front of her, shifting her back with a firm hand.

The men's grins faltered when they saw him. John's stance was coiled, dangerous, like he'd already decided how the fight would go. The hammer hung low at his side, but his grip was almost tight enough to splinter the wood.

"She said no," he told them, voice steady but vibrating with something darker beneath. "Now get off her property."

For a moment, no one breathed. Then the men traded a glance, muttered something under their breath, and backed down the porch steps before heading for their truck. A moment later, the engine roared to life and they sped away.

The silence that followed rang louder than the saws and hammers ever had. Teresa's breath caught when she realized John was still standing rigid, the hammer raised half an inch like he was waiting for another excuse.

"John," she said softly. She touched his arm. "They're gone."

It took him a beat to blink, like coming up for air. Slowly, his grip loosened around the hammer. His shoulders sagged, and he swore under his breath.

"I didn't mean to scare you," he said, voice hoarse.

"You didn't," she lied gently. "You protected me."

Their eyes met, and for the first time, she saw not just the strength in him, but the scars that had resulted in that strength.

The encounter with those two men had rattled her. "Do you think they were the ones who tried to break in the other night?"

"Actually, I do, but I don't have any proof. From now on, maybe I should be the one to answer the door."

She nodded, feeling grateful.

John went outside then and a short time later, she heard the sound of the rotary saw buzzing as he cut the molding for the formal dining room.

Carrying paint samples and a bag with brushes, painter's tape, and a roll of paper towels, she went upstairs to the second-floor bedroom that Bubba had wrecked with a sledgehammer. She studied the newly repaired wall. Not a seam or ripple in sight. Once painted, no one would ever know it had been damaged.

She'd narrowed her paint choices to four: heavy cream, soft sea breeze green, dusty rose, and parchment paper tan. Setting the quart-sized cans on the drop cloth, she opened each one, laying a brush beside it. Then she painted 8x8 inch swatches of each color on all four walls. The cream was bright but boring. The tan, equally dull. That left the rose and the green.

She painted larger swatches of both, then, turning slowly, she studied each wall. After studying the fourth wall, she turned back to the first wall and felt a jolt of surprise. The rose section on the first wall had been painted over in green.

She spun toward the side wall and caught a paintbrush—hovering in midair—brushing green paint over the rose swatch.

Irritated, she took the paintbrush for the rose paint and made a new rose section on the wall.

"I like this color," she said aloud.

The roll of paper towels lying on the floor nearby was lifted into the air by unseen hands. It rotated, unwinding sections of paper towel as it did. Then two sections of towel tore away from the roll and it dropped to the floor. The torn-off sections floated across the room to the wall where they began to wipe off the fresh rose-colored paint. Then the green paintbrush rose and laid down a fresh coat of green.

Uncle Bill. He was a stubborn ghost, and apparently, he liked the color green.

She studied the wall a moment longer. "Fine," she muttered. "You win. I'll paint this room green. But I'm painting the other one rose, so if you don't like it, I don't care."

Though she tried to sound huffy, she couldn't deny the green was growing on her. After sealing the paint cans, she gathered the brushes and went downstairs to rinse them.

Then she stepped outside to check on John. He was shirtless, cutting a board on the miter saw. She stopped to admire the view.

John Morris was handsome—but not in a glossy magazine way. He wasn't pretty. He was solid, sun-browned, and the way his muscles flexed with each movement left no doubt he'd stayed fit in prison. Standing there shirtless, sweat gleaming across his shoulders, he looked like someone out of a fantasy she hadn't known she had.

She was so caught up in staring that she didn't notice when the saw stopped.

When she finally noticed the silence and dragged her gaze to his face, she found him watching her—smiling slightly, as if he knew exactly what she'd been thinking.

"How's it going?" she asked, trying for casual.

"Good. You?"

"I've picked a paint color—well, Uncle Bill picked it. Long story. Anyway, I'll need to head to town for supplies soon, but I thought I'd see if you need help."

"Actually, yeah. I could use a second set of hands to hold the molding while I nail it in place."

"Perfect. I can manage that."

He grabbed several shorter boards and handed them to her. "Can you carry these inside? I'll grab the rest."

Entering the dining room with the boards, she set them down, then stood to study the space. She hadn't settled on a paint color yet, but she wanted it to feel warm and inviting. A place for laughter and comfort.

John laid his boards beside hers, then picked up a long one.

"I marked them on the back," he said, showing her the pencil lines. "This one goes along the top of the far wall."

"Okay, let's do this."

"Can you hold this a sec?" he asked, passing the board to her.

While she held it, he crouched to open a box of finishing nails, sliding four between his lips and slipping a handful into his pocket. He tucked the hammer into his waistband, then straightened and took the board from her, checking the markings.

He lifted it toward the ceiling. "Hold it here."

Teresa stepped in—only to find him blocking the spot where she needed to stand. Seeming to realize it, John took a step away from the wall without removing his hands, creating a small space for her. She slipped between John and the wall, her back brushing against his chest. Her hips pressed into his.

The contact made her breath catch.

His warmth was solid, surrounding. Her arms brushed his as she lifted them to steady the board. When he let go, the board slipped. Instinctively, he laid his hands over hers, pressing the board—and her hands—firmly into place.

She froze.

The air grew thicker, charged.

"Can you handle it?" he asked, voice low.

Her brain short-circuited. "Wh-what?"

"The board," he said, with the hint of a smile in his tone. "Can you hold it while I nail it in?"

"Oh. Right. The board. Yes. Got it."

His chuckle was barely suppressed as he stepped away, but the warmth of his body lingered.

She closed her eyes and rested her forehead against the wall, feeling heat suffuse her cheeks. *Please let the floor swallow me whole.*

John hammered two nails at each end, then added a few more along the center. "One down, seven to go."

They worked another hour to finish the molding. By the time they were done, Teresa desperately needed an ice-cold shower.

Standing beneath the spray a few minutes later, she let the warm water course over her as she ran soap over her body. Unbidden came the fantasy of John's hands touching her, caressing her.

Becoming overheated, she twisted the hot water knob to reduce the temperature, but accidentally turned the knob too far. When she tried to turn it back the other way, it wouldn't turn. She gripped it tighter and applied force. At first, the knob resisted, but then it suddenly gave way and spun freely around and around.

Damn it.

She hurriedly stepped back as the shower water turned ice cold and then twisted the cold-water knob to shut it off. That knob also came off in her hand.

Of all the luck! The ice-cold shower was supposed to have been figurative, not literal.

She was still covered in soap and needed to rinse off, but the water was growing bitterly cold. She reached up to tilt the showerhead down, but then it, too, broke off in her hand.

Water was suddenly spraying everywhere. She yelped as it blasted her in the face and held up her hands to block it.

"Teresa? Are you okay?"

It was John. He was at the door.

"Water's going everywhere," she yelled back. "I can't turn it off."

Before she could tell him not to, he'd opened the door and come into the bathroom. Teresa scrambled to grab the shower curtain and hold it against her as John reached past her. He slammed his fist down on the diverter pin, and all the water started coming out of the faucet instead of the showerhead.

"Oh," she said, wondering why she hadn't thought to do that herself. "Thanks."

He turned to her. "You're welcome." His words died in his throat as his gaze dropped and his eyes grew saucer-wide.

Confused, Teresa gazed down at herself. "Oh, my God," she yelped, finally realizing the shower curtain she was using to cover herself was clear and doing nothing to hide her bits and pieces. "Don't look! Turn around!"

He immediately did as she ordered, and she dropped the shower curtain to retrieve the towel hanging nearby. As she reached for it, though, her eyes strayed to the mirror, where her gaze met his. "Close your eyes!" she screeched, grabbing at the towel. Only the towel she grabbed wasn't nearly big enough to cover her.

"It's a damn hand towel!" she moaned, her face heating with mortification.

"What can I do?" he asked, his eyes still closed.

"Get out and see if you can shut the water off," she told him, bending over in hopes the short towel would cover more of her.

Without opening his eyes, John turned for the door, but misjudged his direction and ran into the door frame.

"Ow!" he muttered, staggering back and holding a hand up to his nose. To his credit, his eyes never opened, and he readjusted his trajectory and finally made it through the open doorway.

With the water still pouring into the tub, Teresa stepped out and closed the door. Then she searched through the cupboard until she found a full-sized towel, which she wrapped around herself. Finally, she eased herself down to sit on the toilet lid and covered her face with her hands.

She was so embarrassed, she wasn't sure how she'd face him again. The only solution was to never leave the bathroom. Ever.

At that moment, the flow of water into the tub slowed, sputtered and then stopped altogether.

John had found the water shut-off. Knowing he must still be outside where the cut-off valve was located, she opened the door and hurried as fast as she could with wet feet to her bedroom.

Fortunately, that last dousing of ice-cold water had rinsed most of the soap away, so once she dried off, there was no lingering soap film covering her skin. As she pulled on clean clothes, she heard John walk past her room, on his way to the bathroom, she surmised.

She finished putting on her clothes and, with the damp towel in her hand, headed for the bathroom, where she found John using another towel to dry the floor. Unsure what to say, she simply stood there and watched him work.

"Any chance you know how to fix the shower?" she asked.

He looked up at her and grimaced. "If it's a plumbing issue, no. You'll need to call a plumber. If it's just a case of old hardware, I can probably figure it out after watching a video or two."

"I'll run into town and buy replacement hardware," she said. "Maybe we try that first and if it doesn't work, then I'll spring for a plumber."

"Sounds good."

"All right then. While I'm in town, I'll pick up something for dinner. Any preferences?"

He seemed to consider it, then said. "Cheeseburger and fries sound good."

She nodded. "Yes, they do." She started to leave but turned back to him and gestured to the bathroom. "Sorry about—all of it. I didn't mean to deny you a shower."

"No worries. And you didn't deny me a shower. You merely delayed it. As soon as we finish eating, I'll replace the hardware and, if we're lucky, we'll be back in business."

She shook her head. "I don't know what I would have done without you."

"I have a feeling you would have figured it out, but I'm glad I'm here to help." He cleared his throat. "I should apologize for barging into the bathroom like I did, but I can't honestly say I'm sorry about it. A man never regrets getting to see a beautiful woman wearing nothing more than a see-through shower curtain."

Heat flushing her cheeks, Teresa wasn't sure how to respond, so she simply turned and rushed away. As she started down the stairs, she thought she heard his soft laughter.

Chapter Twelve

The trip into town had taken her almost an hour.

"I'm back," Teresa called out as she set the two bags of food on the kitchen table.

"I'll be right down," John's voice floated down to her from upstairs.

When she'd reached the hardware store, she'd called The Waterin' Hole, a local bar and grill, to place their dinner order. Then she'd gone inside the hardware store where luck had, once again, been on her side. Parker was working and when she'd told him about the shower head and water knobs breaking, he'd known exactly what she needed. He'd even shown her the tools she'd need to install the parts, and after checking them against a mental list of what was in her toolbox at the house, she'd purchased a set of Allen wrenches.

Then, she'd headed over to The Waterin' Hole to pick up their to-go order.

"The food smells great," John said, coming into the kitchen.

"We should eat it while it's hot." She grabbed two cans of Diet Coke from the refrigerator and offered him one.

"Sure, thanks." He took the can from her, popped the top and took a long swallow. "Yeah, that hits the spot."

"Good." She set her drink on the table and went back to the refrigerator. "I wasn't sure what you like on your burger, so I told them to skip the condiments and put the veggies on the side." Taking the ketchup, mayonnaise and mustard out of the refrigerator, she carried them over to the table and then took the seat across from him.

She smiled and dug into the food bag. Pulling out the top Styrofoam box, she set it in front of him. "I wasn't sure how you liked your burger, so I had them put the cheese, pickles, tomato, onion and lettuce on the side."

"Thanks." He opened the box and inhaled deeply. "Smells great."

For the next couple of minutes, they ate in silence. Teresa started on her fries first, while they were still hot and crispy, not realizing until that moment how hungry she was. She figured from the way he was eating, he had been just as hungry.

Halfway through her cheeseburger, Teresa started feeling like a fat tick on a lazy dog; she was so full.

"Can I ask you a personal question?" John asked.

"You can ask," she replied and was happy to see him smile at the implication that she might not answer his question.

"Fair enough," he said. "You said your mother disappeared when you were little." She nodded. "Does that mean your father raised you?"

She shook her head. "He actually disappeared when my mother did. Everyone assumed they left together."

"I'm assuming the police investigated your parents' disappearance. Did they ever discover anything?"

"Are you asking if there was any sign of foul play?" He nodded. "No, which they thought was strange. There was nothing out of place. Everything was exactly where it should be—except my parents."

"What does that mean—everything was where it should be?"

"The house was clean, spotless." She frowned. "In fact, I don't think I'd ever seen it that clean before, except if we were expecting company." She thought back. "I wonder if they were expecting someone to come over that day after I went to school? Maybe that person abducted them."

"Neither of your parents mentioned company coming over?"

"No. Well, I didn't actually talk to Mom that morning. She was still in bed. Dad said she was exhausted, which makes sense since she was up all night cleaning. I remember waking up once, wondering why she was cleaning so late at night."

"You didn't get out of bed to check?"

She tried to bring more of the memory to the surface. "I think I was coming down with a cold or something. I was so tired that I actually fell asleep while eating dinner. My dad woke me up just long enough to go to bed."

"How was your dad that morning?"

"He seemed fine. He made me chocolate chip pancakes and then drove me to school." She sighed, trying to rein in a sudden wave of sadness. "That was the last time I saw him."

"Were their cars in the garage when you got home?"

"No, but they both worked. That's why I didn't call anyone right away. Not until after it got late. That's when I called my grandparents."

"What about work? Did they show up at their respective jobs?"

She frowned, wondering why she'd never thought to ask that question before. Then she remembered. "They disappeared on a Thursday. Mom had a part-time job as an office assistant and didn't work Thursdays and Fridays. Dad—I don't remember what he did. My grandmother would never talk about him other than to say he was a 'no-good drunken bum.' She didn't like him much." She'd been picking at the Styrofoam of the food container but now looked at him. "You ask questions like a cop or a private investigator."

"Sorry," he apologized. "I have a naturally inquisitive mind, and I don't like questions with no answers."

"Me, neither. One reason I moved back to Las Palomas was because I was hoping maybe, if they were dead, they'd come visit me as ghosts." Again, she shrugged. "Which I guess my mother did, in a way. She came to see you." She fell quiet as the implication of that hit her. "I guess that means she's really dead."

"I'm sorry," he said. "But there might be another explanation. We can't know for sure."

She smiled, feeling the familiar melancholy settle over her. "I just wish I knew the truth."

Chapter Thirteen

Teresa floated in that weightless place between sleep and waking, where thoughts felt thin and slippery.

At first, there was only the sound—muffled voices bleeding through the dark. A woman's voice, sharp but breaking around the edges. A man's, low and rough, each word carrying a hard edge she couldn't quite understand.

She tried to focus, but the words themselves kept drifting away, like scraps of paper pulled by the wind.

Then came a dull, sickening thunk—not loud, but heavy. Followed by a quick gasp that cut off too soon.

Then, as is often the case in dreams, time jumped forward, and the air carried a new scent thick with the sharp, acrid bite of something chemical. Bleach. It stung her nose even as she lay still, not daring to move.

The voices had quieted. In their place came a strange, rhythmic hum, deep and mechanical like a vacuum cleaner pushing back and forth.

Her heartbeat grew louder in her ears. Then a shadow moved in the space beyond her half-closed eyes—tall, deliberate, blocking the sliver of light under a doorway.

The hum stopped. Silence pressed in.

Her body felt heavy, her limbs unresponsive, as if she were sinking into the bed. Something tugged at the edges of her thoughts, urging her to lay still, to stay quiet.

And then—nothing but the fading scent of bleach and the ghost of a voice muttering words she couldn't make out.

Teresa woke with a start, her breath quick and shallow. The dream slipped away almost instantly, leaving only a faint chemical sting in her nose that had no place in the waking world.

It made sense, she supposed. In telling John about her parents' disappearance, she'd brought the memory of them to the forefront of her subconscious. Of course, she would dream about them.

She lay there a few more minutes, listening to the sound of her breathing, giving her heart rate and nerves a chance to calm down. Then she reached over and turned on the bedside lamp. There was no point in pretending she would fall back asleep, and it was much too early to start on the next renovation project. The sun wouldn't be up for another three hours.

Stacking her two pillows so she could lie against them and be propped up, she picked up her Kindle from the nightstand. When it was closer to dawn, she would go downstairs and relax by baking breakfast muffins. Until then, she would read.

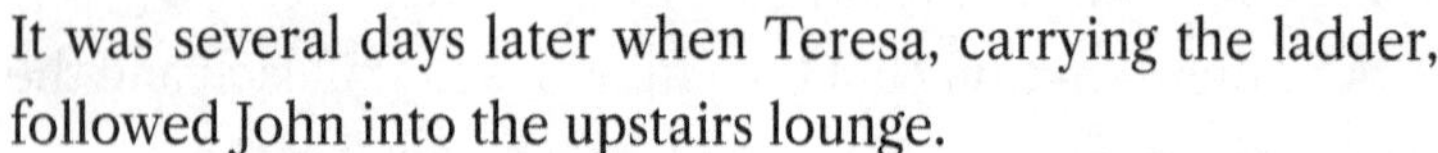

It was several days later when Teresa, carrying the ladder, followed John into the upstairs lounge.

John set the two ceiling fan boxes he'd carried up on the floor and then looked around. "This room is really looking good."

Teresa paused to look around. "I love it."

They'd torn down the wall separating two of the up-stairs rooms because neither room, by itself, had been large enough to be a bedroom. Now the space was perfect for an upstairs common room where guests could gather to watch TV, play cards, read or whatever. They'd spent the morning putting up the crown molding and even though it was well past lunch time, all that was left was to replace the two original light fixtures with ceiling fans and change out the electrical outlet and light switch faceplates. Neither Teresa nor John had wanted to stop their forward momentum to eat lunch, so they'd agreed to keep working and eat later.

"Let me help you with that," John said, taking the ladder from her. She watched him set it up beneath the first of the two lights.

"Are you sure you wouldn't rather I hired an electrician?" She looked around the room as if, at any second, a live wire would drop from the ceiling and electrocute her.

He went over to the open toolbox and started digging around for a Phillips-head screwdriver. "An electrician will cost you a fortune, and there's really no need to hire one." He grabbed the screwdriver and a pair of wire cutters and stuck them in his back pocket. "I turned off the power to this room at the breaker box." He crossed to the closest light switch and flipped it up. When the light fixture remained dark, he flipped the switch down and crossed to the far end of the room to repeat the process. The fixture at that end also remained dark. "See? We're all good. Plus, I watched a couple of videos on changing out light fixtures last night. It doesn't look that hard."

"Famous last words," she muttered.

"I think the hardest part is going to be on you. I'll need you to hold the ceiling fan close to the ceiling so I can connect the wires."

"Sure. No problem." *How hard can that be?*

Harder than she expected, as it turned out. Removing the old light fixtures had been easy. Now, after only five minutes of standing with her arms raised above her head, the ceiling fan felt like it weighed a thousand pounds.

"You almost done?"

"Yeah, unfortunately, it's not as easy as the videos made it look. The color of these old wires isn't the same as in the video. The last thing we need is for me to connect the wrong wires together. One spark and this entire house could go up in flames. Of course, maybe at this point, you'd rather have the insurance money?"

"Don't even joke about that," Teresa moaned. "Because I think I forgot to put the insurance payment in the mail. If the house burns down now, I'm not sure it's covered."

"You're kidding?"

Feeling his gaze on her, she looked up to meet his. "I wish I were." Her arms now burned from the lack of circulation, and she tried to bite back a groan of pain. "Are you finished? I don't think I can hold this much longer."

As if her words triggered a reaction, her arms began to shake.

"Hold it still," he ordered her.

"I can't." And it was true. She'd never had much upper-arm strength, and holding the fixture above her head for so long had completely zapped what little she had. "Oh, crap!" Her arms finally gave out, and she lost her grip on the fixture. She dodged to the side, praying the fixture didn't hit her on the way down—only, it didn't fall.

"Thanks," she muttered, assuming John had caught it. "Can you hold it a few minutes while the circulation returns to my arms?"

He glanced down at her, looking perplexed. "Hold what?"

She stepped closer to take a better look. Sure enough, the ceiling fan was suspended in place, exactly where she'd been holding it.

Above her, John swore. "What the hell?"

She thought he looked a little spooked and smiled at the pun. "Thank you, Uncle Bill. I appreciate you holding that for me."

She felt a warm breeze against her face and knew she'd been right. Uncle Bill was there with them.

"See? Having a ghost in the house comes in handy."

"If you say so," he muttered, pausing for a moment before finally turning his attention back to the light fixture.

He worked a few minutes longer while Teresa watched him, pacing around the room and swinging her arms back and forth to speed up the circulation.

"Okay, I think I've got it," he finally said. "Let me screw it into the receiver plate enough to hold it in place. Then, I'll run down and turn on the power. We'll see if I connected it correctly. Um, Uncle Bill, could you hold it a little higher?"

Teresa felt a burst of satisfaction as the ceiling fan moved closer to the ceiling.

"I'll be damned," she heard John mutter.

John was still feeling shocked a few minutes later as he headed outside to the breaker box. Having a ghost help with the renovation work was a first for him.

Remembering the phone in his hand, he spoke into it. "Almost there."

Teresa, still back in the common room with her phone, replied, "Okay."

Reaching the breaker box, he flipped the switch for the upstairs room. "Power's back on."

Over the phone, he heard a whoop of delight. "It's working!"

He had to admit to feeling a burst of satisfaction, probably due more to not disappointing Teresa than to successfully hooking up the ceiling fan, though there was some satisfaction in that as well, considering the job had been slightly harder than he'd expected.

"All right, I'm turning the power off again so we can hook up the second one."

"Okay," she said.

An hour later, both ceiling fans were hung, and John was just screwing the last faceplate into place while Teresa carried the ceiling fan boxes, now containing the original lights, outside to the garage. At first, he'd thought new faceplates were an unnecessary expense, but after he finished and stood to study the room, he had to admit they added a nice finishing touch.

"Oh, wow!" Teresa exclaimed, walking into the room. "I love how this room turned out. I can hardly wait to see it with furniture."

"Do you have any?"

She smiled. "I do. It's in the next room."

"Let's get it."

"Really?"

She looked so eager, he couldn't bring himself to say no. "Yeah, might as well. We can't work on that room until it's empty."

For the next half hour, they carried two couches, three stuffed chairs and a wooden card table with chairs into the room. Then John obediently moved the furniture around until Teresa was satisfied.

"Perfect," she finally said, excitement filling her tone.

He moved to stand beside her and surveyed the room. He had to admit, with the furniture in place, the room felt warm and inviting.

"Oh, my God!" She clapped her hands together. "I can't believe this room is actually finished!" She turned and wrapped her arms around him, giving him a hug. "Thank you so much for your help. I don't think I'd ever have gotten this far without you."

For a stunned moment, John simply held her, all too aware of her slender form pressed against him. He'd been trying so hard to ignore his growing attraction to her. Teresa, he knew, had no idea how beautiful a person she was, both inside and out, but if he kept holding her this close, she'd know exactly how attractive he found her soon enough.

That might prove embarrassing to both of them, so he reluctantly released her and stepped back.

"Sorry," she said, misinterpreting his move.

"No, please. Don't be. I'm just really sweaty and gross."

She waved her hand in the air. "I don't care about that. I'm dirty, too."

"What do you say we go out to dinner tonight? We can celebrate our success."

"Oh, I'd like that. My treat, though."

"We'll see," he told her. "You worked just as hard as I did, so maybe we should go Dutch?"

"We'll discuss who's paying later. You can have the shower first," she offered.

"That's okay." He grinned at her. "I've learned that you take longer to get ready than I do."

She cocked her head to one side and grimaced. "You're right. Okay, I'll go first."

"All I ask is that you leave me some hot water this time."

"I can do that." Giving him a smile, she left the room.

By the time Teresa and John walked into The Waterin' Hole, the dinner crowd was just gathering. They found an empty table off to the side where they hoped they could be alone, but the surrounding tables started filling up fast. The server came, and while John ordered a celebratory beer, Teresa ordered a margarita.

"Hey, you two. Mind if we join you?"

Teresa looked up to find Chad Lucero and Steve Guilbert standing there. She stood and gave each man a hug, before turning to John. "Would you mind if they joined us?" She realized asking him in public put him on the spot, but he only shrugged.

"As long as you're okay with it."

She turned back to the two men and gestured to the empty chairs at their table. "Please. Join us."

Once they did, Teresa made introductions. "John, you and Chad have already met, and this," she said, gesturing, "is Steve Guilbert. He and Chad work together at the police department. Steve—this," she gestured to John, "is John Morris. He's been helping me renovate my grandmother's house."

Chad held his hand out to shake John's across the table. "Mr. Morris, it's good to see you again."

"Call me John." He finished shaking hands with Chad and held his hand out to Steve. "Nice to meet you."

They shook hands.

"Chad, Steve and I all went to high school together," Teresa said, sensing there was about to be an awkward silence and wanting to avoid it.

The server arrived, bringing John and Teresa's drinks.

"What brings you two into town?" Chad asked after the server left to fill his and Steve's drink orders.

"We're celebrating," Teresa told them. "We finished one of the larger rooms upstairs, and it looks fantastic. John did such a great job of, well, of pretty much everything."

Chad looked from Teresa to John and back again. "That's great. Congratulations."

"With the way things were going with Bubba, I didn't think I'd ever see a room get finished."

"Bubba Raleigh?" Steve asked.

"Yeah, you know him?"

Steve frowned. "Yeah. I've responded to a couple of calls involving him, mostly public intoxication and disorderly conduct."

"He's the worst handyman I've ever worked with," Teresa said. "Do you know he did more damage to my house than actual repairs?"

"I can't believe you hired him," Chad muttered.

She glared at him. "At the time, he was the only helper available. Of course, maybe next time, you can give me a heads up before I hire someone who's going to be trouble?"

Chad had the decency to look chagrined. "I promise."

"How's the house coming?" Steve asked. "With all the renovation you've been doing, I figured by now you'd have found the diamond."

Teresa scowled. "You know perfectly well there's no diamond."

"What's this about a diamond?" Across from her, John looked confused.

The server appeared with their food before Teresa could answer him, so she waited until the server left.

"It's just an old wives' tale, nothing more." Knowing that wouldn't be enough to satisfy his curiosity—and knowing if she didn't finish the story, Chad or Steve would—she continued.

"Back in the early 1900's, the Meyers house was a Bed and Breakfast owned and operated by my maternal great-grandmother. Some of its more infamous guests in the 1940's were Donny Rangel, a small-time gangster; Donny's fiancée, Sarah, and his brother, Bobby. The day before they arrived in town, Donny and Bobby stole the Stanford diamond—a one-hundred forty-nine carat canary yellow diamond owned by the Hugh Stanford family.

"They came to Las Palomas to meet up with Sarah. Well, one night, Donny was arrested for drunk driving. When he was taken into the station and fingerprinted, the police learned an APB had been issued statewide for him and his brother. When asked where his brother was, Donny claimed that Bobby and Sarah had run off to Mexico together. And he denied knowing anything about a stolen diamond. The police searched him and the B&B, but they found nothing."

Chad shook his head. "With a talented lawyer, Donny probably would have walked free, but then he did something stupid."

John raised an eyebrow in question.

Steve picked up the tale. "He pretended to be sick, and when a newbie cop checked on him, Donny grabbed the man's gun and tried to shoot his way out."

"He ended up getting shot himself," Chad said. "But not before killing several officers and the department's receptionist. Yolanda Glossop. Today, she haunts the old courthouse and is known as the Pink Lady—because the day she died, she was wearing a pink blouse and sweater." To Teresa, he said, "You'll have to take John there."

Teresa looked over at John, whose narrow-eyed expression suggested he wasn't entirely buying the suggestion that the courthouse was haunted. She was struggling with something to say when she saw his gaze flick up to something behind her. A moment later, she felt a hand on her shoulder, and when she looked up, Zelda was standing there, smiling down at her.

"Hello, all," she greeted them, bending low to give Teresa, Chad and Steve each a side hug. Following her was Cindy Pecoraro, another old friend from high school.

"Hey, Zelda. Cindy," Chad greeted them.

"I didn't know you were back in town," Cindy said to Teresa, after giving her a hug. "It's so good to see you again."

"Hey, Cindy. It's good to see you, too. I've only been back a couple of months."

"She's turning her grandmother's house into a B&B," Chad volunteered.

"That's so cool." Cindy's gaze flickered to John, and Teresa hurried to make introductions.

"Cindy, this is John Morris. He's helping me with the renovations. John, this is Cindy." She gestured to the entire group. "We all went to high school together."

"It's nice to meet you, Cindy," John said.

"Cindy's husband," Zelda added, "is in Houston for work, so Cindy and I decided to make it a girl's night, starting with a couple of drinks here at The Waterin' Hole. Unfortunately," she looked around the crowded room, "it looks like everyone in town had the same idea."

"Take our seats," Chad offered, pushing away from the table and gesturing for Steve to do the same.

"Are you leaving?" Zelda asked, sounding disappointed.

"No. I think I know where we can find a couple of extra chairs. If the server comes back while we're gone, order me another beer, will you?"

"Sure thing—and thanks," Zelda said, now regarding Chad warmly. Teresa wondered if there might be something more than a casual friendship between them.

"Steve, you want another beer?" Chad asked, interrupting Teresa's thoughts.

"Yeah. That'd be great."

Chad looked at Zelda, who nodded. "Got it."

The two men walked off, and as Zelda and Cindy took the vacated chairs, Teresa saw John raise his hand to signal the server. After their drink order was placed, Chad and Steve reappeared, each carrying a chair over their heads as they wove their way through the crowded room.

Moments later, the six of them were sitting around the table, drinking and conversing like old friends. John listened to their stories and smiled but shared very little about himself. Teresa understood why. If the others thought it was odd, they said nothing.

A couple sitting at the table beside them finally left, and before anyone could sit there, Steve dragged the table over to butt up against theirs, giving them a little more room.

No sooner had they spread out than another couple approached their table.

"Y'all have room for two more?"

Teresa looked up at the sound of the familiar voice to see two more of her old friends standing there.

"Always," Teresa replied with a smile. Then, turning to John, she made the introductions. "John, this is Elise and Diego Juarez. They own and operate the Double R Ranch outside of town. Elise and Diego, this is John Morris. He's helping me renovate Grandmother's house."

They exchanged greetings and the server was summoned once again to take Elise and Diego's drink order.

"Chad, how's Sam doing?" Elise asked after the server left. Then she turned to Teresa. "You heard Sam was shot when the police confronted JD and his drug dealers? I still can't believe they were transporting their drugs across our property."

Teresa felt chagrined. "I heard." She turned to Chad. "And I should have asked about her sooner." Then, to John she said, "Sam—short for Samantha—is another high school friend and also Chief of Police, currently out on medical leave." She turned back to Chad. "How's she doing?"

"Better. I expect she'll be back at work in the next week or so."

"That's terrific," Elise said.

Diego turned to John. "So, what's your story?"

John's gaze narrowed. "What do you mean?"

Diego shrugged. "I don't know. Where're you from?"

"I grew up in Amarillo, then spent some time in Huntsville," he replied, not bothering to elaborate.

"How'd you two meet?" Elise asked, then glanced at the others. "Sorry. Maybe this is old news?"

"No, I'm curious as well," Cindy piped in.

Teresa inwardly groaned. The way she and John had met wasn't exactly normal—at least, it wouldn't have been normal in any other town. "John gave my mother's ghost a ride into town."

Everyone except John, Chad and Zelda looked confused.

"I remember your mom and dad left town when you were a kid," Diego said. "But I hadn't heard she'd died. I'm sorry."

"Yeah, it was news to me, too," Teresa said.

"Did you get to see her?" Elise asked.

Teresa shook her head. "No—and I don't know why she showed herself to John and not to me."

Elise gave her a sympathetic look. "I'm sorry. I know how you feel." Her father had died recently, and Teresa took the comment to mean that she hadn't seen her father's ghost. She offered Elise a genuine smile.

After that, the conversation turned to stories from their high school days.

Hours passed, and it was late when the conversation finally hit a natural lull. Diego and Elise excused themselves so they could visit friends sitting at another table. After they said goodnight, Zelda stood and announced she was headed to the ladies' room. Cindy stood and went with her.

"Guilbert—you're up!" someone shouted.

The voice sounded as if it had come from the back corner. When Teresa looked that way, she saw that a game of darts had ended, and a man was gesturing at Steve.

Steve pushed away from the table. "Finally. Game of darts anyone?"

"No, thanks," Teresa said. Her throwing skills left much to be desired, and the last thing she wanted to do in this crowded bar was take out someone's eye.

"I think I'll sit this one out, too," Chad said.

Steve looked over at John. "Dude, don't leave me hanging."

John looked over at Teresa, raising an eyebrow in question.

"Yeah, sure. Go play," she urged him, giving him a playful shoulder bump.

Giving a shrug, he stood and followed Steve across the room.

"What's going on? You love playing darts." Teresa asked, pinning Chad with a look. "Did you set this up?"

He gave her a knowing smile. "I might have asked Steve to lure John away if an opportunity presented itself. I wanted a chance to talk to you privately."

Teresa glanced around the crowded room. "I'd hardly call this private."

"Close enough. Look, I'll make this fast before everyone gets back. It looks like you and Morris are getting along well, but I wanted to make sure that's actually the case."

"Yeah. Everything's great. He's been such a big help."

"He's not said or done anything to make you feel uncomfortable?"

"No. And, if you've noticed, he only had one beer tonight. Then he started drinking Coke."

"I noticed that," Chad admitted.

"Chad, I think John's a good guy who made a horrible mistake and paid for it. I hope you'll give him a chance and not hold his past again him."

"If you trust him, then I'm willing to give him a chance," he told her. "But if you ever have any problems, call me."

She nodded. "You know I will."

Chapter Fourteen

"Your friends are nice," John said as they drove back to the house in his car.

"Thanks. I'm kind of surprised to find so many living here. It seemed like we could hardly wait to get out of town after we graduated, so it's funny to see everyone coming back."

"I'm quickly learning that Las Palomas is unique. After growing up here, I would imagine almost any other place might seem a bit—" he paused, struggling for the right word. "Mundane?"

She chuckled. "You're probably right. How many towns can boast they're the Grand Central Station of the spirit world?"

"If I hadn't experienced it for myself, I wouldn't have believed it." He smiled. "Not only do you have a resident ghost, but an infamous gangster once stayed at your house. For the right demographic, that makes your B&B attractive." A dim glow up ahead caught his attention. "Did you leave the upstairs lights on?"

"I can't remember," she admitted, sitting up straighter as she stared at the house out the front windshield. "Maybe?"

She didn't sound sure, and he didn't want to frighten her by telling her he knew for a fact that they'd only left on the kitchen light downstairs.

They were still a couple of houses away, but he pulled the car over to the side, shutting off the headlights. If someone was inside the house, he didn't want them to know he and Teresa had returned.

He turned to her. "Stay here and call the police, just in case."

"What are you going to do?"

"I'm going to check out the house."

She placed her hand on his arm, stopping him. "I don't think that's a good idea. What if someone broke in and they're still there? We should both wait here until the police arrive."

He placed his other hand on top of hers, trying to ignore how perfectly their hands fit together. "I'll be fine. There weren't many good things about prison, but I learned how to take care of myself," he assured her. He gave her hand a gentle squeeze before pulling away. "You have your house keys?"

She nodded and reached into her purse to find them. Then she handed them to him.

"Stay here," he told her, taking the keys. She looked like she wanted to go with him, but nodded. He handed her his car keys. "Lock the door after me."

He got out of the car and quietly pushed the door to, making as little sound as possible. As he approached the house, he had to make a decision. Enter through the front door or the back?

He figured that whoever had broken into the house had gone in through the back door, so he headed around to the back of the house.

When he reached the back door, his heart rate spiked. The door stood open, and he knew damn well that he and Teresa hadn't left it open.

Moving quietly, he entered through the kitchen's back door. As he moved through the kitchen, he pulled a knife from a kitchen drawer. Then he walked as quietly as he could through the front living room, cringing when he saw damage to one of the walls. Someone had taken a sledge-hammer to it, leaving a gaping hole. Anger surged through him, knowing how upset Teresa would be. They'd nearly finished that room.

He reached the stairs and peered up. There was no one standing at the top, so he started up. The hallway when he reached it was empty. He crept down the hall, stopping before each doorway to check the rooms. Two of the rooms had sustained damage.

When he reached the newly finished common room at the end of the hallway, his heart plummeted. There were new holes in two of the walls. Teresa would be heartbroken. She'd been so excited to have finally finished a room. Now this.

He shoved his anger aside and continued to the stairs that led to the third floor. So far, he'd not heard any sounds coming from up there, but that didn't mean there wasn't someone waiting for him.

Halfway up the stairs, he caught the muted sound of a car door shutting outside. He hoped that meant the police had arrived and not that Teresa would be following him inside.

He'd only been on the third level once before, when Teresa had given him a tour of the house. It consisted of a single room.

Unlike the first and second floors, there was little damage to this room. Looking up at the attic access panel in the ceiling, he saw it was closed. He didn't think anyone could have climbed up there and, from the top, retracted the folding ladder and closed the access panel.

"Morris?"

Chad's shout floated up to him from the first floor.

"I'm on the third floor. There's no one here. I'm coming down," he shouted back.

He didn't bother turning off the lights. It was possible Chad would want to dust for fingerprints. Plus, Teresa needed to see the damage. He hated how upset she was going to be.

When he reached the second floor, he ran into Chad coming down the hallway holding a flashlight. "You on duty again?"

Chad nodded. "We're all doing double and triple duty these days. What about the house? Anything taken?"

"I don't think so, but Teresa will need to check her things to see if anything is missing. They sure did a number on the walls, though. Most of the rooms have new holes in them. Might have been kids."

"I don't think so," Chad said, echoing John's earlier words.

"Why not?"

"No spray paint."

John realized he was right. It didn't mean it couldn't have been kids, but usually in those circumstances, the kids left behind their mark.

"Teresa said something about the lights being on, but they were off when you left?"

"That's right."

"That was careless of our vandals," Chad said, "but might be good news for us. Could be they left some prints behind."

John sighed. It was going to be a long night. "I'd better get downstairs before Teresa comes in and sees all this damage."

"Too late."

John looked past Chad in time to see Teresa round the corner of the stairs to the second floor. She looked a bit shell-shocked.

"I'm going to call in a team to dust the place," Chad said before John could respond. "Try not to touch anything. Teresa, I need you to look around and let me know if anything is missing."

She nodded without taking her gaze off John. Chad gave him a sympathetic look before he turned and left them to go downstairs.

"How bad is the damage up here?" she asked once they were alone.

"We have a few more holes to patch," he told her, trying to make light of it.

She sighed. "I'll run into town tomorrow and buy more drywall. How many sheets do you think we need? Two? Three?"

He would have given anything to avoid answering her but knew he couldn't. "More like ten to twelve."

Her eyes grew wide as she stared at him. "What?"

Before he could answer, she started down the hall, stopping at each doorway to check out the damage to the rooms. He followed her, knowing the damage to the common room would hit the hardest.

When they reached it, she stood inside the doorway and slowly looked around the room. Fortunately, whoever had been there hadn't cared about the furniture and had shoved it aside. Everything was coated in drywall dust but was otherwise unharmed. The walls, on the other hand, were a sorry sight with their large gaping holes and pieces of drywall dangling from strips of paper.

Standing behind Teresa, he waited for her reaction. After a moment, when she'd been quiet for too long, he stepped toward her, needing to see her face.

The sight of silent tears coursing down her cheeks was nearly his undoing. Without thinking about what he was doing, he gathered her into his arms, gratified when she wrapped her arms around his waist and laid her head against his chest. Unsure what to say, he simply held her and let her cry.

After several long moments, the tears seemed to stop.

"I can't do this anymore," she mumbled against his chest. "It's too much."

"No, Baby. This is just a speed bump. Half those rooms we hadn't even started on."

"But the common room," she sniffed. "It was finished."

"There is nothing they did I can't fix," he promised, giving her a gentle squeeze. "By the end of tomorrow, that room will be beautiful again."

"Why would anyone do this to my house? I don't understand."

"I don't know," he told her honestly.

He loosened his embrace when she pushed away enough to look up and meet his gaze. "Do you think they'll be back?"

Once again, he had to be honest. "I don't know, but I promise you they won't be back tonight. And tomorrow, I plan to install security cameras so if they come back then, we'll know who they are."

Teresa's shoulders slumped. "I can't afford security cameras."

"I can."

She shook her head. "You don't need to spend your money on my house."

"No," he agreed. "I don't. Which is what makes it such a beautiful gesture on my part." He winked when she looked at him to let her know he was teasing her.

"Do you even know how to install security cameras?"

"I'm sure I can find a video on it. Now, let me escort you to your room where I will wait while you look through your stuff to make sure nothing is missing. Then we'll report back to Chad."

It was almost two in the morning when John left Teresa sitting at the kitchen table to go find Chad. He found the officer on the second floor, standing outside the common room.

"How's Teresa doing?" Chad asked.

"She's still a little freaked out," John admitted. "Do you need us to stick around? Teresa's about to pass out, she's so tired. I think the adrenaline is wearing off."

"Where do you plan to go?"

"I called Ruby Mae. She's got an available room. I booked it for Teresa."

"What about you?"

John shook his head. "I'll come back here and stay—unless you're planning to seal off the house as a crime scene?"

"No. I don't see the point. Nothing was taken. I had my guys dust the light switches and tools for prints. Maybe we'll get lucky."

"Any idea when your team will be through?"

"They're wrapping up now."

"Okay. I'm going to run Teresa over to Ruby Mae's and then I'll be back. I want to be here in case whoever did this comes back."

Chad gave him a pointed look. "Be careful."

John nodded. "I will."

They said their goodbyes, and John went into Teresa's bedroom. Earlier, while he'd waited for her to search through her stuff to see if anything was missing, he'd studied her room. It was surprisingly empty. Either she had very few possessions or she was storing those possessions elsewhere. Either way, it meant that he didn't have to look too hard to locate a small suitcase. He grabbed the folded clothes sitting on top of the antique dresser and placed them into the suitcase. He hadn't wanted to dig through her things, so he hoped the stack of clothes contained a change of underwear.

There was a phone charger plugged into the wall and a Kindle reader on the nightstand, so he added both to the suitcase before heading to the bathroom. Since they shared a bathroom, he knew she kept all of her toiletries in a bag with nothing scattered across the counter. He grabbed the bag and took it back to her bedroom and placed it inside the suitcase. Satisfied that she had enough to get through one night, he closed the suitcase and carried it downstairs.

He found her bent forward over the kitchen table, head resting on her arms, eyes closed. From the sound of her heavy breathing, he knew she'd fallen asleep. He hated to wake her, but he couldn't let her sleep in that position.

"Teresa?" He placed a hand on her shoulder and gave her a soft shake. "Wake up, honey."

"Wha-what?" She stirred, looking at him through barely cracked eyelids.

He placed his hand under her elbow, helping her to her feet. "Come on. I'm taking you to Ruby Mae's."

She was too tired to fight him, and with his help, got to her feet. Then his words must have sunk in because she shook her head. "No, I can't afford to stay there."

"My treat," he told her. "You can't stay here. Your room is covered in fingerprint powder."

"Oh."

She scrunched up her eyes as if she were trying to understand what that meant. Knowing that once she did, she might argue with him about leaving the house, he steered her outside to the car.

They were on their way to Ruby Mae's when her brain must have finally caught up with his words.

"I should stay and clean the house," she complained. "A friend of mine in San Antonio got robbed and after they dusted her place for prints, that black powder was everywhere. She was still cleaning it up a week later."

"You'll get your chance to clean," he assured her. "After you've gotten some sleep."

She was quiet, and he knew she was coming up with a new argument. He nearly smiled when she suddenly blurted out, "I can't stay at Ruby Mae's. I don't have clean clothes. Everything's back at the house."

"I packed a suitcase for you."

That caught her off guard. "You went through my stuff?"

"No. I grabbed the stack of clothes off your dresser and put them in a suitcase for you. Hopefully, there's something there you can change into. And before you ask, I also packed your phone charger, your Kindle reader and your toiletry bag."

"Oh." She sounded surprised. "Thank you." She'd been staring out the front windshield but now turned to look at him. "What about you? Did you get a room?"

He shook his head. "No, and it wasn't because I couldn't afford it. I want to go back to the house and make sure we don't get any more uninvited guests."

"That's not right," she argued. "You also need your sleep, and it could be dangerous staying there at the house alone. I insist you stay at Ruby Mae's tonight as well."

Her words warmed him. "Ruby Mae had only one room available."

"Oh." She fell silent and out of the corner of his eye, he noticed she was chewing on her bottom lip. After a long moment of silence, she said, "I don't mind sharing. I'm sure the room has two beds."

"It doesn't. I asked." He didn't know why he was even allowing her to pursue this line of thinking when he'd already decided to stay at the house, but there was a part of him that was curious.

"You could sleep on the floor. Or ..." There was a long pause. "We could share the bed."

This last was said so softly, he almost didn't hear her.

"You're asking me to share your bed?"

He caught her peering at him in the dark. "Yeah. I mean, we're both adults. And it's just sleep. Right?"

He smiled. "Can I be honest with you?"

"Um, sure." She didn't sound totally convinced.

"When you and I finally share a bed, I can assure you the last thing either of us will do is sleep. But this is not something we're going to discuss at three o'clock in the morning after dealing with a break-in."

"I can't think of a better time to make that decision," he thought he heard her mumble, but she had turned to look out the passenger window and he couldn't be sure.

A few minutes later, they had reached Ruby Mae's. John carried her suitcase as they walked up the front walkway.

Ruby Mae greeted them at the door with a welcoming smile. If she was feeling put out at the lateness of the hour, she didn't let on. John knew he was leaving Teresa in excellent hands as he left the B&B. Ruby Mae would mother Teresa and make sure she was comfortable.

Before he left, he promised to pick her up when she called to say she was ready, but encouraged her to sleep in.

Returning to the house, he found that most of the police cars and vans had left. Only Chad's truck remained parked out front.

"I'm surprised Teresa didn't come back with you," he said when John stepped into the house.

"I think if she hadn't been so exhausted, she might have tried harder," John admitted. "But she doesn't need to be here tonight. She's been under enough stress already. Besides, Ruby Mae will look after her tonight. That will give me time to clean up the place before she returns."

"All right then," Chad said. "I'll leave you to it."

John walked him to the door. "You'll let us know if you get any hits on those prints?"

"Yep. And call me if you get any more visitors."

"Will do." The men had stepped outside and stood on the front porch. After shaking hands, John waited on the front porch until Chad drove away. Then he went inside.

Looking around, he took a deep breath. Despite her promise to sleep late, John knew Teresa wouldn't stay away long. He had a lot to do and not much time to do it in. Well, this wouldn't be the first night of sleep he'd missed and likely wouldn't be his last.

Going into the kitchen, he brewed himself a cup of coffee. When it was done, he took it upstairs. After stopping to change clothes, he carried the coffee down the hallway and stood before the open door to the vandalized room. There was so much damage.

Where do I even start?

CHAPTER FIFTEEN

Where do I even start?

Bobby Rangel stood in the dim hallway, breathing shallowly through his nose, the tip of his index finger poised an inch from the painted wood of Sarah's door. The Meyers B&B creaked and settled all around him, old bones popping in the darkness; the faint aroma of last night's pot roast still haunted the air, mixing with the chemical tang of furniture polish and the sour sweat he'd worked up running interference for Donny all day.

Donny. His older brother snored like a lawnmower with a slipped belt—every third inhalation skipping, catching, then launching into a stuttering crescendo that echoed through the upstairs. Donny's door was closed, but Bobby couldn't shake the feeling that his brother's presence seeped out under the gap and onto the threadbare carpet like a toxic fog.

It was stupid what he was doing. Risky, even by Rangel standards. If Donny found out he was slinking around in the middle of the night, hovering outside his fiancée's bedroom, he'd tear Bobby apart, marrow and all. But Bobby couldn't make himself leave; he had to talk to her. Had to see her. Had to ... something. He didn't know what.

He pressed his ear to the door. For a long minute, nothing—then, the faintest rustle of bedsheets, the gentle groan of bedsprings. Sarah was awake. Or maybe she slept lightly, maybe she never really slept at all, not after everything Donny had done. The thought made Bobby's stomach knot.

He forced himself to count to ten, then, barely more than a whisper, he rapped on the door. *Tap. Tap.* He listened. Silence, but not the suffocating kind—just a hush, a pause. He tried again. *Tap. Tap.*

This time, there was a response. Footsteps, careful and quiet, padded to the other side. The crackle of a lock, then a hinge squeaking just enough to open the door two inches.

Light from inside bled out across the hallway floor in a thin, uncertain line. Sarah's face appeared, half-obscured by shadow, her hair falling loose and dark around her shoulders. She looked at him with eyes too tired for the hour, but alert—curious, but not afraid. Never afraid of him.

"Bobby?" Her voice was soft enough to be a secret.

He nodded once, not trusting his own voice. He couldn't help glancing over his shoulder at Donny's door, even though he knew Donny had drunk so much he would sleep through an air raid.

Sarah opened the door wider, just enough for him to squeeze inside if he wanted. Her white nightgown was old-fashioned, high at the collar, but even in the gloom he could see the bruising along her jaw where Donny had tagged her a week ago. It made his hands want to strangle something, mostly Donny.

"Is everything all right?" she whispered.

"No." He swallowed. "Can we talk?"

She hesitated only a second before stepping aside, silent and barefoot on the scuffed wood floor. The room smelled faintly of her—soap, talc, a hint of floral perfume she must have applied out of habit, even out here in the middle of nowhere. It made his heart ache.

As he slipped into her room, Bobby paused and listened one last time for Donny's snore. Still going, a lullaby of monsters. He exhaled and shut the door behind him, careful with the latch.

The room was barely wide enough for both of them. Sarah hovered by the window, arms folded loosely at her waist, head tipped as if bracing for trouble. Bobby stood by the door, back pressed to the wood, heart knocking double-time. He didn't know where to put his hands, so he stuffed them deep in his pockets, shoulders rolled forward to make himself smaller, less threatening. In the pocket of his slacks, his lucky marble clicked against his thumbnail. The marble was a little token of luck, a thing he'd carried since he was a kid, before he realized you make your own luck in life.

A nightstand lamp burned low, casting soft gold across the bedspread and onto Sarah's face. She looked like something out of a dream he'd had a hundred times and never remembered except as a feeling in his chest when he woke. He tried to swallow, but his throat was sandpaper. He'd rehearsed what he wanted to say all night, and now the words tasted bitter. "I didn't mean to wake you."

"I wasn't sleeping."

He believed her. Her eyes never looked rested, not even when they laughed. He wished he could've given her one good night's sleep, just one, before everything went to hell.

They stood like that, silent, for what felt like an eternity. The only sound was the hum of an electric fan on the dresser, which wasn't doing anything to cool the sweat gathering under his collar. He looked at her, really looked, and wondered what she saw when she looked back. A screw-up with dirt under his nails and a criminal for a brother. Probably nothing good.

"Sarah, I ..." He couldn't get it out. He dug deeper, into the place where words usually came from. All he found was mud. "I know I shouldn't be here. It's just—"

She cut him off, gentle. "If Donny finds out, he'll be mad."

"Donny's always mad." It slipped out before he could catch it, and he watched her flinch. That was Donny's legacy: bruises you could see and some you couldn't. "Sorry. I just meant—" He trailed off, suddenly embarrassed.

She moved closer, just a step, but enough that he caught the scent of her shampoo. "Why did you come?"

Why had he come? He didn't even know. Maybe it was that he'd caught her crying in the parlor earlier, face pressed to her palms so hard he thought she'd bruise herself. Maybe it was how she said his name, Bobby, with a kind of hope behind the fear. Maybe it was how Donny called her "Baby Doll" like she was a toy, and Bobby hated the way toys always ended up broken.

Or maybe it was because he'd never wanted anything as badly as he wanted her, and wanting was the only thing he was good at.

He risked a glance at her, hoping for a sign—some green light, however dim. Instead, he saw the lines of worry around her mouth, the way she bit her bottom lip and hid her hands in the folds of her nightgown. She was scared, but she hadn't sent him away.

He stepped away from the door, moved toward her, slowly, like he might scare her off if he moved too quickly. He stopped an arm's length away.

His chest cracked open, just a sliver, and all the words he'd held back came tumbling out at once. "Donny doesn't deserve you, Sarah. He never did. I know he's my brother, and maybe I shouldn't say it, but it's the truth. You could do better. You could—" He paused, knowing he should return to his room without saying another word; and yet, knowing he wouldn't. Instead, he met her gaze, steady as he could manage. "There're things you don't know."

They fell silent, the only sound that of the fan's ticking as it oscillated. Outside the window, a cicada buzzed once and went quiet. Somewhere down the hallway, Donny's drunken snore rose and fell like the low grumble of an engine about to stall.

Sarah was the first to break the quiet. "You're scaring me, Bobby."

"I don't mean to." He took a cautious step closer, then stopped, hands still buried deep in his pockets. "But you need to know who Donny really is."

"I already know who he is." Her hand lifted as if to touch her bruised jaw and then dropped just as quickly. "Or I'm starting to."

"No," Bobby mumbled. "You think you know. But it's worse than you think."

She looked at him again, a little more guarded now. "Then tell me."

He hesitated. The truth weighed heavy in his chest, but it needed air. He wasn't just doing this for her anymore. He was doing it because the lie was killing him too.

"You've seen the papers, haven't you?" he asked. "About the Stanford diamond?"

Sarah frowned. "Of course. It's everywhere—radio, headlines. The biggest jewel heist in years. Why?"

Bobby's breath hitched. He looked at her like it might be the last time she'd ever look at him without hate in her eyes.

"We stole it," he said. "Donny and I."

Sarah moved, almost absently, to the edge of the bed and quietly sank down until she was perched on the edge of it.

She didn't blink.

Didn't breathe.

The only sound was the fan, spinning on like it didn't give a damn.

Then, her mouth parted. "What?"

CHAPTER SIXTEEN

John blinked. "What?"

He'd been at the hardware store as soon as it opened in order to purchase more supplies. Hefting a box of drywall screws onto the counter, he'd been fishing for his wallet when Parker, the clerk, caught him off guard.

"The diamond." Parker grinned. "You find it yet?" He didn't wait for John's answer. "Word is it's still hidden somewhere in that old B&B you're working on. You know, the one Donny Rangel stayed in back in the forties."

John stared at him, momentarily stunned. "Donny's brother ran off with the diamond," he finally said, repeating the story he'd heard the night before.

"No," Parker argued. "Some high school kid was digging through the historical records from the old jail. Found a report written up by one of the guards the night before Donny was killed. It didn't get much attention at the time because, well, he died the next day in the shootings. But according to this guard, he overheard Donny talking to his cellmate about how Bobby and Sarah never found the diamond and had to take off without it. So *ipso facto*, the diamond must still be in the house." He chuckled, sliding John's receipt across the counter. "Hell, if I were you, I'd keep an eye out."

John forced a vague smile and pocketed his change. "Yeah. Sure."

He left the store with his supplies, but the words stuck like splinters under his skin. By the time he loaded the truck, curiosity had gnawed its way past caution.

He wondered ...

Later that morning, Teresa stood frozen in the doorway of the second-floor common room, expecting to see wreckage. Instead, she saw half the damage repaired—patches of fresh drywall, seams neat and square, and a new sheet waiting against the far wall, but there was no sign of John.

She called his name.

From inside the wall came a scuffle. A moment later, John's face appeared in the opening, lit by the glow of his flashlight. When he saw her, he grinned.

"Good morning. How'd you get here?"

"Ruby Mae," she said, still dazed. "I brought breakfast and coffee. They're downstairs." She looked around. "You've been busy. It looks great. I can't believe you got so much done."

He smiled. "I didn't want you to have to come home and deal with it."

She shook her head. "It's really remarkable what you've done here." She turned her gaze back to the hole in the drywall from which he'd just stepped. "Um, what were you doing behind the wall?"

He gave her a too-casual shrug. "Short answer? Looking for the Stanford diamond."

Teresa blinked, certain she'd misheard. "What? That's crazy! We don't even know if the old stories about Donny Rangel are true. And even if they are, the diamond wouldn't be here. Bobby took it when he ran away with Donny's fiancée."

"Yeah. About that." He gestured toward the stairs. "There's something you should know. I'll tell you while we eat. I'm famished."

Later, after he'd told her what he'd learned at the hardware store, she said, "I don't know how much stock you can put into that story."

"But have you honestly searched the entire house for it?"

"Well, no, of course not. I only just inherited it."

"What about your grandparents?"

She shook her head. "I doubt it. Everyone assumed Bobby and Sarah took the diamond. Then Donny died. End of story."

He studied her for a long moment. "I think we should search for it as we work. Just in case. It won't cost us any more time or money." He shrugged his shoulders. "I bet there's a reward for it if we find it. That could help pay off some of your expenses. And if we don't, we can at least let everyone know we've done a thorough search and the diamond's not here."

Because she couldn't disagree, Teresa nodded. "Yeah, okay. I guess we can do that."

They worked all morning, cutting out damaged sections of drywall and searching the space behind for the missing diamond before sealing off the space with a new section of drywall. Teresa didn't know how big the Stanford diamond was or whether it was loose or stowed in some kind of packaging. After all these decades, it could be covered in dust and easily mistaken for a chunk of dirt or a rock.

"You know," she muttered. "This is like searching for a needle in a haystack."

John sighed, nodding. "You're right." Then he fell silent, a thoughtful expression crossing his face.

"What?"

"I was just wondering if your Uncle Bill could help? I know little about ghosts, but I'm assuming he can walk through walls and such? Maybe he could look for the diamond in places we can't easily get to?"

"He's not the most reliable ghost," she said, thinking back to all the times as a kid when she'd tried to interact with him, only for him to go radio-silence on her.

The weight of John's gaze had her glancing over. "What?"

"Would it hurt to ask?"

She sighed. "No, of course not." She gazed off into the distance. "Uncle Bill? Are you here?" She felt stupid talking to space. "There might be a diamond hidden somewhere in this house. Could you help us look for it?"

They both waited expectantly. Nothing happened. There was no sign that the ghost was even around. That didn't mean he wasn't, Teresa knew. She looked over at John, who shrugged.

"Well, it never hurts to ask." He stared at the section of wall they'd just finished searching. "I guess we can replace this wall now."

She stepped over to help him measure the space so they could cut the correct size from the sheet of drywall.

"If you tell me how much you spent on supplies, I'll pay you back."

"Don't worry about it," he told her.

"No, seriously. You shouldn't be spending your money on supplies for my house."

He stared at her for a moment, like he was considering arguing with her. Then he nodded before turning his attention to the tape measure. "I think I saved the receipt. Remind me later and I'll find it for you."

"Okay." As he marked off a measurement, she glanced at her phone and saw it was almost 11:00 AM. "I need to run an errand. How about I pick up lunch while I'm in town?"

"Sounds good. Would you like me to come with you?"

"No, that's okay."

"Then I guess I'll finish mounting this sheet and then patch the seams."

She was grateful he didn't push to go with her. She was going to the bank to ask for more money but had little hope they'd give her any. Their rejection would be hard enough to endure alone, much less with John at her side.

An hour later, Teresa was just as poor heading to Burger King's drive-thru as she had been walking into the bank. Instead of being embarrassed, though, she was mad. Fuming, in fact.

She took deep breaths as she ordered and then paid for the food. Unfortunately, the drive home wasn't nearly long enough for her to get over her hurt and anger, but pulling onto her street and finding cars parked up and down the road while crowds of strangers gathered on her front lawn gave her something new to fume about.

She slowly drove past her house and then took the back alley to her driveway.

She was spotted as soon as she pulled up to her garage. Before she could even get out of the car, it was surrounded by people shouting questions at her. As they pushed closer to the car, she panicked. There was no way she could make it into the house without being accosted. She wasn't sure she was any safer staying in the car.

Then, suddenly, John was there, shoving several people to the side as he made his way to the car. As soon as she unlocked her door, he pulled it open and grabbed her arm. He practically lifted her out of the car, taking the food from her.

"Lock the car," he shouted after kicking the door shut.

She fumbled for her key fob and pressed the button twice to lock the doors and set the alarm. As soon as he heard the blare of her car horn signaling the alarm was set, he shoved the bag of food into her arms. Then he tucked her close to his side with his free arm and steered them through the crowd of people with the ease of a hot knife cutting through butter.

Before panic could get the best of her, they were inside the house.

"You okay?" He was still holding her close, peering down at her. She made no move to pull away, needing to lean into his strength, taking comfort from the warmth of his body beside hers.

"I-I think so. Where'd all these people come from?" She didn't need to ask what they were doing there. "Damn Parker and his big mouth," she muttered.

"Yeah, I'm afraid so."

She sighed and looked up at him. "What are we going to do?"

"For now? Ignore them and keep working. As long as they stay out there and aren't damaging anything, I say let them stay. It's already ninety degrees out there. Let's see how many of them stick around once the temperature hits one hundred. Meanwhile, we'll be inside enjoying the A/C."

She thought about it. She didn't enjoy having all those people on her property, but she could live with it if they weren't doing any harm. As she slowly let go of her upset over being invaded, she grew conscious of John's arm still wrapped around her back. His very nearness set her senses on high alert. Wondering if he was as aware of her as she was of him, she sneaked a peek at him from below lowered eyelashes. Their gazes met, and it seemed neither could look away. How long they stood there; how long they might have stayed like that, she didn't know. Then John removed his arm while clearing his throat and stepped away, giving them both some much-needed space. Though if she was honest, she liked the feel of his arm around her shoulders.

"You get all your errands done?" He asked, turning to lock the back door before joining her at the kitchen table.

"More or less. I went to the bank," she admitted. "They wouldn't lend me any more money. Hank, the bank president, was very nice about it, but I'm apparently overextended." She huffed out a heavy sigh. "He's right, of course. I'm not sure how I'm going to pay back the first loan I took out, much less pay back a second. Then, as I was leaving, Joe Dodd, one of the bank vice-presidents followed me to my car and offered to become my partner! In exchange for half the reward for the diamond's return, he'd provide me the capital I need to finish the renovation. Can you believe it? I don't even know this guy."

She shook her head in disbelief.

"News travels fast," John said.

"Yeah. Anyway, now I hope we find the diamond because even if I can afford to pay for the repairs and restoration, I won't have any operating cash."

He offered her a comforting smile. "Don't worry. Things will work out. While you were gone, I cut out and replaced all the sections of damaged drywall in the rest of the rooms on the second floor. I'm sorry to report that I did not find the diamond. There's nothing more we can do on the second floor until the mud dries."

"Thank you!" She was so lucky to have someone like him helping her. "Let's eat and then we can start on the third floor."

"Sounds like a plan."

CHAPTER SEVENTEEN

JOHN FOLLOWED TERESA AS she led the way up the stairs to the second floor, his full attention on admiring the view of her hips swaying as she mounted each step.

He clenched his hands into fists to keep from reaching for her, drowning in the exquisite pain of unrequited longing.

As they moved along the second-floor hallway, he had to admit that her butt was only one of her many excellent features. Her legs were long and shapely. Imagining them wrapped around his waist nearly caused him to groan aloud. He wished their work didn't require her to wear jeans all the time. He would love to see the way she looked in shorts. The one time he'd seen her bare legs had been when the shower broke, and then, he'd only gotten a glimpse of them before his attention was diverted to her perfect breasts, which she'd covered much too quickly.

The direction of his thoughts was causing his jeans to become uncomfortably tight. He needed to think of something else.

He thought about the lunch they'd shared, but that proved to be an equally dangerous subject. Watching the thoughtful way in which she'd devoured her fries, one at a time. He sighed. Did she know the effect she had on men?

Probably not. Teresa wasn't a flirt, which was just another of the many things he liked about her. He shook his head slightly, surprised at the state of his emotions. He liked her a lot. Was it more than like? He wasn't prepared to answer that. There was a time when he would have made his affections known, put himself out there. That time in his life pre-dated his stint in prison.

"A penny for your thoughts?"

At her question, he realized they'd reached the third floor and were now standing in a large finished room. "Save your money. I wasn't thinking about anything important." He stepped further into the room and looked around. "Was this used as a guest room? It's pretty big."

"This was my great-grandparents living space when they operated the B&B."

He nodded in understanding. "Interesting." He continued to look around the space, something nagging at him. Finally, he walked over to the outer wall and counted his steps to the opposite wall. Reaching it, he knocked on it. "What's on the other side of this wall?"

She looked confused. "What do you mean?"

"This room takes up only about half of the entire floor. Plus, I noticed when I was outside that there are three windows on this floor that look out on the backyard, but this room only has one window." He gestured to the back wall. "Where are the other two?"

"Well, the bathroom and closet are there," she said, gesturing to the two doors on the wall to her right. "I'm almost positive the bathroom has a window."

He opened each door to peer inside, confirming that there was a single window in the bathroom that looked out onto the backyard. The closet, as expected, had no windows.

He went back into the main room and looked around. Since, from the outside, the third floor was the same size and shape as the second floor, and the bathroom, closet and main room only accounted for about two-thirds of the area, that left a lot of floor space unaccounted for.

"Is there another staircase to the third floor?" He'd been all over the second floor and hadn't seen one, but it never hurt to ask.

"Not that I know of."

If there wasn't another staircase, then that meant access to the rest of the third-floor space had to be from this room. He moved back to stand in the middle of the room and studied the left wall.

"If there's an access panel," he told her. "It's going to be in this wall."

He tapped in various spots, listening for—what exactly? He wasn't sure. Something about the crown molding caught his attention. Seams where there shouldn't be any.

He started pressing the wall below the seams and was rewarded when, halfway up the wall, he heard a definite click and felt the wall give slightly. When he eased off the pressure, a section of the wall slid forward.

Smiling, he looked over at Teresa. "Bingo." Gripping the edges of the panel, he pulled it toward him, revealing a doorway into a larger room lit by light shining in from both a side window and the missing backyard window.

Without waiting for her to agree, he stepped through the opening. Teresa followed close behind him into what turned out to be an office, complete with a dust-covered desk, an old rolling office chair with a missing wheel, a metal four-drawer cabinet and stacks of old boxes.

"Oh, my God," Teresa breathed out. "A secret room? How did I not know about this? I would have loved to play in here as a child."

"I think you answered your own question. Your grandparents probably didn't think it was the safest room in the house for you to play in."

"I wonder what's in these old boxes?" She was already moving forward to the first box and opening it. She pulled out folded stacks of cloth. "Hmmm. Looks like table linens." She replaced them and moved to the next box.

Meanwhile, John was more interested in what might be in the filing cabinet. Pulling open the top drawer, he found it filled with ledger books. Taking out the top one, he flipped through the pages. Expense entries for things like food, laundry, cleaning supplies and housekeeping services filled one column while another column reported income from guest stays. These were the financial books from the operation of the B&B.

"When did your family stop operating the B&B?"

"I'm not exactly sure. It was shortly after my grandmother was born, which was in 1950."

He replaced the ledger, and closing the top drawer, opened the second one. This one was also filled with ledgers.

"I think your great-grandparents must have used this space as their office. It was a great location for keeping their records safe. Few people would know to look for an office up here."

"I bet you're right," Teresa replied. "Maybe I should do the same once I open for—" At that moment, she sneezed.

"Bless you," he said. "I wonder," he continued, sounding thoughtful, "if the guest ledgers are here somewhere."

Across the room, she paused in her search through a box to look at him. "You think so?"

"It's possible."

She sneezed again. "I need to get out of here." She barely got the words out before sneezing again. "All this dust is getting to me. Next time I come in here, I'll bring cleaning supplies."

Unfortunately, though they'd looked, they hadn't found the guest ledgers. Disappointed, John closed the filing cabinet drawer and was about to join Teresa at the doorway when he stopped. "Did you hear that?"

"What?"

The sound came again, of metal clanging against metal, followed by male voices raised in argument. Frowning, John headed for the side window. "It sounded like it was coming from over here."

Teresa walked over to join him, and together they looked down into the side yard. Two men with shovels were there, arguing over a freshly dug hole.

"What the hell?" Teresa shrieked. "They're digging a hole in my yard!"

"That's it," John muttered. "Call the cops. I'm going down there to put a stop to this."

Teresa fumbled for her phone as she hurried after him. He was already halfway down the stairs to the second floor when she located LPPD's dispatch number.

"Bev, it's Teresa Thacker," she said when dispatch answered. "I have people at my house, and they're digging holes in my yard!" Still hurrying down the steps, she struggled to catch her breath. "Can you send someone over?"

"Right away," Bev assured her. "Are you in any danger?"

"I'm not, but those men will be if they don't stop digging."

"Don't confront them on your own," Bev advised.

"I won't. John's here with me."

"John?" There was confusion in Bev's voice.

"He's helping me restore the house," she explained. She reached the ground floor and went out the front door. Hurrying around to the side, she spotted John confronting the two men.

"This is private property," he was telling them. "And not only are you trespassing, you're defacing the property. The cops are on their way. If you don't want to be arrested, I suggest you leave immediately."

"No way," one man said. "I'm not leaving here so he can have the diamond."

"There is no diamond," John told him, raising his voice so the gathering crowd could hear him. "Both the house and grounds have been thoroughly searched. There are no diamonds on the property. Bobby Rangel took it with him when he fled to Mexico."

"But according to the historical report, Donny bragged that Bobby never found it," someone shouted from the crowd.

In the distance, Teresa finally heard the blare of sirens growing louder.

"Donny Rangel lied," John told the crowd. "He didn't want to admit that his brother out-smarted him."

The people in the crowd looked at one another. Teresa thought maybe they were trying to decide if John was telling them the truth. From the street, the sound of sirens ended, and a second later, Teresa heard car doors slamming shut. When she looked around, Chad and Steve were walking toward them. She went to meet them halfway.

"Coming here is becoming a habit," Chad greeted her, taking in the crowd. "Town gossip spreads fast."

"I guess. Now these lunatics," she gestured to the two men with shovels, "are digging holes in my yard!"

"I'll go talk to them. Do you want to press charges?"

Part of her wanted to say yes, but pressing charges would mean filling out paperwork and creating ill-will. In the end, it would probably do more harm than good. "Not if they'll leave peacefully and promise not to return."

"Sounds good." Chad gestured to the two police officers who'd just arrived in a second police car. They followed him around to the side of the house where the two arguing men, John and the rest of the crowd, were still gathered.

Teresa watched Chad say something to John, who then walked over to join her. They stood in the front yard while Chad and his officers talked to the crowd.

A moment later, the crowd began to disperse.

Chad walked over to join John and Teresa. "I'm going to hold the two digging in your yard at the station for a while, just to make a point. I'll send a couple of cars to patrol the neighborhood throughout the day, in case you get more uninvited guests."

"Thanks," John told him. "We appreciate that. Between the vandalism and unwanted attention, it's really interfering with our work."

"No problem," Chad replied. "By the way," he added, turning to speak directly to Teresa. "My request for a cadaver dog team was granted. They're coming out tomorrow. It's a team of four dogs and their handlers. They'll sweep the entire area where John picked up your mother's ghost. I'll let you know if we find anything."

Teresa felt her heart skip a beat. "Can I come out and watch?"

"Of course, but don't get your hopes up. I don't know how long the dogs will be out there searching before they find something. If they find something."

Teresa was disappointed. "I understand."

As if sensing the emotions running through her, John reached out and ran his hand gently up and down her back, offering comfort.

Chad, who noticed the intimate gesture, arched a brow but said nothing. "Call me if you have any more trouble." Then he headed for his truck.

"Okay. Thanks."

She and John remained out front until Chad drove away.

"You okay?" John asked her when they were alone again.

"Yeah." She took a deep breath. "It's all just a lot to take in, you know?"

"Yeah, I get that, but you don't have to face it alone. I'm here if you need me."

The offer surprised and pleased her. She smiled up at him. "Thank you."

He smiled back and then, by silent agreement, they walked back into the house to continue their work.

CHAPTER EIGHTEEN

TERESA TUCKED A LOOSE strand of hair behind her ear as she and John crossed the front lawn and stepped onto the faded flagstone path leading next door. The afternoon sun slanted through the maple leaves, casting mottled shadows over Mrs. Petrie's rose-clad gate. Teresa hadn't talked to her elderly neighbor in a while and simply wanted to check on her.

Climbing the steps to the front porch, she rapped gently on Mrs. Petrie's pale green door. The single knock went unanswered. Teresa waited a moment, then tried again, louder this time, in case Mrs. Petrie hadn't heard her the first time.

Still nothing.

Frowning, she left the porch and walked to the back of the house to peer through the dusty garage window. Mrs. Petrie's cherry-red sedan sat parked inside.

John joined her at the window. "Everything all right?"

Teresa let him see her concern. "I don't know. If she's home, why didn't she answer the door?"

"Let's knock on the back door," he suggested. "Maybe she's in the kitchen and didn't hear us."

Their footsteps crunched on the grass as they walked around to the back door. Teresa knocked once more. This time, a faint, anguished cry drifted through the crack beneath the threshold.

"Mrs. Petrie?" Teresa called, peering through the door window. The kitchen appeared empty. She knocked again. No answer—only that low cry again. Teresa tried the doorknob but found it locked.

Without hesitation, John used his elbow to break a bottom window-pane. The jagged edges gleamed in the late-day light as he reached past them, unlatched the lock, and pushed the door open.

They hurried inside. The family room was in disarray—a vase toppled on the rug, its trio of white lilies wilting across the threadbare carpet. In the center of the room, Mrs. Petrie lay curled beside her broken rocking chair, one mahogany rocker and leg splintered in half. She peered up at them as they entered. Her face was flushed and she was grasping her hip, but still managed a small, rueful smile.

"Don't you move," Teresa said, her voice sharp with fear. "You could have hit your head."

"I didn't," Mrs. Petrie muttered, though her breathing was labored. "Just hurt my pride. I used to laugh at those TV ads," she whispered, voice tight. "The ones with the old ladies who fall and can't get up. Now look at me."

John was already on the other side of her, his big hands steady as he helped guide her into the nearest chair. Teresa fetched a glass of water and set it in front of her, watching closely for any signs of disorientation.

"You scared the life out of me," Teresa admitted, more softly now. "You've got to be careful."

Mrs. Petrie gave a little laugh that sounded more like a sigh. "You fuss just like your mama used to."

The words caught Teresa off guard. "You knew my mother?"

"Knew her?" Mrs. Petrie's gaze drifted to the window as if she were watching some old scene play out in the glass. "Child, she was sweet on my Daniel for a time. Thought one day she'd be my daughter-in-law. Those two ... they laughed at the same jokes, shared secrets in the garden. I thought it was a sure thing."

Teresa blinked, absorbing the revelation. She'd never once pictured her mother in this kitchen, never considered the kind of connections she'd forged in Las Palomas before everything fell apart.

"What happened?" she asked, her voice careful.

Mrs. Petrie's lips turned down in a sad smile. "Daniel died. It was the summer after your mother graduated high school. Daniel was driving back from Brownsville when an eighteen-wheeler ran a stop sign. He was killed instantly. They found a diamond ring in his possession. An engagement ring. The store receipt had that day's date, and we all assumed he had gone to Brownsville to buy it for your mother." She sighed. "Such a shame. They were so in love."

It sounded like a great romantic tragedy, but Teresa had her doubts. If her mother had been that much in love with Daniel, then why had she married Roger Thacker a short two months later? She kept her thoughts to herself, however.

"It looks like the leg and rocker on this chair gave out," John commented, breaking into her thoughts.

Mrs. Petrie's eyes grew teary. "That chair ... my husband built it the week we were married. Right outside in the garage. I hate to get rid of it, but I don't suppose there's any way to fix it."

John took her hand and gave it a squeeze. "Let me see what I can do."

Mrs. Petrie's smile was feeble and she seemed to grow frailer right before Teresa's eyes, causing her to make a decision. "I'm calling an ambulance," she said, fishing her phone from her pocket. When Mrs. Petrie didn't argue with her, she knew she'd made the right decision.

She arranged transport to the urgent-care clinic in town and minutes later, the EMTs arrived.

"I'll follow you over in my car and stay with you," Teresa promised the woman as they lifted her onto a gurney. To John, she said, "We should call Marshall to come back out here and fix her window."

"We don't need to bother him again," John told them, "I can buy a replacement pane and install it."

John watched as, moments later, the paramedics left, Teresa following behind them in her truck. He walked back to Mrs. Petrie's garage door, lifted it, and was greeted by the warm, dusty scent of sawdust and aged timber. The two-car space was crowded with lathes, band saws, and planes—dusty but in good condition, proof that Mr. Petrie had tended them with pride. John's heart leaped. Before prison, he'd been a hobbyist woodworker, his hands were accustomed to coaxing form from raw wood.

He ran a finger over a jointer's iron bed, then drifted from tool to tool, making a mental list of what he'd need: safety glass for the back door, wood glue, clamps, replacement wood. Closing the door when he left, he strode off toward his car, his pulse quickening with excitement.

A few minutes later, he was at the hardware store. Parker eyed him warily, but when John explained the delicate rocker and its sentimental owner, the man's expression softened. Soon the counters were piled with glass pane, dowels, wood and a fresh pot of waterproof glue. Bags in hand, John climbed back into his car and headed to the grocery store.

As he headed back to Mrs. Petrie's house, Teresa called to let him know the elderly neighbor was stable, though she'd need X-rays and a couple of hours under observation. She worried aloud about leaving her alone.

John's voice was calm. "Don't worry. I've got things under control." Teresa thanked him, relief easing her tone.

Back at Mrs. Petrie's house, John set to work. He donned safety goggles, swept away shards of broken glass from the threshold of the backdoor, and fitted the new pane with patient precision. Then he hauled the battered rocker into the garage workshop. He adjusted blade heights, ran each splintered piece through the jointer, and glued broken joints, clamping them with perfect pressure to dry overnight. A window air-conditioning unit hummed overhead, filling the air with a cool, dry breeze as John labored quietly, a cheerful tune playing through his head.

By the time Teresa returned with Mrs. Petrie—walking slowly, her arm in a sling but her spirit lighter—John was in Mrs. Petrie's kitchen, stirring simmering sauce over her range and arranging fresh salad on the countertop with vegetables he'd bought earlier. Resting in the kitchen corner was a carved, slender wooden cane, its handle gently curved and sanded smooth.

John hurried outside to help Teresa get Mrs. Petrie into the house. Their warm smiles and thanks when they realized he had dinner ready for them was one of the most rewarding moments of his life, second only to the warm hug and kiss Mrs. Petrie bestowed upon him at seeing the cane.

Then the three of them gathered around the kitchen table, laughter and conversation punctuating each course of pasta and warm bread. The evening was a picture-perfect scene of homey comfort. Mrs. Petrie sitting at the table, cane leaning against the table leg, John clearing dishes, Teresa doling out pain medication and tucking a quilt around Mrs. Petrie's shoulders.

Later that evening, as Teresa helped the older woman to bed and she finally laid back against her pillows, Mrs. Petrie sighed contentedly. "I could get used to nights like this."

Teresa would have stayed, but Mrs. Petrie insisted she return home to sleep in her own bed. So she bent to kiss the older woman's cheek. "I'll check on you first thing in the morning," she promised before leaving with John to return to her own home.

Chapter Nineteen

THE NEXT MORNING, TERESA awoke feeling anxious. Today, the cadaver dogs would look for her mother's remains. She didn't know whether or not to hope they'd find them.

After getting dressed, she and John checked on Mrs. Petrie, who was no longer wearing the sling and assured them she was a bit bruised, but otherwise fine. She'd proved her point by making them breakfast.

After helping to clean and put away the dishes, Teresa and John had returned to her house to paint the walls of the second-floor common room.

Normally, Teresa found painting to be relaxing, but today it only gave her more time to think about what the cadaver dogs might find.

"Why don't I finish up here?" John finally suggested, coming to stand beside her, taking the paintbrush from her.

That was when she realized she'd simply been standing there, holding it, but not actually using it. Looking around, she saw that John had finished painting two walls in the time she'd partially painted one.

"I'm sorry." She felt guilty for slacking on the job. "I just can't seem to keep my thoughts on work today."

"It's understandable. Today has the potential of being a big day. Are you going to go out there?"

She shook her head. "I'd just be in the way. Maybe I'll go downstairs and bake some muffins."

He smiled. "I like that idea, especially if I get to have some of them."

She smiled back, relieved he wasn't upset about her bailing on him. "Of course, though don't get too excited. I'm thinking of trying out a new recipe."

"Then I'm happy to serve as your guinea pig."

"Thank you, John. I really appreciate this."

"No worries."

She had just reached the first floor when there was a knock at the front door. Surprised, all she could do for a moment was stare at it while her thoughts spun out of control. She hated that all the recent publicity and problems made her afraid to open her own door.

The knock sounded again, startling her from her thoughts.

"John!" she hollered, hoping he'd hear her over the sound of the music.

A second later, he was coming down the stairs. "I heard the knock. Want me to get it?"

"No, I just want you here as back-up."

"You bet." He went to stand off to the side where he'd be out of the way.

She opened the door. A man she didn't know stood there, dressed in a business suit and looking a bit wilted in the ninety-degree heat.

"Hello," he greeted her with what struck her as a well-practiced smile. "Would you be Teresa Thacker?"

For half a second, she considered lying to him and telling him Teresa wasn't home, but that was only putting off the inevitable.

"I'm Teresa. Can I help you?"

"I hope so." He held his hand out for her to shake.

Images raced through her head of him gripping her hand and yanking her off balance so he could attack her. She really needed to stop watching *Forensic Files*, she thought, slowly extending her hand to shake his, reassured because John was close enough to intervene if necessary.

"I'm Tom Kobbel."

"The investment banker," she said, as his name registered.

"That's right. I'd like to make you an offer I think you'll find hard to refuse. May I come in so we can discuss it?"

"No." Then, because that had sounded rude, she elaborated. "I'm sorry if someone told you I was interested in selling my house or taking on a partner, but I'm not."

"Oh." His smile faltered, but he quickly recovered. "I understand you're renovating the house and, without getting too personal, you're strapped for cash. What I'm proposing to you is a partnership with an eighty-twenty split in profits.

In exchange, my company will provide the capital to finish all of your renovations."

"Eighty-twenty, huh? Let me guess, you get the eighty percent? And probably want eighty percent of the control over operations?"

"Well, since we are providing the bulk of the capital ..." He let the rest of the sentence hang.

"You know there's no diamond hidden in the house, right?"

"Excuse me?" He had the decency to look confused.

"Please. It's been all over town. I don't see how you could have avoided hearing about the Stanford diamond being hidden in the house, but it's not. With all the renovation we've done, we would have found it. So, if you're offering to invest in my house hoping to find the diamond, you can forget it."

He held his hands up, palms facing her. "No. I just returned to Las Palomas this morning and must have missed that story. I assure you, Miss Thacker, that's not why I'm here. My company is interested in putting a hotel in town but, so far, we've been unable to acquire suitable property."

"I appreciate you stopping by, Mr. Kobbel, but I'm not interested in your offer."

She started to close the door, but he put a hand out to stop her. Before she could get mad, he held up his hand to signal he meant no harm and with his other hand, reached into the breast pocket of his suit coat and extracted a business card, which he held out to her.

"In case you change your mind."

As soon as she took the card from him, he turned and went down the front porch steps. Teresa closed the door and locked it before going to stand next to John by the front window.

"That was, uh, interesting," he said, watching Mr. Kobbel climb into his car and drive away.

Teresa sighed. "I wish they'd all go back into the woodwork they crawled out of."

"He seemed harmless enough."

"I guess."

John turned to her and placed his hands on her shoulders. "It'll be okay."

She was so damn tired of the stress, so when he offered her this small measure of comfort, it was more than she could resist. Stepping closer, she rested her forehead against his chest, then worried the moment might turn awkward, until she felt his arms slip around her and pull her close.

He lowered his head until she felt his breath against her hair. "It'll be okay. I won't let anything bad happen."

He'd spoken so softly, she wasn't sure if she was supposed to hear his words, but she had and was more grateful than she could tell him for the sense of security they gave her. She knew she should step back, put some distance between them. Instead, she slipped her arms around his waist, and they stood there for a long moment just holding one another.

The moment ended far sooner than she would have liked.

"I should get back upstairs and finish those walls," he told her, his arms still wrapped around her.

She nodded against his chest. "I know." She eased back enough to raise her head and meet his gaze. "Thank you."

"For?"

For holding me. "For everything."

He smiled down at her. "My pleasure. Now, get to work, or were you just teasing me with the promise of a new muffin recipe?"

She smiled. "I wasn't teasing."

"Then off we go." John left her to head up the stairs.

Teresa stood at the bottom, unabashedly admiring his backside as he climbed. Then, with a much lighter heart than she'd had earlier, she went into the kitchen to bake.

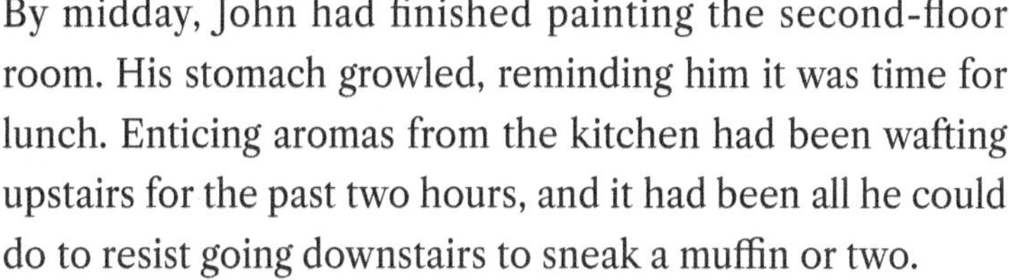

By midday, John had finished painting the second-floor room. His stomach growled, reminding him it was time for lunch. Enticing aromas from the kitchen had been wafting upstairs for the past two hours, and it had been all he could do to resist going downstairs to sneak a muffin or two.

As he finished covering his wet paint roller and brush with plastic wrap to prevent them from drying out, he wondered what new recipe Teresa had tried. The woman certainly knew how to bake, that was for damn sure.

His mouth was practically watering by the time he went downstairs.

"Something smells fantastic," he announced, walking into the kitchen.

Teresa was just pulling a pan of muffins from the oven. She carried it over to the side counter, where dozens of freshly baked muffins sat on cooling racks.

After she set the pan on the counter, she looked up. "You want to try one?"

"Absolutely!"

She gestured to the cooling rack, and he helped himself. She watched him as he peeled the paper wrapper away and took a bite. Fruit flavors burst in his mouth, making his tongue tingle.

"Oh my God," he moaned. "This is fantastic. What kind of muffin is it?"

"Fruit Loop."

"Excuse me?"

"It's a Fruit Loops muffin. You know—like the cereal? After I started mixing the ingredients, I realized I was out of fruit, and I didn't feel like running to the store, so I improvised. Which reminds me, we're now out of cereal."

"That's okay. I'm happy eating these for breakfast." He looked at the muffins sitting about. "Although I'm not sure even I can eat this many."

She shrugged. "It doesn't matter. Thanks for letting me come down and bake. It helped take my mind off what was happening with the search team."

"I guess you haven't heard from Chad?" He reached for another muffin.

She shook her head. "Not yet." Then she dropped her gaze, looking embarrassed. "I'd really like to go out there and watch."

He considered it. "It might help you feel better to see what they're doing," he agreed. "You want company?"

"While I welcome the company, if you're offering because you're worried about me, then don't. I'm fine. I just want to watch the dogs work."

"If you're sure you're okay going out there alone, then maybe I'll run into town. I ran out of paint upstairs and thought I'd go pick up a couple more gallons."

"We're out already? Damn. I was really hoping those first couple of gallons would go further."

"The walls are really dry, and they're soaking up the paint like a sponge."

She reached into her pocket and pulled out the few loose bills she had on her. It wasn't nearly enough to purchase the paint, so she found her phone and took her credit card from the holder on the back of the phone case. She held it out to him, but he shook his head.

"Keep it. You might need it. I'll buy the paint, and you can pay me back later."

"Oh, okay." He thought she might have sounded hesitant, and he understood. He knew money was tight for her. It was a matter of pride for her to pay for this renovation herself. She hadn't counted on the recent vandalism eating into her funds. "Thanks." She looked around the kitchen. "You're probably hungry. Can I make you a sandwich?"

"You'd do that for me?"

"Sure."

"Then yes, please. Some of that ham and cheese, if we still have it. You going to have one, too?"

She rubbed her stomach. "I might have sampled one too many muffins as I was baking them. I'm stuffed."

He chuckled, imagining her eating muffin after muffin. Going to the fridge, he took out the ham, cheese, mayo and a bottle of water, and then carried them over to the counter where she stood before two slices of bread sitting on a paper plate. He held a water bottle out to her, but she shook her head. So he kept it for himself and then stood nearby and watched while she made his sandwich. He could have made it himself and had considered telling her so, but she seemed to want to do it and really, when was the last time he'd had someone do something nice for him?

As he watched her work, he nibbled on another muffin, finding it nearly impossible to resist eating them. As he ate, an idea slowly took form. Today might be the perfect day to see if the idea had merit.

"Here you go," Teresa said when she'd finished, handing him the paper plate with his sandwich.

"Thanks." He took a bite of it, chewed and swallowed. "Why does the sandwich taste so much better when you make it?"

That earned him a smile, and he found he enjoyed making her smile.

They sat and talked while he ate. When he was done, he helped her place the now-cool muffins into gallon-size baggies.

"We'll never eat these," she complained, looking at the twenty bags before them. "Plus, I still have four bags of raspberry crumble muffins left over. Maybe I should take a couple of bags out to the crew working the dogs."

"Maybe not," he suggested. "The smell of the muffins might distract the crew and the dogs."

"Good point. Okay, maybe I'll freeze some. I'll decide when I get back." She brushed her hands against her jeans. "I feel like I have flour everywhere. I'm going upstairs to change and then I'll head over to the site where the dogs are working."

"Sounds good. I'm going to make a list of all the supplies we need, and then I'll head into town. I'll lock up when I leave."

"Great. I'll see you later, then."

CHAPTER TWENTY

JOHN PURPOSELY TOOK HIS time making a list, waiting for Teresa to leave the house. If this new idea of his didn't work, it might be better if she never knew about it.

After changing into a clean pair of jeans and a shirt, he went downstairs. He remembered seeing a medium-size box outside in the garage. After retrieving it, he carried it into the kitchen and placed fifteen of the gallon bags filled with the fresh muffins inside. He then carried the box out to his car.

His first stop after arriving in town was the hardware store. He gave them his list of supplies and told them he'd be back in an hour to pick them up. Then he drove to Ruby Mae's B&B.

Carrying two of the gallon bags, he went inside.

"Hello, John." Ruby Mae, seated behind the reception desk, greeted him. "How are you?"

"Hi, Ruby Mae. I'm doing well, thanks. How are you?"

"I'm fine, thank you." She frowned. "I hope you're not looking for a room. I'm afraid I'm full at the moment."

"No, I'm still staying at the Thacker house. I'm here for another reason." He placed the bags of muffins on the desk before her.

"What's this?"

"I don't know if you knew this, but Teresa is an accomplished baker. She baked these fresh this morning. I want to leave them here, hoping you will share them with your guests. Teresa is considering operating a small boutique bakery out of her house, providing fresh baked goods to businesses such as yours." He held up his hand before she could say anything. "I know you do a lot of your own baking, but as busy as you are, I'm sure that if you knew you could provide your guests with quality baked goods without having to spend hours in the kitchen yourself, baking them, that might be of interest to you?"

She gave him a narrowed look out of the side of her eye as she pulled a bag towards her. He nodded when she glanced at him, silently asking permission to open it.

He watched with growing excitement when she held the open bag under her nose to smell the muffins, and her eyes opened wider in surprise.

"How much?" She asked him.

"These bags are complimentary, but additional bags are available for a fee."

As soon as the words left his mouth, she reached into the bag and pulled out a muffin. Peeling the paper cup away from the bottom of the muffin, she broke off a piece and popped it into her mouth.

John practically held his breath as she chewed and swallowed.

"Well?" He finally had to ask.

"This is extremely good," she admitted. "What kind is it?"

"We call these Fruit Loop Muffins."

"Interesting. Do you have any other flavors?"

"Everything Teresa makes is fantastic. One of my other favorites is her raspberry crumble." Phrased that way made it seem like he'd sampled a lot of her baking when, in fact, he'd only had the two types, but he had confidence that Teresa could bake just about anything. "If you decide you want to order more, call me." He wrote his cell number down on a piece of paper. "Until we can expand our business, I'll only be able to sell the flavors we have on hand."

"How much?"

This was the tricky part. Charge too much and no one would buy any. Charge not enough and Teresa would do a lot of work for nothing. "How about ten dollars for a half-dozen, twenty for a dozen?"

She considered it and then nodded. "Okay. I'll put them out for my guests, but I can't promise anything."

"That's all I can ask. You have a good day." He gave her a wave and left the B&B, but not before noticing that she had taken another bite from the muffin.

After leaving the B&B, John drove into downtown Las Palomas. He made the entire block around the city park, studying the various storefronts. He spotted one that looked promising and parked his car. Grabbing a couple more bags of muffins, he headed into the quaint shop called Katherine's Kozy Korner. Judging from the art on the windows, this was both a book shop and coffee bar. He went inside the shop and stopped. The aroma of freshly brewed coffee hit him and he considered taking up permanent residence because it smelled so good.

There were several people in the shop, sitting at various tables. A couple were bent over their laptops while they enjoyed their coffee. Others were reading while they drank coffee. There were even a few people browsing the titles of the books shelved along the side walls. It was an inviting space, John thought.

Near the back of the room, an older woman stood behind the counter. Dressed in a long, vibrantly colored broom skirt and peasant blouse, her long dark hair fell loose about her shoulders. He thought she looked like a 1970s hippie.

"Hello," she called to him with a smile as he drew closer. "Welcome to Katherine's Kozy Korner. I'm Katherine. I don't believe I've seen you in here before."

"Hi. This is my first time in your establishment, but hopefully not my last. I don't know what kind of coffee you're serving, but it smells great."

"It's my own blend. Would you like a cup?"

"Yes, please. I think I have to try it."

He sat at one of the bar stools at the coffee bar while she poured him a cup.

"Sugar, sweeteners and creamers are over there." She set the coffee mug before him and gestured to the small side counter.

"Thanks." He added sweetener and creamer, then took a sip, being careful since it was hot. "Wow! This is great. What do I owe you?"

"First cup is on the house."

He nodded in acknowledgeable. "Thank you." He took another sip, aware that she was studying him.

"You're the young man helping Teresa Thacker with her house, aren't you?" she finally asked.

"I am." He waited to see if her attitude toward him changed. If she knew he'd recently been in prison, the attitude change was inevitable.

"How are the renovations coming?" Hearing her casual tone, he realized that she either didn't know he'd been in prison, or didn't care. Probably the former.

"Slow. We've had problems with vandalism."

She shook her head and muttered something under her breath that sounded a lot like "demons," but maybe he was mistaken.

"What do you have there?" She pointed to the two bags he'd placed on the counter.

"Freshly baked muffins." He opened a bag and held it out to her. "Have one. They're worth it," he encouraged when she seemed about to hesitate.

She reached in and pulled out a muffin. She went through the ritual of peeling back the paper cup and then broke off a piece of muffin, which she popped into her mouth.

Once again, he was gratified to see her eyes light up as she swallowed.

"Dang. Those are tasty. You made these?"

He laughed. "Me? No, I can't bake. Teresa made these. She's one heck of a baker."

"Mother," Katherine called to an older woman who'd just appeared from a side hallway. "You've got to try these." To him, she said, "John, I'd like you to meet my mother. This is Mrs. Parrish."

John held his hand out to her. "Mrs. Parrish, it's a pleasure to meet you."

"John is the young man helping Teresa restore her family home," Katherine explained to her mother. "Taste this." She broke a piece of her muffin off and handed it to her mother. "Teresa made this."

The older woman popped a bit of muffin into her mouth, chewed, and swallowed. "Oh, my," she exclaimed. "That is quite tasty. You know, I bet this would go well with your coffee."

"I have to confess," John told them. "That's kind of why I came in here. I noticed you sell a few food items, but no baked goods. Teresa is exploring the possibility of starting a side bakery business, which she would operate out of her home. I'm going to leave these muffins with you to keep or sell to your patrons. If you decide you're interested in ordering more, you can call me. Right now, we're operating more like a bake sale than an actual business. We're happy to sell you as many of the muffins of the day as we have on hand. As business expands, we'll secure a food license, and you'll be able to order the quantities and flavors you want." He shared the same pricing he'd quoted to Ruby Mae, glad when neither of them balked at the cost.

He left the bookshop a few minutes later with a feeling of optimism and a reference to the cafe across the block.

By the time John returned to the hardware store an hour and half later, he was out of muffins and had four potential future clients. Both the cafe and one of the gift shops had expressed an interest in the muffins.

He loaded gallons of paint and supplies into his trunk and headed back to the Thacker house, intending to get right back to work, but as he hit the long stretch of road leading through town, he reconsidered.

He knew where Teresa was and could only imagine how hard it might be to watch cadaver dogs work a site, not knowing if they'd find her mom's remains or not.

His knuckles tightened on the wheel. He'd only been hired to patch walls and fix windows, but that line had blurred days ago. She wasn't just his boss anymore.

Exhaling, he flipped on his blinker. Instead of turning toward the house, he swung the car back onto the road that led out of town.

He wasn't sure if it was the memory of Marie's ghost, his own instincts, or something deeper, but the pull was the same. Teresa shouldn't be alone right now.

He pressed down on the accelerator, heading for her.

Reaching the spot a short time later, he pulled in behind the other cars parked along the side of the road. He wasn't sure exactly where Teresa was, but he saw her truck and knew she was still here, somewhere.

Exiting his car, he walked toward the group of people gathered nearby. He found Teresa standing with Chad, Zelda and a woman with blond hair pulled back in a ponytail that he'd not yet met. Teresa was the first to spot him, and a smile lit her face.

"Hey, John. What are you doing here?" she asked, coming toward him.

"I got curious. Thought I'd come see what's going on." He wasn't about to confess his concern for her in front of all these people.

"I'm glad you came. You know Chad and Zelda, but I don't think you've met Sam Hunter, our police chief." She gestured to the blond woman. "Sam, this is John Morris. He's staying with me and helping me renovate the house. He's also the one mother appeared to."

Sam reached out to shake hands with him. John thought she looked pale, but then remembered hearing she was recovering from a gunshot wound.

"It's nice to meet you," he told her.

"Same here," she replied. "Did Teresa just say her mother's ghost appeared to you?"

"That's right."

"You seem pretty calm about it," she observed.

"Do I?" He gave a half shrug. "I wasn't, at first, but between giving Marie a ride, and Uncle Bill's ghost haunting Teresa's house, I guess the shock of knowing ghosts exist has worn off."

At that moment, several of the dogs started barking, drawing their attention.

"Sounds like they found something," Chad said. "I'll go over and see."

John turned to Teresa. Her gaze was locked on the dogs and their handlers. He could only imagine the thoughts running through her head. Wanting to offer moral support, he stepped closer to her.

Chad returned a few minutes later, a grim expression on his face. "They found human skeletal remains. Right now, we have no way of knowing how long they've been buried there."

A stunned silence met his announcement.

Then Teresa asked, "How many bodies?"

"One so far, but there could be more buried underneath it or nearby. We've got a forensics team coming to exhume the remains. And the dogs will keep searching the area."

"Did the body have any ID on it?" Sam asked.

"Not that they've found. The clothing is in pretty bad shape. There's not much left of it." He turned to Teresa. "I'm sorry. The remains will go to the county's forensics lab, and as soon as I'm done here, I'll call Neela Tompkin." To John, he added, "She's the only dentist in town. She took over the practice when Dr. Bush retired. I'll see how far back her records go. Maybe we'll get lucky and your parents will have dental x-rays on file." He paused. "Sam? Zelda?"

The two women, who had been staring off at the recovery team, seemed to startle at the sound of their names.

"Anything you want to add?" Chad asked them.

The women exchanged looks. John thought he saw Sam shake her head, but it was so subtle, he could have been mistaken. He was more interested in what Zelda had to say since she was the one who could see auras, wasn't she?

"There are too many people here," she said, as if guessing the direction of his thoughts. "Too many auras. The area is looking like a child's fingerpainting." She turned to Teresa. "I'm sorry. I wish I could be more help."

Teresa looked so lost that John put his arm around her waist and pulled her close, as if by doing so, he could shield her from the pain he was sure she was feeling. He'd acted before thinking and immediately worried that maybe shouldn't have shown such intimacy, especially in front of the others. Instead of shrugging him off or moving away, though, she moved closer, giving him a grateful look.

"We should head back," he told her. "Why don't I drive you? We can come back and get your car later."

If he had been expecting an argument, he didn't get one. She simply nodded.

"Give me your truck keys, Teresa," Chad said. "I'll have one of my men drive your truck back to your house later."

Digging into her pocket, she found her keys and handed them to him. Then she let John lead her to his car.

She was silent as he pulled onto the road and stared out the window for much of the drive home.

"How're you doing?" he asked as he finally pulled the car onto their street.

"I'm okay, I guess. I don't think I realized just how much I hoped they wouldn't find anything. As long as they didn't, I could pretend they were still alive."

"That might still be the case," he warned her. "Those remains could belong to a drifter or some other unfortunate soul." Though it would be hard to argue her mother was still alive if the ghost he picked up was Marie. Who else would have had her locket?

He didn't press the point though as he pulled the car into their driveway—when had it become *theirs* and not *hers?*—and turned off the engine.

"Why don't you go on inside and relax? Maybe soak in a hot bath. I know that standing out there all afternoon, waiting for them to find something, was stressful."

"What about you? What are you going to do?"

"I ran to the hardware store earlier, so I'm going to unload the car. When you're done in the bathroom, I might take a quick shower. Then we can talk about what we want to do for dinner."

"Oh, wow. I hadn't realized how late it was. I can help you carry in supplies," she offered.

"Thanks, but I've got this. Go take a hot, relaxing bath. You'll feel better."

Knowing he was right, she thanked him and went inside. She headed directly upstairs and started filling the tub with water. While she waited, she looked through her clean clothes until she found something comfortable to put on after her bath.

When the tub was full, she climbed into it. She'd debated how hot to make the water and was glad, now, that she'd opted to make it just warm enough to relax her aching muscles. Leaning back, she closed her eyes, letting the warm water relax her, and cleared her mind, freeing it of all thoughts.

She came awake suddenly when there was a knock on the bathroom door.

"Teresa? You okay in there?" John's concerned voice sounded through the door.

"Yes, sorry. I think I fell asleep."

"No worries," he called to her. "I ordered pizza for us. Hope that's okay."

"Yeah, absolutely," she said, realizing now that the water had grown cool. "I'll be out in a second."

She listened to the sound of his retreating footsteps, then quickly bathed. After dressing in her clean clothes, she dropped her dirty clothes on top of the pile of other dirty clothes in the corner of her room.

She started down the hallway, stopping outside John's open doorway.

"I'm out. Sorry again for taking so long."

"No worries. Pizza should be here in about twenty minutes," he assured her. "If it comes before I'm done, though, I already paid for it, including a healthy delivery tip, so you don't need to worry about giving the driver any money."

"John, I should pay for your meals, not the other way around."

"You can get the next one," he told her as he stepped past her into the hallway. "See you downstairs in a few minutes."

Teresa left him to head downstairs, musing at how comfortable she felt around him. It was like they'd known each other for years instead of days.

When she reached the kitchen, she pulled out paper plates, napkins, red pepper flakes and Parmesan cheese and carried them over to the dining table. She grabbed a couple of water bottles from the refrigerator and added them to the other items.

Then she sat down at the table to wait for the pizza to arrive. It was when she was gazing around the kitchen, lost in thought, that she noticed the missing bags of muffins. Had John put them away?

She crossed to the pantry, but a quick search came up empty. She hadn't noticed any muffins in the refrigerator when she'd retrieved the water bottles, but she checked it again anyway. Next, she checked the freezer. When they weren't there either, a horrible thought occurred to her.

What if John had lied to her earlier when he'd told her the muffins were good, not wanting to hurt her feelings, and as soon as she'd left, he'd thrown them away?

Unable to shake the depressing thought, she checked the trash can, pulling out the trash on top in case he'd buried them further down.

"What are you doing?"

Teresa spun around to find John, his hair freshly washed, standing in the doorway holding a large pizza box in his hands.

"Um. I didn't hear the doorbell ring," she said, evading the question.

"It didn't. I saw him arrive when I came down and met him at the door." He carried the pizza box over to the table and set it down. "What were you looking for in the trash?" He asked again.

She felt her face flush. "I thought maybe you told me my muffins were good to spare my feelings and then threw them out as soon as I left."

"What?" He looked horrified. "Why would you think that?"

She gestured to the clean kitchen counters. "Because they're all missing."

Now he looked embarrassed. "Yeah, about that."

"You didn't eat them all yourself, did you?"

"No, nothing like that." He gestured to the table. "Why don't we sit down and eat while the pizza's hot? And I promise to tell you what happened to your muffins and hope you'll forgive me."

That didn't sound good, but with the aroma of the pizza filling the kitchen, Teresa realized she was famished, so she nodded her agreement and took her seat.

For the next twenty minutes, they ate in silence. Finishing her third slice of pizza, hunger abated, Teresa couldn't wait any longer. Her imagination was filling her head with too many scenarios.

"Okay, John. What happened to my muffins?"

He set his unfinished slice of pizza on his plate and wiped his mouth. "First, those muffins were outstandingly good. Easily as good as the raspberry crumble ones you made the other day. You are a talented baker, and you seem to enjoy baking."

She nodded. "Yeah, I love to bake."

"Good. That's what I thought. Well, maybe there's a way for you to supplement your finances by selling baked goods."

"What?"

"I decided to find out, so I took your muffins into town and dropped them off at several businesses. I sort of led the owners to believe that you were considering opening a bakery, and this was a test run. The bags of muffins I left were free samples, but if they want more, they'll need to purchase them for twenty dollars a dozen."

He paused, but she hardly noticed. Her brain was spinning. It had never occurred to her that anyone might be interested in buying the muffins she loved to bake.

"Do you think anyone would actually pay for my muffins?"

He smiled at her. "I do, but we'll have to wait and see."

"I suppose I could make several types and have them ready, but that's a lot of inventory to have on hand, and they won't stay fresh long."

"I thought of that. Initially, the deal is they take whatever flavor muffin you've made that day, and we'll fill the orders until we run out. Then they'll have to wait until the next day if they want more."

She considered the possibilities. "I could wake up early and have several dozen muffins ready to go by seven in the morning."

"And I'd be more than happy to deliver them."

She shook her head, grasping for a dose of reality. "No one's going to buy muffins from me."

"Maybe they won't," he agreed. "But then again, maybe they will. What if tomorrow we both get up early? You can bake while I work on the house. The worst thing that happens is that we both lose an hour of sleep, spend a dollar or two on ingredients and end up with a lot of muffins to eat by ourselves."

She thought about it and then smiled. She could think of a lot worse ways to spend her morning than baking. "Deal."

He smiled, picked up his unfinished slice of pizza and continued eating. While he chewed, Teresa picked his brain on what flavor muffin he thought she should make and then raced around the kitchen to see if she had the right ingredients. Since neither of them had gone to the store for anything more than a couple of needed items, it didn't take them long to settle on cinnamon crumble. She worried the flavor would be too common, but John assured her that nothing she baked could ever be common.

After dinner, they worked together to clean up the kitchen. John went around making sure all the doors were locked and then, together, they headed up the stairs. It was late and tomorrow would come early.

"Good night," Teresa said when they reached his door.

"Good night, Teresa. I hope you sleep well."

"Thanks. I'll see you in the morning."

She went off to bed, surprised at how much lighter her heart felt, but later, as she slid beneath the covers, a chill of unease threaded through her.

CHAPTER TWENTY-ONE

LAS PALOMAS, TEXAS
AUGUST 3, 1945 12:05 a.m.

A chill of unease threaded through Bobby at seeing Sarah's reaction.

"He tricked me, Sarah. Told me he needed a ride. Said he had a quick job, nothing illegal, just a pickup. Next thing I know, we're on the road out of Houston. There's a dead guard at the bank, a gun in the glove box and a diamond the size of a walnut in Donny's pocket."

"You're lying."

"I wish I were."

Her hands trembled as they clutched at the edge of the bedspread. "He... he wouldn't..."

"He would. And he did. And now he's planning to run. Mexico. That's why he wanted you here. He's not taking you on vacation. He's disappearing."

She shook her head, blinking hard. "No. No, he wouldn't do that. Not to me."

Bobby's voice dropped, rough and low. "Yeah, he would."

He looked down, then met her eyes once more.

"You were never supposed to know."

And with that, he opened the door and slipped into the dark hallway, leaving the soft click of the latch behind him—and a silence that screamed louder than anything he'd ever said.

Sarah sat frozen on the edge of the bed, her fingers still curled around the bedspread where Bobby had left her. The fan spun lazily on the dresser, stirring the hot air, but she didn't feel it. Didn't hear it. Not really.

We stole it. Donny and I.

The words echoed, sharp and unreal, bouncing around in her skull like marbles on tile.

"No," she whispered, but there was no one to hear it. Not even herself, really.

Donny was hot-tempered. Donny was reckless. Donny could be cruel.

But this?

A diamond? A gun? A dead guard?

She pressed her palms to her knees, trying to keep from shaking. Her thoughts moved like syrup—slow and sticky, every step forward pulling another memory up from the muck.

The sudden trip. The urgency in his voice when he'd called and asked her to meet him in Las Palomas. Trust me, Baby Doll. We're getting a fresh start.

Fresh start.

Her gaze drifted to the nightstand, where Donny's silver cigarette case lay half-open. She stared at it for a long moment before snapping it shut.

A fresh start built on blood.

Sarah rose from the bed like a sleepwalker, her legs moving before her mind could catch up, and crossed the room to lock the door. Her fingers hesitated at the bolt, trembling—not from fear, but from the brittle edge of resolve hardening inside her. On the other side of the door, she could hear Bobby's footsteps as he moved down the hallway. He'd taken a chance coming to her, telling her the truth.

She touched her jaw, where the bruise was still tender.

And then, as the pieces began to fit—quiet, deliberate, undeniable—a single tear slipped down her cheek.

She didn't wipe it away.

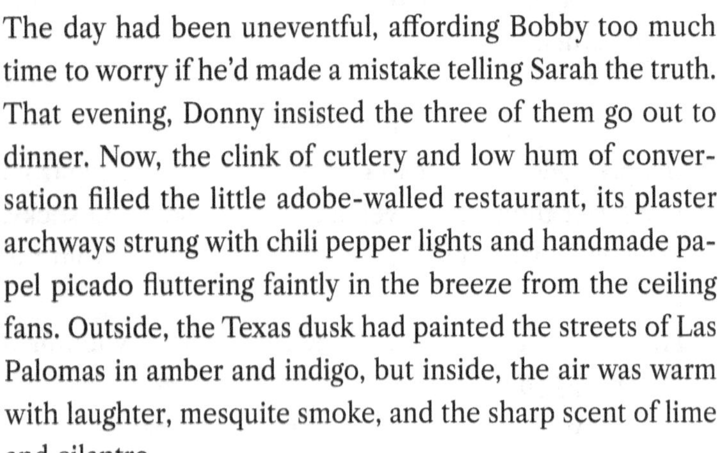

The day had been uneventful, affording Bobby too much time to worry if he'd made a mistake telling Sarah the truth. That evening, Donny insisted the three of them go out to dinner. Now, the clink of cutlery and low hum of conversation filled the little adobe-walled restaurant, its plaster archways strung with chili pepper lights and handmade papel picado fluttering faintly in the breeze from the ceiling fans. Outside, the Texas dusk had painted the streets of Las Palomas in amber and indigo, but inside, the air was warm with laughter, mesquite smoke, and the sharp scent of lime and cilantro.

Donny cut a striking figure at the corner table. Dark hair slicked back, white shirt crisp beneath his charcoal vest, he had a grin that could pass for charm if you didn't know better—and the entire dining room didn't. He leaned across the table, talking animatedly to the young waitress as she poured his drink, flashing that easy smile that made people like him before they understood why they shouldn't.

"Gracias, sweetheart," he said smoothly, raising his glass.

The waitress blushed and scurried off. Donny chuckled and turned back to his companions. "You see that? Polite and popular. Not bad for a guy just passing through."

Bobby didn't answer. He picked at his enchiladas, barely tasting them. Every bite stuck in his throat. His eyes kept drifting to Sarah, who sat across from him, quiet and straight-backed in a pale blue dress. She hadn't spoken much since they arrived. Hell, she'd not spoken much all day. Not to Donny, not to him. Just small nods, faint smiles, as if her words were locked somewhere deep where no one could reach.

Donny didn't notice. Or maybe he didn't care.

He reached across the table, laid a hand over Sarah's. "You know, I was thinking earlier, babe. We've been through a lot, you and me."

Sarah didn't move. Her fingers stayed still beneath his.

Donny went on, oblivious or pretending. "And I figure, what's the point of waiting? Life's short. You gotta grab what makes you happy, right?"

Bobby's fork froze halfway to his mouth.

Donny reached into his pocket and pulled out a small, black velvet box. He popped it open with a flourish, revealing a diamond ring. Not *the diamond*, of course. This one was modest—suitable for a proposal, not a fencing deal.

Sarah blinked, startled. "Donny—"

But he was already taking her hand.

"No speeches," he said, sliding the ring onto her finger. "No big fuss. Just me, you, and forever."

She opened her mouth, but no sound came out. She hadn't even said yes.

Didn't matter.

Donny shot to his feet and turned toward the other diners. "Hey, everyone—raise a glass, would ya?" he called out, voice booming. "This beautiful woman just made me the luckiest guy in the world. We're engaged!"

A few people clapped politely. One older couple cheered. The waitress from earlier, now frowning, brought over a complimentary flan with a candle jammed in the center.

Bobby stared at the ring on Sarah's hand like it was a brand.

Sarah looked down at it too, unmoving. Her face gave nothing away. Not shock. Not joy. Not even fear.

Just silence.

Donny sat down again, grinning like a king. "Told you I had something special planned," he said, lifting his glass in a private toast to her. "Mexico, Baby Doll. That's where we'll get married."

Sarah blinked. "I thought we were just going to vacation there."

Donny's grin widened. "Surprise," he said, like it was the punchline to a joke. "We'll find a place—somewhere real nice. I'm about to come into some money, and I've got big plans. You'll love it down there. Sunshine, beaches, a house with a little garden, maybe even a porch swing. Just the two of us."

Sarah nodded slowly, but her eyes didn't leave the ring.

Back in the kitchen, as if coming from far away, Bobby heard dishes breaking.

CHAPTER TWENTY-TWO

As if coming from far away, Teresa heard dishes breaking. She tried to ignore the noise, hoping it would go away. She was so tired. All she wanted to do was sleep. Hoping to block out the noise, she rolled to her side, but the noises grew louder.

Shouting.

Angry, violent words.

The dull smack of flesh hitting flesh.

A woman weeping.

A growing sense of danger, of something being wrong. Once again, she struggled to awaken. Her body felt weighed down.

Then she heard a woman's terrified scream, abruptly cut off.

Then, blessed silence.

Sleep claimed her once again.

An indeterminate passage of time later, a roaring, sucking sound dragged her awake.

A short while later, a pungent odor filled the air, burning her nose and lungs.

Then, just as suddenly, the blessed silence returned.

The odor dissipated—but not the sense of wrongness.

Everything faded into nothingness until the entire sequence started over again, like an annoying song stuck on repeat.

This time the voices were louder, vaguely familiar.

The sense of danger was stronger.

Flesh beat flesh.

Dishes shattered.

A woman cried out in pain.

The dull roar of a motor mixed with an acrid odor.

She struggled to awaken. Dragging open her eyes, Teresa fought past the lingering fog of the nightmare and realized she was in her own bed. She took several long breaths to steady her nerves.

It was only a nightmare. About to reach out to turn on the bedside lamp, she froze when she spied a menacing figure standing in her bedroom doorway. Light from the hallway spilled in behind him, casting him in shadows so dark she couldn't see his face.

The sense that she might be in danger shot through her. Her heart raced, but she knew she had to hold perfectly still. She couldn't let him know she was awake. Through slitted eyes, she watched the figure in the doorway, hardly daring to breathe. After what seemed like an interminably long time, the figure receded into the hallway, and she heard a bedroom door down the hallway softly close.

That's when she came fully awake. Sitting up in bed, she reached for the lamp beside her bed and turned it on. Instantly, the shadows receded into the corners.

She scanned the room carefully, looking for anything out of the ordinary. Everything looked fine until her gaze fell on the bedroom door.

It was closed, as it had been when she'd gone to bed. There was no way anyone could have been standing in the doorway just now.

Had she even been awake?

She'd been having the same nightmare for the past several nights. The appearance of the figure in the doorway, however, was new.

She didn't know what any of it meant.

Checking the time, she saw that it was too early to get up. She turned out the lamp light, lay back in bed and started counting backwards from ten, because that relaxation technique had worked for her in the past. Quickly realizing that wasn't going to work, she started over from one hundred. Eventually, her body grew relaxed. Around the count of sixty-five or sixty-four, sleep overtook her.

Then the nightmare started over again.

Angry, violent shouting.

Flesh pounding flesh.

Dishes exploding.

A woman's frenzied cry, suddenly quieted.

An overwhelming sense of danger; drawing closer and closer, until—the danger was there! Familiar and terrifying. Standing in the doorway. Coming for her.

A woman's scream pierced the night.

Teresa was violently yanked from the depths of her slumber, her own scream still reverberating in her ears like a haunting echo. Looming above her was the same shadowy figure she'd seen earlier. He had come for her.

She lashed out blindly, her fists flailing against the figure.

"Ow!" The figure exclaimed, recoiling slightly. "Jesus, Teresa, it's me, John. I'm not going to hurt you. You had a bad dream. Stop hitting me."

The familiar cadence of John's voice sliced through the lingering haze of her nightmare, and Teresa collapsed back onto the bed, her heart racing. Fear clung to her, exhaustion tugged at her limbs, and an overwhelming sense of embarrassment washed over her.

"I'm so sorry, John. Did I hurt you?" Remorse filled her tone.

"No. You hit like a girl," he replied, his tone light and teasing, drawing a smile to her lips as he'd no doubt intended. "Must have been one hell of a dream."

"It was." Even as the details faded, the nightmare haunted her.

"Mind if I sit?" he inquired gently.

Now fully awake, Teresa's eyes had adjusted to the dim light, allowing her to see him gesturing toward the bed. "Of course." She shifted her legs, making space for him beside her.

"Want to tell me about it?" He settled next to her, becoming a comforting presence.

She considered it, then decided. *Why not?* "I don't really remember it," she admitted, her voice soft and uncertain. "Just bits and pieces."

"Tell me those," he encouraged gently. "The more you talk about it, the less scary it will seem. Believe me, I know what I'm talking about."

She realized then that going to prison had been a deeply traumatic ordeal for him. She was an idiot. *Of course it had been.* He was a good man who had made a grave error in judgment, leading to dire consequences. He'd been thrust into the harsh world of hardened criminals—killers and truly evil men. The men who starred in real-life nightmares.

"I'm sorry." Her voice was barely more than a whisper. "What was it like in prison."

"Scary," he admitted. "But I learned how to get along, but not before getting the crap beat out of me and nearly dying."

"Oh, my God. I had no idea. It must have been horrible for you."

"It was, but we're not going to talk about me right now." His tone was firm yet gentle. "I only meant that I know it helps to talk about it."

So she recounted what fragments she could remember. Voices clashing in heated argument. The sharp, jarring sounds of violence. The shattering of dishes. A woman's sobs echoing through the chaos. The cacophony of noise and the acrid smell that lingered.

"The worst part was the suffocating awareness of being in danger. I knew I needed to run away, but it was as if I was trapped, unable to wake up."

"With all the attention your house has been getting recently, and the vandalism, it's reasonable to think your nightmare results from that stress. But I'm curious, in the nightmare, did you get the sense that you were the woman screaming?"

She thought about it for a moment, then shook her head. "No. It wasn't me."

"Interesting." The word rolled off his tongue with a thoughtful air that piqued her curiosity.

"What are you thinking?"

"Could it be a memory?"

"Of what?" Her mind raced with possibilities.

"That's what we have to figure out," he said, his voice steady and reassuring. "You should take a few minutes to write out as many of the details of your nightmare as you can remember. Tomorrow, we can study them and see if we can draw any conclusions."

She heaved a deep sigh, her breath shaky as she released it. "Might as well. I doubt I'll be falling back asleep tonight," she admitted, her voice tinged with doubt.

"You have something to write on?" he persisted, his determination unwavering.

"I don't think so." She glanced around the dimly lit room.

"I'll be right back." He left the room before she could ask where he was headed, then returned a minute later carrying a notebook and pen. He held them out to her, a silent offering.

"I don't want to take your notebook from you," she tried to argue, not wanting to impose.

"It's fine. I can buy another one," he replied with a shrug, dismissing her concern.

Realizing he wasn't going to relent, she reluctantly took the notebook and pen from him. "Okay. Thanks."

She scooted back in the bed, settling herself with her back against the headboard. Reaching over, she flicked on the bedside light, casting a warm glow across the room. It was only then she noticed John wasn't wearing a shirt, his muscles faintly illuminated by the light. Why couldn't she dream about that instead of the terrifying images that haunted her?

"You okay now?"

At that moment, she realized that if she said she was, he would go back to his room. Icy fear snaked through her, twisting in her stomach, remnants of the nightmare rushing back, vivid and unsettling.

"Would you stay with me for a little while?" Her voice trembled slightly, and her cheeks flushed with warmth, acutely aware of what he might be thinking. "Not for anything intimate, just ... I don't want to be alone right now." She shifted to the far side of the bed, her fingers delicately plucking a pillow from the stack behind her and placing it at the head on the vacant side. "Maybe you could stay until I've finished writing?"

John regarded her thoughtfully, his gaze steady, before giving a slow, considerate nod. "Sure, I'll stay for a while. Until you've finished writing."

She flipped back the covers from the side of the bed clos-est to him, the fabric rustling softly in the quiet room. "This might take some time. You might as well be comfortable," she suggested gently.

He paused, but then climbed into bed beside her. Only then, as his presence cast a calming aura, easing her frayed nerves, did she realize the full weight of the tension and stress the nightmare had left in its wake.

"Thank you." She spoke so softly she worried he might not have heard her.

"No problem." She thought she heard him reply as he rolled away from her.

Feeling more at ease, though still acutely aware of the very appealing man beside her, she opened the notebook. It was brand new, the pages untouched, crisp and inviting, ready to absorb her thoughts. She began to write, the pen gliding smoothly across the paper, her focus deepening with each word.

Time slipped away unnoticed, and when she eventually finished her notes, fatigue settled over her like a gentle wave. John had drifted to sleep long before, his rhythmic breathing providing a soothing backdrop. It seemed almost cruel to wake him, and selfishly, she chose not to. If he was upset with her for letting him sleep, she'd deal with it in the morning. Right now, she craved a night of undisturbed rest.

Carefully, she placed the notebook and pen on the night-stand, extinguishing the soft glow of the bedside lamp. With deliberate care not to disturb the sleeping form beside her, she eased herself down into the bed, her body finding a comfortable spot next to him.

For the first time in what felt like ages, Teresa closed her eyes, her heart lightened by the comforting presence beside her. No more bad dreams would haunt her that night.

Chapter Twenty-Three

John came awake slowly, all too aware of the warm body pressed against his side. Teresa. The steady rhythm of her breathing told him she was still asleep. Her arm lay across his chest, her legs tangled with his as though she had sought him out in the night.

His pulse kicked at the closeness, at the softness of her curves pressed against him. There was no hiding his response beneath the covers. Would she wake embarrassed? Or horrified?

Or ... would she feel the same inevitability he did—that this moment had been building from the instant they met?

He'd resisted for her sake, reminding himself of the job waiting in El Paso and the life he might claim elsewhere. His deadline for leaving was approaching fast. How long did he have? A week? Maybe two? But lying here with her now, he wasn't sure he wanted anything beyond this bed, this woman.

She stirred, her hand flexing against his chest. He braced for her to pull away, but instead her fingertips lingered, feather light as they traced across his skin.

"Good morning." Her hushed voice was barely more than a whisper.

"Good morning," he murmured back. He longed to pull her closer, but his arm was pinned and he didn't dare shift.

Her head lifted slightly, then dropped back to the pillow. "Is that a mouse under the covers? Or are you glad to see me?"

A grin tugged at his lips. "Oh, I'm very glad to see you. Does that bother you?"

"Only if you don't plan to do anything about it." She pressed nearer, her breasts through her thin nightshirt brushing his arm, her words teasing yet edged with invitation.

That was all the encouragement he needed. He rolled until he hovered above her, bracing himself with one arm, the other hand sliding up to cup her cheek. Her eyes pulled him under, steady and sure.

"I'm going to kiss you now," he warned softly.

"Morning breath alert," she said, wrinkling her nose. "Speaking for myself, I don't mind, but you might."

He gave a low laugh. "I don't give a damn." His smile faded into urgency. "If I don't kiss you right now, I might explode."

"Well then, you'd better—"

Her words broke off as he captured her mouth with his. Slow at first, savoring. Then deeper, more insistent, as if the days of restraint had broken all at once. Teresa's arms slid around his neck, pulling him closer, kissing him back with a fervor that matched his own.

It felt like a dream she never wanted to end. His mouth trailed from hers to the curve of her jaw, down to her throat, leaving shivers in its wake. She arched against him, her breath coming in quick gasps, every nerve strung taut with want.

"John ..." Her whisper carried all the longing she couldn't put into words.

"Teresa." His forehead pressed against hers, his voice rough with need. "I want you—but I need to do this right."

Her heart stumbled. Then she remembered. "Desk drawer," she blurted, pointing across the room.

His eyes searched hers, questioning, then he slipped away long enough to dig into the drawer. Relief flickered across his face when he found what he was looking for.

Moments later he was back, covering her again, his touch tender, reverent, as if he'd been waiting his whole life for her.

Time blurred. What began with laughter and teasing turned to whispers and gasps, to a closeness that left them both trembling.

At last, they collapsed together, tangled in sheets and each other, hearts still racing.

"That was ... nice," Teresa said breathlessly, a teasing light in her eyes.

"Just nice?" he asked, mock-offended.

She chuckled. "Actually, it was incredible."

"Damn right it was." He kissed her again, soft and lingering. Then he pulled back with a rueful grin. "We're out of supplies, though. I'll run into town later." His gaze softened, searching hers. "Assuming you're up for a repeat performance?"

"Absolutely," she said without hesitation.

His answering smile was pure relief. "Good." He pushed up from the bed. "You want the shower first?"

She sat up, tousled hair framing her flushed face. "We could shower together."

He groaned, shaking his head. "Rain check. If I get in there with you, we'll never make it out again."

She laughed, knowing he was right, though disappointment tugged at her. "Fine. Then you should go first. I need to wash my hair, which always takes a little longer."

"Okay, if you're sure. While you shower, I'll go start breakfast. After that, we can check the third floor—see what secrets your grandmother left hidden."

She flashed him a wicked smile. "Before or after we run into town?"

"After," he answered immediately. "Definitely after."

"Exactly what I thought."

The smell of eggs and bacon reached Teresa long before she stepped into the kitchen.

"Sure smells good in here." She grabbed a mug from the cabinet and started the coffee.

"Great timing," John said, sliding scrambled eggs onto two plates already lined with crisp bacon. He set one in front of her and sat.

They ate in silence for a few minutes, both hungrier than they realized.

"This is really good," she said at last.

"I'm glad. After that last time, I wasn't sure how they'd turn out." He watched her a beat too long. She dabbed at her mouth, suddenly nervous.

Then he cleared his throat. "I need to tell you something, and I don't want you to freak out."

Her stomach sank. For a split second, she was sure she knew what was coming. He'd had time to think about the heat between them earlier that morning, and now he was going to tell her he regretted it—that he'd changed his mind about staying.

She set her fork down, bracing herself. "You're leaving, aren't you?" The words came out tighter than she'd intended.

Surprise flickered across his face before he leaned forward, voice steady. "No. Nothing like that. I'm not going anywhere, Teresa. Especially not now." His gaze held hers until the knot in her chest loosened.

"Okay," she whispered, relief flooding through her.

He gave her a small smile. "Good. Then let me finish before you try to guess again."

She pressed her lips together, determined to keep quiet this time.

"I got a call this morning—"

"I knew it," she blurted, unable to stop herself. "They found more skeletal remains."

"Teresa," he said, half laughing, half scolding. She bit the inside of her lip hard.

"The call was from Kathy's Café. Your muffins sold out in under an hour. She wants three dozen more for tomorrow."

She blinked at him, stunned. "They want to buy muffins?"

"They do. And it's not just Kathy. Two more orders came in by text."

"How many so far?"

He winced as if bracing for her reaction. "Six dozen."

"Holy cow."

"I may have oversold this new venture," he admitted. "Tell me if I need to call and scale it back."

"No—don't." Her surprise bloomed into delight. "This is incredible."

"So ..." He tilted his head. "Can you bake that many?"

She mentally scanned her pantry. "Yeah, I think so. I'll need more flour, sugar, butter—maybe another muffin pan or two. I should make a list." She looked up. "When do they want them?"

"I told them I'd deliver later today, so they're set for morning. Is that enough time?"

"It is. But it means I'm not much help on renovations."

"Don't worry about it. I'll work on what I can."

She smiled. "This muffin thing might actually work."

"I think so," he said, smiling back.

She gathered their plates. "Leave these. I'll have a lot more dishes before I'm done. I'll wash while the next batch bakes." Knowing she'd be paid for the muffins eased the knot in her stomach about buying supplies.

⸺◆O◆⸺

The oven chimed and Teresa straightened, back stiff. She slid out two trays of cinnamon-crumble muffins and set them on cooling racks. Getting paid to do something she loved—the novelty hadn't worn off.

She cracked more eggs, whisked, measured. Cinnamon and brown sugar built a warm cloud around her. The house was quiet except for the whisk's soft scrape. John hadn't returned yet from delivering the six dozen she'd baked earlier; he'd called from town to say more people were asking, so she'd started another round.

She'd just tucked the third batch into the oven when slow, deliberate steps sounded on the back walkway.

A moment later, the door creaked open and Mrs. Petrie came in, white hair twisted neat, cane clicking on the tile. Dressed in a floral housedress and pale pink cardigan, she was the embodiment of grandmotherly competence.

"Good morning, dear," she said, not apologizing for walking in without knocking. "Smells like a bakery. Someone's birthday?" Her brown eyes twinkled.

Teresa grinned. "Only if you count the birth of a new business venture." She gestured at the trays covering every inch of the counter. "I may have overdone it."

"New business, you say?" Mrs. Petrie eased herself into a chair with a small, satisfied sigh. "Renovating the house wasn't enough?"

"That's still the plan." Teresa held up a mug in silent question and, at Mrs. Petrie's nod, stuck it under the Keurig and started a fresh cup of coffee. "But until the backyard money tree blooms, yielding thousands of dollars, I'm running a side hustle to help pay the bills. If I sell muffins to the shops in town, it keeps me afloat another month."

"How very clever," Mrs. Petrie said.

"It was John's idea," she admitted, removing the fresh cup of coffee and handing it to Mrs. Petrie. "Cream or sugar?"

"Nothing, thank you," she replied, cradling the mug. "That John is a smart one. And a hard worker, too—this house is really shaping up nicely, from what I can see. You should find a way to hang onto that boy!"

She joined Mrs. Petrie at the table, but didn't comment. They sat a moment, the radio humming softly. Mrs. Petrie eyed the muffin mountain. "Business must be good."

Heat climbed Teresa's cheeks as she rose. Placing several of the fresh muffins on a plate, she carried them over to the table and set them down. "I might have made too many. Please, take as many as you want," Teresa said, sitting.

Mrs. Petrie leaned in conspiratorially. "Have you tried the grocery store bakery lately? Frozen dough from Houston." She wrinkled her nose. "Last week I bought a Danish. I'm not convinced it was food."

"That's what I'm counting on," Teresa said. "People around here remember when things tasted real."

"My mother's blackberry muffins," Mrs. Petrie said, gaze going wistful. "Berries from the ditch behind the house. I haven't had one that good since the '60s."

"Did she write down the recipe?"

"Maybe." Mrs. Petrie tapped the table, thinking. "I kept Mother's and Gran's recipes, though I hardly use them." She weighed Teresa with a look. "Want to see?"

"I'd love to."

Mrs. Petrie finished her coffee and levered herself up with her cane. "Don't go anywhere," she commanded, and disappeared out the back door.

Fifteen minutes later, Teresa was pulling the last batch of muffins from the oven when Mrs. Petrie returned, carrying an ancient metal index box the color of faded sky. She set it down like contraband.

"Don't judge the box," she warned. "It's survived several generations, four moves and three floods." She flicked open the lid and thumbed through the cards, fingers still nimble. "Chess pie, corn casserole, cucumber and onion salad ... ah." She drew a battered card, its edges soft and yellow. "Blackberry Buckle Muffins."

Two hands had written the recipe: one in a neat, upright script; the other in bold lettering filling the margins. Smudges of dried batter freckled the corners.

"Mother always said the secret was lemon zest and just enough buttermilk to make the batter sing." She slid the card across. "Copy it if you like."

Teresa took it reverently. "It looks amazing. Are you sure? People can be protective of family recipes."

Mrs. Petrie patted her hand. Her skin felt like worn cotton. "I'm sure. You're the closest thing I have to a granddaughter. I want someone to keep it alive."

Emotion rose so fast Teresa had to blink it back. "Thank you. I'll do it justice."

"You better. And if you ruin it with chocolate chips, I'll haunt you myself." She let that hang, then winked. "Everyone needs a specialty. Maybe this puts your muffin business over the top."

Teresa pressed the card to her chest, smiling. "I'll try it as soon as I can. Maybe next week's special."

"Good girl." Mrs. Petrie stood and walked to the back door pausing in the doorway. "You and John should come for supper sometime. I love cooking, but not just for myself."

"We'd be thrilled," Teresa said—and meant it.

She watched her neighbor shuffle out the door, her recipe box tucked under her arm like a secret weapon. Warmth settled in Teresa's chest, heavier and sweeter than cinnamon.

She looked at the card again, already tasting the muffins. This was how traditions survived—not just in faded ink, but in passing them down, one woman to another.

Could this day get any better?

CHAPTER TWENTY-FOUR

LAS PALOMAS, TEXAS
AUGUST 3, 1945 8:30 p.m..

Could the day get any worse?

Sarah was still trying to get over the shock of Donny's proposal, wondering how she could give back the ring without angering him.

"Now this is how you end a perfect evening," Donny said, pouring whiskey into a tumbler with a heavy hand.

They were back in the sitting room of the Meyers B&B. A brass lamp cast amber light over the worn rugs and floral-patterned chairs, shadows stretching long across the wood-paneled walls. The other guests had long since retired to their rooms, leaving the house quiet except for the distant ticking of the grandfather clock and the clink of glass as Donny helped himself to the small liquor cabinet near the fireplace.

"Food, fanfare, and fiancée." He threw Bobby a look over his shoulder and smirked. "Ain't that right, baby brother?"

Bobby didn't respond. He stood near the window, arms crossed, watching the streetlamp flicker through the lace curtain like it might offer some escape.

Donny flopped into the overstuffed armchair and let out a theatrical groan, kicking off one shoe with a grunt and leaving it lying sideways on the rug.

"Hell, my feet are killing me," he muttered. He stretched his legs out in front of him and looked toward Sarah, who sat stiffly on the edge of the settee, hands folded tightly in her lap.

He nodded at her. "Come rub 'em."

Sarah blinked. "What?"

"My feet, sweetheart." He took a slow sip of whiskey. "They hurt. Long day. You wanna make your fiancé happy, right?"

"I—I'm tired, Donny. Maybe we should just go upstairs—"

Donny's smile vanished. He leaned forward and set the glass down with a thud.

Bobby straightened. "She said she's tired."

Donny's gaze slid over to him, calm and venomous. "Stay outta this."

Bobby took a step forward. "Be reasonable, Donny—"

Donny stood. In one slow, deliberate motion, he reached behind his back and pulled a gun from the waistband of his pants. He let the barrel dangle from his fingers, casual as could be, like it was no more important than a cigarette.

"Now see," he said, voice low and measured, "this is what happens when people forget who's in charge."

Silence dropped over the room like a lid on a coffin.

Donny turned back to Sarah, tilting his head. "You wanna argue with me too, Baby Doll? Or are you gonna do your job and rub my damn feet?"

Sarah's eyes dropped to the floor. Then, slowly, she rose and crossed the room. She knelt before him, fingers trembling as she reached for his other shoe and pulled it off. The smell of leather and sweat hit her nose, but she didn't flinch. Not yet.

She began to rub gently, her hands working over the socks, careful and steady.

Donny leaned back again and closed his eyes, smug satisfaction etched on his face.

But it didn't last.

"You're doing it wrong," he snapped suddenly, opening one eye. "Hell, it's like you're petting a dead cat."

"I—I'm sorry—"

He lifted his foot and shoved it hard against her chest.

Sarah lost her balance and fell back onto the rug with a soft gasp.

Bobby was at her side in an instant, crouching to help her sit up, his hands under her elbows. "Are you okay?"

Donny stood over them, glass in one hand, gun still dangling from the other.

"Get out," he growled. "Both of you. I don't wanna look at either one of you tonight."

Bobby looked like he might argue—but Sarah touched his arm.

"Let's go," she whispered, not looking back at Donny.

They rose together and left the sitting room without another word.

Behind them, Donny slumped into his chair again, took another long drink, and muttered to no one, "Damn ingrates."

The door clicked shut behind them as Bobby followed Sarah into her room. A pale sliver of hallway light cut across the floor before he turned and gently eased the door closed, muffling the creak of old hinges. The silence that settled was thick with what hadn't been said downstairs.

Sarah stood near the bed, arms wrapped tightly around herself. Her dress, now slightly rumpled, swayed with her shallow breaths. Bobby hesitated just inside the room, watching her shoulders tremble.

"Are you okay?"

She didn't answer right away. Then, in a voice sounding small and raw, she said, "He pushed me like I was nothing. Like I was a dog that disappointed him."

Bobby's throat tightened. "You're not nothing. You never were."

She turned toward him, eyes glistening but dry. "I can't stand him, Bobby. I don't even want to pretend anymore."

Without thinking, Bobby closed the distance and wrapped his arms around her. She melted into him, the tension in her shoulders unraveling as he held her close. He pressed his cheek to her hair and closed his eyes, letting the quiet fill them like a prayer.

"I should've stopped him," he murmured.

"You did enough," she whispered. "You stayed."

For a long moment, they stood like that, just breathing the same air. Then Sarah tilted her head back, just enough to meet his eyes.

The kiss happened like rain—soft at first, then sudden. His lips met hers, and the ache in his chest fractured into something fiercer, something whole. Her fingers curled into his shirt, pulling him closer. For a moment, nothing else existed but the warmth of her mouth and the desperate, silent promise in their touch.

When they finally pulled apart, breathless and blinking, Sarah was the first to speak.

"I want to leave," she said. "Now. Tonight."

Bobby nodded, already halfway to agreeing, but then something cold and familiar tugged at the edge of his conscience.

"I want that too," he said. "But I can't—not yet."

"Why?"

"Because of the Stanford diamond."

Sarah shook her head. "Forget the diamond. Who cares about it? We can just go. Start over."

Bobby stepped back, running a hand through his hair. "I wish we could. But as long as it's still out there—I'm still out there. I'll always be looking over my shoulder. I'll never be free to enjoy a life with you if I'm spending every day waiting for someone to figure out what I helped him do."

She stared at him for a long beat, then gave a small nod, defeated but understanding.

"I know where he hid it," Bobby said. "In our room, beneath a baseboard. If I can get it back, turn it in—maybe I've got a shot at starting clean."

Sarah nodded again, already reaching for her bag. "Then get it and let's go."

Bobby shook his head. "Can't. He'll stop us. Tomorrow night, I promise. I'll take Donny into town for drinks after dinner. We'll play a couple of hands of poker, then around eleven, I'll tell him I'm not feeling well and head back. Hopefully, he'll want to stay. I'll come back, grab the diamond and we can leave." He paused. "Just in case I can't ditch Donny, maybe you'd better meet me out back. If I'm not there by eleven-thirty, leave without me."

Sarah didn't like waiting, but she nodded. "All right. Tomorrow night, then."

She walked him to her bedroom door but stopped him before he could turn the knob. Rising onto her toes, she leaned in to kiss him again. "Be careful," she whispered when the kiss ended. Then she stepped back and watched him slip out.

CHAPTER TWENTY-FIVE

"I have an idea," John said as they finished lunch. The kitchen smelled of muffins, warm and sweet, the kind of scent that made the old house feel safe and homey—like it belonged to another life entirely.

Teresa narrowed her eyes. "This isn't another money-making scheme, is it? Because I don't think I can handle one more of those."

He gave a short laugh and shook his head. "Nothing like that. I was thinking we could spend the afternoon looking for the guest registers. We can see if Donny really stayed here and, if so, which room he used. That'd give us a place to start."

The words struck Teresa like a blow to the stomach. For a fleeting, terrible moment, doubt whispered in her mind. Had she been wrong about John? What if all this time—his kindness, his steady presence—had only been a cover for his actual goal? The diamond?

But almost as soon as the thought formed, she knew it wasn't true. The John she knew wasn't a liar or a thief. He was honest—sometimes painfully so. He'd stood by her, not for what she had, but for who she was. And if she admitted the truth to herself, she was falling in love with him. The idea of his walking away and never coming back was more than she could bear.

Still, something of her turmoil must have shown on her face, because he crossed to her quickly. His hands settled gently on her arms, his gaze searching hers.

"Don't do this, Teresa. I thought we'd moved past doubting each other." His voice was rough with hurt. "If you really think I'm here for the diamond, just say the word. I'll pack my things and go. You'll never have to see me again."

The lump in her throat swelled, stealing her voice. Her silence made his hands fall away. He stepped back, disappointment etched across his features.

"Wow," he exhaled. "Okay. If that's how you feel…" He turned.

"Wait, please!" The words tumbled out, and she grabbed his arm before he could step away. "I'm sorry. I do trust you—I do. And I don't want you to leave."

He turned back, lifting her chin so she had no choice but to meet his gaze. "Are you sure?"

"Yes." Her voice was steady now, but her heart was anything but. His nearness made her breathless, every nerve taut, hoping he might kiss her—and fearing that he wouldn't.

Then he did. He gathered her into his arms, his lips claiming hers in a kiss that silenced every lingering doubt. She melted against him, letting the warmth of his embrace and the tenderness of his mouth sweep away her fear. When at last he drew back, his breathing was as uneven as hers.

"You make me want to carry you upstairs and keep going," he murmured, his lips brushing her temple, a crooked smile tugging at his mouth. "But—"

"But we have work to do," she finished for him, smiling even as her pulse still raced.

"To be continued later?"

"Definitely."

He pressed a quick kiss against her forehead before releasing her.

"As I was saying before we got sidetracked—if we can find the registers, we'll know if Donny stayed here and, if so, in which room. If he hid the diamond here, that room is the best place to look. And if he didn't stay here, then we can make that public, and maybe people will finally stop tearing this place apart looking for something that isn't here. My chief concerns are putting an end to the vandalism and keeping you safe. And if by chance we find it, returning it to its rightful owner would settle things once and for all—and the reward could give you a cushion until the B&B is ready to open."

His concern for her, more than the diamond, warmed her in ways she couldn't explain.

"And who knows," he added, "maybe we'll discover someone else famous once stayed here. That could get the historical society invested in preserving this place. Maybe even help you secure a grant."

His enthusiasm was infectious, tugging a smile from her. "Where do we start?"

"The attic. It's the only place we haven't searched."

Hand in hand, they turned toward the stairs.

John steadied the ladder as Teresa climbed up first, her hand reaching for the string dangling from the lone bulb. She gave it a tug, and the attic flickered to life in a weak yellow glow. The air was hot and stale, thick with the scent of cedar and dust. Shadows stretched long across the rafters, sharp and unfamiliar.

Teresa pulled herself the rest of the way through the hatch and glanced around. "Not much up here."

John followed, ducking his head through the opening and brushing dust from his shirt as he stood. His gaze swept over the sparse contents—a few stacks of boxes, some old linens piled in the corner. "Guess your grandmother wasn't much of a pack rat."

She made a face. "That doesn't sound like her at all."

He crouched beside one of the nearest boxes and pried it open. Inside were strings of tinsel, ornaments wrapped in tissue, and a battered angel for the top of a tree. "Christmas decorations," he muttered.

Teresa lifted the lid on another box. "Thanksgiving," she said, pulling out a ceramic turkey. She set it gently back down and dusted her hands. "Well, that's ... festive, but not very helpful."

Before John could reply, a faint scrape echoed from the far side of the attic. One of the stacked boxes shifted, sliding forward just enough to draw their eyes.

John froze, straightening slowly. His eyes narrowed on the box, then flicked toward her. He didn't say anything, but Teresa caught the flicker of tension in his jaw.

"Uncle Bill," she whispered.

John gave her a look, but didn't argue. He crouched beside her as she pulled the box over and opened it. Inside was an album, filled with newspaper clippings carefully tucked into sheet protectors, yellowed but neatly preserved.

She flipped to the first page and felt her chest tighten. It was her mother—smiling in her high school cheer uniform, pompoms in hand, the caption crowing about the big game. "I didn't even know Grandma kept this ..." Teresa murmured, brushing her fingertips against the plastic.

The floorboards were dusty, but Teresa sank down cross-legged anyway, the album balanced in her lap. She turned page after page, smiling faintly through the sting in her eyes.

Then, as she lingered on one clipping tucked inside the album, the page flipped sharply of its own accord.

Teresa blinked, then frowned. "Hey—give me a second."

Another page turned on its own.

"Really?" she muttered.

Another page turned, more insistent.

Teresa steadied the book and let her gaze fall to where the page had opened. Not her mother's picture this time. This one was of Felipe Velasquez. The article described his years documenting oral histories, preserving folklore, and warning that "local legends should not be forgotten."

John came over, crouched beside her, and leaned close as she tapped one of the clippings tucked behind a page.

"Who's that?" he asked.

"Felipe Velasquez," Teresa said. "He's sort of the unofficial town historian. He's been collecting oral histories and preserving folklore for years."

John's brow furrowed slightly. "Why would Uncle Bill want us to see this?"

"I don't know," Teresa admitted. "But maybe it means Felipe's worth talking to."

They exchanged a thoughtful look, but the moment carried no urgency. John eventually pushed back to his feet. "Well, maybe he's a lead. In the meantime, we should keep looking."

Teresa nodded, closing the album carefully. She started to rise when, without warning, another album rose from the box, tilted forward, and tumbled to the floor at her feet. Dust puffed into the air as the cover fell open.

The pages began flipping on their own.

Teresa's breath caught. She leaned closer, scanning as the flipping slowed and finally stopped. Several clippings covered local events and festivals ... and then she saw it. Her eyes widened. "John—come look at this."

He crouched beside her again, and she read aloud, "Felipe Velasquez is asking townsfolk to donate memorabilia for his historical collection, particularly items related to the late 1800s and early 1900s."

She looked up at him, her voice tight with realization. "Do you think ... maybe Gram donated the guest registers to him?"

John exhaled, glancing at the clipping and then back at her. "There's only one way to find out."

Teresa closed the album, brushing dust from her palms. "We need to go talk to Felipe."

"We'll go see him tomorrow." John offered her a steadying hand up. "Before it gets too late in the afternoon, I need to run those muffins into town and pick up supplies. You want to tag along?"

"Yeah, I do. Thanks."

Together they headed back toward the ladder.

Above them, the lightbulb flickered once, and the album pages gave a faint rustle—as if Uncle Bill approved.

CHAPTER TWENTY-SIX

The back porch light flickered, and from somewhere in the darkness came the rustling of leaves. Like a ghost stirring, Sarah thought, checking her watch again. 11:39 p.m.

Bobby was late.

She'd promised to leave if he wasn't there by 11:30, but she'd lied. She was leaving without him, but the minutes were dragging out like the final notes of a dying song. The backyard was off-limits to guests due to the construction. Unsafe after sunset, the B&B owner had warned earlier that week.

"So we can host parties out here once the weather cools," Mrs. Meyers had said with a laugh, gesturing to the chaos with a kind of pride.

Sarah didn't feel like laughing now.

The yard was a disaster zone. Jagged stacks of scrap wood leaned like broken ribs against the side of the house. Rusted tools lay abandoned in the weeds. A cement mixer loomed near the porch like a gutted beast, and the freshly poured concrete stretched out across the patio in a dull, wet sheen—untouchable and dangerous.

Mosquitoes buzzed near her ears, drawn by the sweat clinging to the back of her neck. Every creak, every distant clatter from a shifting board made her flinch.

She bit her lip and glanced again toward the house.

Donny had jumped at the chance to go into town for drinks with Bobby, and the two had left hours ago. Sarah had played her part, feigning a headache to stay behind, her bag already packed and ready.

Bobby had promised. If I'm not there by 11:30, you go without me.

But she couldn't. She wouldn't.

Her shoes scraped softly along the narrow edge of the patio as she turned and paced again, careful to avoid the wet concrete. The darkness clung to the edges of the yard, thick and pressing. Trees cast tall, tangled shadows across the lawn, and the air hummed with the tension of something about to break.

She checked her watch. 11:42.

How long could she wait before the window slammed shut forever?

Then—crunch.

She froze.

Somewhere to her left, dry grass shifted. Not the wind. Something heavier. Footsteps.

She held her breath, listening.

Snap.

Behind her.

She turned sharply, eyes searching the line of trees beyond, heart thudding like a war drum. Her voice, when it came, was a fragile thread of sound.

"Bobby?"

A long pause.

Then—

"Afraid not."

The words slid from the dark like a blade, smooth and sharp and cold.

Sarah's heart stopped.

From the shadows, a figure stepped forward, the faint yellow glow from the back porch catching the glint of metal in his hand. Her breath caught as the gun came into focus, gleaming in the low light like a promise already kept.

Donny.

She didn't scream.

She didn't move.

Her mind scrambled for a lie, a reason, anything—but nothing came. Her thoughts scattered like dry leaves in the wind.

Then there was a flash—brief, brilliant, final.

And everything went black.

CHAPTER TWENTY-SEVEN

Hours later, they returned to the house, a few dollars richer, thanks to the muffin sales, loaded down with four ceiling fan kits which they'd purchased from the hardware store, and sated from a dinner at the local Italian restaurant. They placed one ceiling fan kit into each of the second-floor bedrooms.

"It's getting late," John said when they were done. "I'd rather replace these light fixtures when it's daylight."

"Good, because I'm exhausted. I'd like nothing more than to crawl into bed and watch TV until I fall asleep. I guess that's not going to happen though."

Turning to her, John saw the exhaustion written on her face. Even the circles under her eyes seemed to have grown darker. "Oh, I think we can work something out. The TV downstairs isn't that heavy. Why don't you go take a hot bath? I'll bring the TV upstairs and set it up in your room. We can watch TV in bed."

"I like the sound of that."

She hurried down the hall to start the bathwater, so he headed downstairs. He went around checking the doors and windows to make sure everything was locked. Then he carried the TV upstairs to Teresa's room.

He had to do some minor rearranging of furniture before he could set the TV on top of the small desk and plug it in.

When Teresa finally finished her bath and walked into her bedroom, he was sitting on her bed, dressed in the T-shirt and shorts he usually wore when lounging around.

Her smile seemed almost shy, and he found that endearing.

Dressed only in her nightshirt, she turned out the room lights and crawled into bed beside him.

"What do you want to watch?" he asked her.

"I don't really care," she admitted. "I just want the background noise."

"Okay." He searched through the channels until he found reruns of *Everybody Loves Raymond*. Watching television wasn't what he really wanted to do, but he respected the fact that she was tired and tried to be content lying beside her.

Before the opening credits finished scrolling across the television screen, Teresa was sound asleep. She'd scooted close enough that her head rested against his arm. For the entire duration of the show, he held perfectly still, not wanting to risk disturbing her and having her roll away from him.

When the episode ended, he debated on leaving the television on or turning it off. He left it on and then, as quietly as he could, started to get out of the bed.

He stopped moving when Teresa grabbed his arm.

"Are you leaving?" Her voice sounded husky from sleep.

"I didn't want to assume you'd want me to stay."

"I do."

He didn't have to be told twice. He stood only long enough to pull the covers back so he could join her beneath them. Then he turned off the TV and settled back against the pillows. When she moved close, he slipped an arm around her so she could rest her head on his chest.

He'd never known such contentment before and thought he could lay there forever, just holding her. Those lonely and sometimes terrifying nights spent in prison seemed like nothing more than a long-ago bad dream.

He listened to the sound of Teresa's breathing, trying to memorize every nuance of this moment. Only when he could no longer hold his eyelids open did he surrender to sleep.

Consciousness was slow in coming to Teresa. The first thing she was aware of was a feeling of being well-rested. That in itself was monumental. She couldn't remember the last time she'd slept so well. Definitely not since she'd returned to Las Palomas.

She cracked an eyelid and saw that morning light was spilling through the cracks in the blinds, confirming she had slept through the night.

Feeling a need to stretch like a cat, she froze before moving a muscle, realizing she was draped over a hard, firm body.

John!

He'd stayed with her through the night and was still there, in her bed.

"Did you sleep all right?" His voice, sounding low and tender, still startled her.

"You're awake."

Below her head, his chest rumbled with soft laughter. "I am."

"Have you been lying there, listening to me sleep?"

"Guilty as charged."

She didn't even try to sound offended because she wasn't. "That's nice. I like waking up next to you."

He gave her a squeeze. "I like waking up next to you, too."

"I can't believe it."

"What? That I like sleeping with you?"

She gave an embarrassed huff of laughter. "Well, yes, that too, but I can't believe I slept through the night without having a nightmare. You must have chased them all away."

"I think you're giving me too much credit, but on the chance you're right, then I'm glad to be of service."

She pushed herself up until she could kiss his cheek. "Thank you," she whispered.

He caught her to him and, turning his head, kissed her long and hard. "Speaking of being at your service," he said when the kiss finally ended.

"If you're thinking I'm going to tell you no," she finally said when he continued to gaze at her expectantly. "You're mistaken."

Further conversation was aborted as the kissing resumed. Even worries about things like morning breath were soon forgotten as clothes were shed. Teresa was glad they had left one of the boxes of condoms in her nightstand so there would be no unnecessary delay while John ran to his room to grab a box.

For the next thirty minutes, all worries about the house renovations, money, or finding the diamond were forgotten as they made love.

Finally, the two broke apart and lay on the bed, feeling fully rested and sexually sated.

"I could stay here forever," Teresa mumbled, mostly to herself.

"I know what you mean," he said, giving her a gentle shove in the opposite direction before he rolled out of bed. "But I'm afraid we have muffins to bake, fans to mount and a diamond to find."

"From your lips to God's ear," she said, crossing to her dresser to pull out clothes. John was pulling on the same shirt and shorts he'd slept in. He didn't have any other clothes in her room to wear, and it occurred to her to suggest that if they were going to keep sleeping together, he might want to keep his clothes in her room. She could easily clear out a couple of dresser drawers for him to use. She remained silent though, suddenly insecure about their relationship. After all, there was still a job waiting for him in El Paso and he had said nothing about staying.

Seemingly unaware of her thoughts, now dressed, he headed for the door. "I'll see you downstairs in a few." He went out the bedroom door but then, a second later, he was poking his head back through. "What do you think about moving my dresser into this room? There's plenty of room for it, and it would be more convenient for me to have my clothes in here, but I don't want to rush you."

Teresa felt like her heart was about to burst with joy. "I'd say that's a great idea. Maybe we move it in after breakfast?"

"Deal." Then he was gone, headed down the hallway. "Last one downstairs does the dishes," his voice floated to her from down the hallway.

Teresa, who had been basking in the joy of being in a committed relationship, shook herself from her stupor. She didn't mind cooking, but she hated doing dishes. Grabbing the first outfit she found in her drawer, she was still trying to pull it on as she hurried down the stairs.

Chapter Twenty-Eight

After dropping off that morning's muffin orders, Teresa and John drove out to Felipe Velasquez's house. The gravel crunched beneath the tires of her old truck as she turned off the highway and pulled up to the adobe house tucked beneath a tangle of mesquite trees. Bone and copper wind chimes clinked lazily in the hot breeze.

John climbed out and squinted up at the sun-bleached roof. "Place has character," he said, glancing at the wind chimes with a raised brow.

There weren't many adobe houses left in town, making this one unique. Teresa thought it a fitting residence for their town historian.

She lifted her hand to knock, but before she touched the weathered wood, the door creaked open. Felipe stood in the doorway, thinner than she remembered, his sharp gaze softening when he saw them. His arms, bare beneath rolled-up sleeves, carried faint bruises and scratches.

"Señor Velasquez," Teresa said gently. "I'm sorry to arrive unannounced." She glanced pointedly to his arms. "Are you okay?"

He glanced down, almost as if surprised to see them. "Just wrestling my demons, *mija*. Nothing I can't handle."

"Mr. Velasquez, this is John Morris. He's helping me renovate my grandparent's house." At the introduction, John reached past Teresa to shake the older man's hand. "We were hoping we might talk to you," she added.

Felipe waved them inside. "Come in. Come in. I'm always happy to receive visitors. And please, call me Felipe."

He led them into the family room, which smelled faintly of cedar and dried sage. Worn furniture and shelves lined with framed photos gave the space a lived-in warmth. They sat together—Teresa and John on the couch, Felipe lowering himself into an armchair with the stiffness of advanced age.

Except he's not that old. Early seventies?

For a few minutes, they exchanged small talk. Teresa asked about his son, Gabriel, and Felipe's face brightened.

"He's doing well," Felipe said, a touch of pride in his voice. "Works for the state these days—criminal profiler, behavioral analyst type. Travels a lot, studying men who've lost their way." He paused, eyes fixed on a picture of Gabriel on the shelf. "Funny thing, though ... he didn't need to leave home to find that."

The words hit a little too close. Teresa's thoughts drifted to Sam and the bullet she'd taken—how close she'd come to dying. Then, as always, her mind veered toward the deeper scar—the one left behind by her parents' disappearance. Fifteen years later, and still no answers. Yet ...

"Yeah," she said softly, almost to herself. "Sometimes the darkest things are the ones that grow in your own backyard.

Felipe's gaze shifted to her and lingered for a moment, then slid to John before he asked, "I always appreciate a friendly visit, but what brings you?"

Teresa hesitated, then leaned forward. "John and I have been looking for the old guest registers from the Meyers B&B. We searched everywhere in the house but can't find a thing. My grandmother was big on preserving history, so it occurred to me she might have donated them to you?"

A spark lit Felipe's eyes. Slowly, he pushed himself up from his chair. "Come with me."

He led them down a narrow hallway to a room lined with bookshelves, stacked boxes, and cloth-bound ledgers. Old photographs hung on the walls, their sepia tones faded with time. *This*, Teresa thought, *must be his historical library.*

Felipe crouched stiffly beside a stack of crates, scanning the faded ink scrawled across their lids. "Yes. She gave them to me. Said she didn't want them collecting dust."

He tugged one box forward and opened it. Inside were leather-bound books, tied bundles of papers, and even a few rolled-up blueprints. Pulling out another box, he opened the lid. This one held menus and photographs.

Teresa swallowed hard at the sight. "These are incredible. I'd love the chance to go through them."

Felipe smiled faintly. "Normally, I'd say sit and stay as long as you like, but I have somewhere I need to be this afternoon. Better you take them with you. I'll stop by later this week to collect them."

John gave a short nod. "We'll make sure everything stays safe."

Teresa helped John carry the boxes back through the house and out to the truck, noting the way the paper smelled faintly of dust and age. John used rope he found behind the front passenger seat to tie the boxes so the lids wouldn't come off during transport.

As they worked, Felipe stood in the doorway, one hand braced against the frame, watching them. His shoulders slumped in a way Teresa had never noticed before. He looked smaller somehow, fragile in the afternoon light.

Thanking Felipe again, she climbed into the truck, unable to shake her concern for the older man. Maybe he was sick? She didn't know, but it would be rude to ask. Whatever was happening to him, she couldn't shake the feeling that Felipe Velasquez, the town's guardian of stories, was fighting a quiet battle of his own—and losing ground.

⚬

By the time they returned home, John was already getting muffin orders for the next day. So Teresa spent the afternoon in the kitchen, baking muffins, while John studied the guest ledgers and blueprints Felipe had entrusted to them. She might have finished much earlier but she'd accidentally burned the first batch and been forced to throw them out and start over. The incident left her worried about the success of this new venture, but she pressed forward and kept baking.

When she finished the last batch, she walked over to where John stood at the table. "So? Did you find anything?"

John tapped one of the open books. "I did. Donny and Bobby Rangel—Blue Room. Sarah Holloway—Yellow Room."

Her pulse jumped. "So the rumors were right. They really did stay here."

"Yeah," he said, "but I don't remember seeing a blue or yellow room upstairs. Do you?"

She shook her head. "No. They were all painted off-white by the time I moved in here as a kid. I have no idea which one used to be the Blue Room."

He spread out the blueprints, tracing neat lines with his finger. "Felipe gave us these too—renovation plans from 1945. I was hoping for a clue, but none of the rooms are labeled by name. And I didn't see any hidden spaces or false walls. Everything lines up." He looked up at her. "You know what that means?"

Teresa blew out a breath. "We'll have to check every room."

"Let's be logical about this," John said. "Bubba punched holes in half the walls upstairs, didn't he?"

"Yes." Her mouth tightened. "And now I have to wonder if he was really making repairs—or just looking for the diamond."

"If he had been looking, and the stone was hidden in the walls, he would've found it."

"Unless Bubba was too inept to know he had," Teresa countered, though without much conviction.

John gave her a wry half-smile. "Possible. But think about it—back in the 1940s, hiding a diamond inside a wall would've been hard to pull off without someone noticing, especially in a guest room. A loose floorboard would've been easier, and less suspicious."

Her gaze shifted toward the ceiling as she thought about the upstairs rooms. "I think the floors are original, but I can't swear to it."

"Let's find out."

A few minutes later, they were upstairs. John crouched down and ran his hand across the boards, tapping lightly in several spots. "Looks original to me."

"Then that's where we start."

Teresa bent down beside him, ready to help, but John stopped her with a look. "Why don't you go deliver muffins while I handle this. I'll work through the floors one room at a time."

She hesitated. "Are you sure? I don't like the idea of you doing it alone."

"I'll be fine," he assured her, already testing another spot on the floor.

Reluctantly, Teresa nodded. "All right. But don't go tearing the place apart without me."

He gave her a quick grin. "Wouldn't dream of it."

With one last look at him crouched on the floorboards, methodical and focused, she headed back downstairs.

The upstairs hall fell quiet, except for the soft thud of John's knuckles on wood. He shifted a few boards, patiently listening, measuring. Then, just as he leaned back to reach for his pry bar, it slid a few inches across the floorboards, turning until its handle pointed directly at the window. looking out over the patio

John sat back on his heels, jaw tightening. "Old houses," he muttered, though the words rang hollow. His gaze lingered on the glass panes overlooking the patio below.

He shook his head, forcing himself back to work, but as he tested the next seam in the floor, a strange unease lingered. When things like that happened, it was harder to argue against the house being haunted.

CHAPTER TWENTY-NINE

LAS PALOMAS, TEXAS
AUGUST 4, 1945 11:39 p.m.

Bobby took the stairs two at a time, his heart pounding in his throat. It had taken him longer than expected to ditch Donny in town. Now, he wasn't sure which outcome he dreaded more—finding Sarah still waiting, or discovering she was already gone. If she had left for the bus station without him, she was safe. That was all that mattered.

But God help him, he wanted—needed—to see her one more time.

He reached the third room on the left and knocked. No answer.

His fingers closed around the knob. It turned easily.

He stepped inside, scanning quickly. Her suitcase and purse were gone.

A rush of relief. She must've gone ahead. That was good. Smart. Safe.

Unless …

Unless she was still out back, waiting.

He crossed to the window and yanked back the curtain, eyes cutting through the darkness. At first, nothing—just the mangled backyard, cast in crooked shadows by the porch light. Then, movement. A flicker of fabric at the far edge of the yard, near the tree line.

A skirt?

He waited. Seconds later, a figure emerged—slender, familiar.

Sarah.

Relief mixed with urgency. He was already late. There was no telling when Donny would stumble home from the bar.

Bobby turned and bolted from the room, hurrying into the one he shared with Donny. His suitcase was already packed, mostly. The rest of his things didn't matter. The only thing that did matter was finding the diamond.

He pulled open the closet door and dropped to his knees. With practiced hands, he reached for the loose floorboard in the back, wedging a coin into the crack. The board gave way with a soft pop.

He reached into the gap beneath—expecting the smooth feel of a leather bag.

Instead, his fingers met empty air.

No diamond.

Heart stuttering, he grabbed his lighter, flicking it on and angling the flame down into the crevice. He tilted it from side to side, hunting the corners.

Empty.

His breath came faster. Donny had moved it.

Didn't trust me. Never did.

He replaced the board, his mind racing. Where would Donny hide it? Somewhere simple. Close. Donny wasn't clever—he was arrogant. He liked easy, fast. He liked control.

Bobby crossed to the dresser and yanked open drawers. He slid his hand beneath the lining, behind loose backs, tapping for hollow sounds. Nothing. He crouched beside the mattress, ran his hands beneath the frame, lifted the edge of the bed skirt.

Think. Think like Donny.

He paused, eyes scanning the room. Then he moved.

Three minutes. Three minutes was all he'd allow himself to find the diamond. No more. If he didn't find it in that time, he would leave without it.

Three minutes later, Bobby stood in the center of the room, chest heaving, sweat sliding down his spine.

It was time to go.

Grabbing his suitcase, he hurried out the front door and around the side of the house to the back. The darkness wrapped tight around him, pressing against his lungs. His breath came shallow. The construction equipment looked like beasts asleep in the yard, shadows bent and twisted under the porch light.

"Sarah?" he called in a loud whisper. No answer.

He was still too far.

He rounded the corner to the backyard, scanning past the uneven slab of wet concrete toward the trees where he'd seen her skirt. His eyes brushed the patio and snagged—something wasn't right. The concrete looked wrong. Not smooth.

Disturbed.

Rutted.

As if something—or someone—had broken the surface.

He turned toward the trees, searching for Sarah, calling her name again. Still no answer.

Then he saw it.

A shape near the tree line. Something small. Familiar.

Her suitcase.

Relief should've come. Instead, dread slithered up his spine. She wouldn't leave her suitcase unattended. Not unless—

"Sarah?" he tried again, his voice tighter now, sharper. "Where are you?"

No reply.

He was moving before his brain caught up. His feet dragged him forward, toward the patio—toward that irregular patch of concrete.

Something had sunk into it.

Closer now, he saw it wasn't just a blemish. It was a body.

Half-submerged. Still. Limp.

His breath hitched.

The dress—blue. The one she'd worn tonight.

No—no no no—

"Sarah!" he dropped to his knees in the wet cement, heedless of the mess, hands sinking into it as he crawled toward her.

Please let her be alive. Let her be breathing. Let her have tripped, fallen, hit her head—

But the moment he reached her, the illusion shattered.

A single, dark bullet hole marred her forehead.

The warmth drained from his body. A scream built in his chest and stuck there.

Footsteps behind him.

He turned.

Donny stepped from the trees, his shirt half-untucked, his face unreadable in the half-light. He held the gun low, at his side.

"You shot her," Bobby accused, his voice cracking. "You killed her. Why? Because she didn't love you?"

Donny stared at him with chilling calm. "No," he said. "Because she loved you."

The gun came up, level with Bobby's chest.

A thunder crack split the night.

Then—silence.

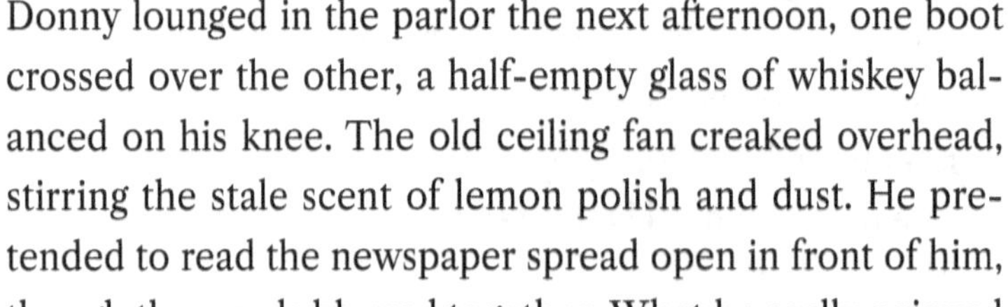

Donny lounged in the parlor the next afternoon, one boot crossed over the other, a half-empty glass of whiskey balanced on his knee. The old ceiling fan creaked overhead, stirring the stale scent of lemon polish and dust. He pretended to read the newspaper spread open in front of him, though the words blurred together. What he really enjoyed was the silence—the kind that came after a job well done.

The sound of tires crunching over gravel drew his attention. Moments later, the doorbell chimed as two uniformed officers stepped into the foyer. Donny didn't bother to move. From his chair, he could see Mrs. Meyers scurry to meet them, wiping her hands on her apron. Two officers stood there, their badges catching the afternoon light.

"We've got a warrant for the arrest of Donny Rangel," one of them said, his tone clipped and professional.

Mrs. Meyers froze, then glanced instinctively toward the parlor. Donny lifted his gaze over the top of the paper and offered her a lazy smile, as if she'd just caught him napping instead of reading.

"Well," he drawled, setting the whiskey down and folding the paper neatly. "Looks like you found him."

The taller officer stepped forward, reading from the warrant. "Murder and theft of a valuable diamond, among other charges. You'll need to come with us."

Donny rose slowly, straightening his cuffs. "Of course, but I assure you, this is all a big misunderstanding," he said with a smirk.

"Where's your brother, Bobby?" the second officer asked, eyes narrowing.

Donny shrugged, casual as ever. "Haven't seen him since last night. He and my girl skipped out on me. Probably in Mexico by now."

He gave a chuckle that had the officers exchanging a look but they remained quiet. One of them stepped behind him and snapped the cuffs in place. Donny didn't resist—he'd expected this. It was all part of the game.

As they led him out the door, he glanced back at Mrs. Meyers, who stood pale and trembling in the foyer. "Don't worry, ma'am," he said, flashing her a grin. "I'll be back to pay my bill."

As he was led to the patrol car, other units arrived.

Probably to search my room, he thought. *Good luck with that.*

He learned later that one of his buddies in Houston had ratted him out. He'd deal with him later.

Now, he sat in a prison cell, arms crossed, a smirk tugging at the corner of his mouth. His arrest was nothing more than a temporary detour, a brief delay in his march toward Mexico and freedom.

"What's your name?" his cellmate asked—a stocky man with a broken nose and the thousand-yard stare of someone who'd seen too much.

Donny turned his head. "Donny Rangel." He wanted everyone to know his name, especially the officer sitting at the nearby desk who kept staring at him with disdain.

His cellmate grunted. "Name's Ortega. Juan Ortega."

Donny barely nodded. He wasn't in the mood for conversation. Not when his brain was working the angles. Not when he was already planning his next move.

Ortega raised a skeptical brow. "They say you're the one who stole the Stanford diamond."

"They got nothing on me, not without the diamond as proof," Donny told him.

"I heard the cops are looking for your brother because he was in on it with you."

"Yeah? Well, they won't find him either," Donny muttered. At Ortega's raised eyebrow, he added, "he skipped town with my fiancée."

Ortega whistled. "Your own brother? Damn. That's cold."

"Yeah," Donny agreed. What he didn't say—but clung to like a secret prayer—was that the concrete had dried by the time the cops showed up at the Meyers house to search for the diamond. The slab being poured was extra tall, which was the only reason he'd been able to leave the bodies there, and he'd taken great pains to smooth the surface so no one would know what lay beneath it.

"What about the rock?" Ortega pressed. "You still got it?"

Donny's eyes narrowed. "I'm sure, wherever it is, it's safely hidden."

They fell quiet and Donny had time to reflect on recent events. Bobby had thought he was so smart, plotting to steal the diamond and then run away with his girl. HIS girl. They might have gotten away with it, too, if Donny hadn't overheard them making their plans.

Two night ago, after he'd pushed Sarah away, he'd gone upstairs to spend a little private time with her, but when he'd reached her room, he'd heard Bobby's voice coming from inside. Surprised and more than a little curious about why his brother would be in his fiancée's room, Donny had pressed his ear to the door and listened unabashedly. The more he'd heard, the angrier he got until he was in a cold, murderous rage. He honestly didn't know what angered him more, that Bobby had pursued Sarah and made her fall in love with him? Or that Bobby, who had done nothing more than drive the getaway car, was planning to steal his diamond? In the end, he'd dealt with both problems.

Donny glanced at the clock. It was time to put his plan into action.

"I don't feel so good," he moaned, hand on his stomach as he leaned forward on his cot.

"Hey, man. You okay?" Ortega asked, sitting up straighter on his cot. Donny's reply was a long, drawn-out moan. Then he leaned so far forward on the cot that he tipped himself over onto the floor, where he lay in a fetal position. "Hey, you?" Ortega shouted, presumably to the cop sitting outside their cell. Officer Garrett, according to his name badge. "There's something wrong with him. He needs a doctor."

Donny heard the scuff of a chair being pushed back and then footsteps. The cop shouted for help but didn't wait for it to arrive before opening the cell door.

When the cop bent over him, Donny was ready. A quick scuffle and Donny had the gun in his hand. Then all hell broke loose.

When it was over, several people lay dead, including Donny. And no one ever found the diamond.

Chapter Thirty

It was late afternoon and between them, John and Teresa had checked most of the second story floorboards. There was still no sign of the diamond.

"I guess it's not here," Teresa said at last, her voice edged with disappointment. They had just finished mounting the last ceiling fan, and she was hot, tired, and more than ready to be done.

John climbed down from the ladder, set his tools aside, and came to stand beside her. His hand found her shoulder in a steady squeeze.

"I'm starting to think you're right. Believing Donny stuffed the diamond in light fixtures was a stretch. He wouldn't have had the tools to dismantle anything, and hiding it in a lampshade where anyone could see it? No way."

"But it couldn't have been anywhere too obvious, either," she countered. "Otherwise, he wouldn't have risked leaving it here while he was in prison. He must've thought he could come back for it."

John tilted his head, considering. "But then why try to break out? If he believed the diamond was safe, why take that risk?"

Teresa lifted her hair from her damp neck, trying to catch a breeze. "Then we have to assume he didn't leave it here. We've checked everywhere a hundred times."

John crouched, resting his elbows on his knees, eyes tracing the room like a blueprint. He forced himself to imagine Donny Rangel's mindset. Desperate for a hiding place, short on tools, carrying only what a man in the 1940s might have in his pockets—coins, maybe a money clip, cigarettes and a lighter, keys, a pocketknife.

"The vents," he said suddenly.

Her eyes widened. "What about them?"

"We pulled the covers when we painted, but did you actually look inside?"

"No." Her gaze darted to the nearest vent. Then she turned back to him, anticipation sparking. "You take this side of the house, I'll check the other."

John grabbed a screwdriver and crouched by the vent. In minutes, the screws were out, and he had the cover free. He dropped to his side, phone flashlight cutting into the dark shaft. Nothing. His disappointment hit like a weight. He replaced the cover, sat back against the wall, and rubbed a hand over his jaw.

The quiet pressed close. A faint sound reached him—like the soft scrape of something shifting along the floorboards. His eyes flicked to the corner, where the baseboard met the window wall. For a heartbeat, he thought he saw a shadow stir there, darker than the rest.

He pushed himself up, eyes narrowing at the trim. The baseboards were original, neatly fitted. Except ... there. The corner block sat just slightly off, the alignment wrong. So subtle most people wouldn't notice. But sitting in the bare room, it stood out like a beacon.

Crossing the floor, he slid the screwdriver tip into the seam. The block gave with a dry sigh, prying loose.

"Teresa!" His voice cracked with urgency.

She hurried in, breathless. "What is it?"

He angled the block aside, revealing a cavity in the drywall. Inside lay a leather pouch.

"Oh my God," Teresa whispered, bending close. "Is that what I think it is?"

"We're about to find out."

With careful pressure, John worked the pouch free. It landed in his palm with a weight that made his pulse quicken. Something hard inside knocked against the sides. His fingers shook as he untied the leather cords. This was it—the discovery that would change everything.

He tipped it into his hand.

A large blue marble rolled into his palm, catching the light.

"What the hell—?" His voice broke, the word caught between confusion and anger.

Teresa's face fell. "That's not a diamond."

Before John could answer, the marble slipped free, dropped to the floor, and rolled in a slow, taunting circle before coming to rest against his boot. The air in the room seemed to shift, just enough to raise the fine hairs on Teresa's arms.

She swallowed hard. "Uncle Bill."

And though the room was silent, she could almost feel the echo of someone laughing at the joke only they understood.

Reluctantly, John reached back into the pouch. His fingers brushed something thin and brittle. Pinching it free, he unfolded a slip of paper, the ink faded but legible.

He read aloud, his voice low.

You won't understand this, but we're returning the diamond. We didn't mean to hurt you, but we couldn't help falling in love. —B

The silence that followed was thick, charged—not just with disappointment, but with the eerie sense that the house itself had been waiting for them to find this.

Chapter Thirty-One

THE NEXT MORNING, TERESA had just pulled the last batch of muffins from the oven and was letting them cool on the counter when there was a knock at the front door.

She started toward it when John appeared at the top of the steps.

"I thought I heard someone knock," he said.

"You did."

"Check who it is before you open the door," he cautioned, coming down a step or two to wait.

She peered through the peephole and then turned back to John.

"It's Chad."

She was afraid of why he'd dropped by, afraid that he'd come to tell her the skeletal remains were not her mother's. More afraid that he'd come to tell her they were.

John must have sensed her unease because he continued down the steps to join her, placing his hand on her arm as she reached for the door handle.

"You're not alone. Whatever he's here to tell you, I'll be by your side."

Not trusting her voice to speak, she simply nodded, mentally braced herself and then opened the door.

"Hey, Chad."

"Hey, Teresa." His gaze flickered past her. "John."

"Come on in." She stepped back to give him room to enter. "You want something to drink? I have coffee and there's tea in the refrigerator."

"No, I'm good, thanks." He lifted his nose into the air and sniffed. "Something sure smells good."

She smiled. "Can I interest you in a muffin?"

"I really shouldn't." He patted his waistline, which appeared to Teresa not to have an ounce of fat on it. "But yes, thanks. They smell great."

"Come on. I'm pretty sure I have extra." Teresa led the way to the kitchen and then smiled when Chad's jaw dropped at the sight of all the muffins cooling on the counter.

"Extra? It looks like you have five or six dozen sitting here. You two must really like muffins."

John chuckled. "Actually, Teresa has been selling muffins to some of the local businesses."

Teresa selected a muffin and set it on a napkin before handing it to Chad. "Why don't you take this to the table? We'll join you so you can tell us why you came over."

John grabbed three bottles of water and carried them to the table, where he handed them out before taking a seat next to Teresa.

When Chad took a bite of muffin, Teresa was content to let him slowly chew and swallow. As much as she wanted to know what he had to say, she wasn't eager to hear it. She uncapped her water and took a long drink.

As he swallowed, Chad gave her a curious look. "Did you sell any of these to Kathy? I had a muffin at her cafe yesterday that was out-of-this-world. And this tastes just like it."

Teresa smiled. "Yeah, Kathy's one of my customers." Those were words she'd never thought she'd say.

"You're one hell of a baker, you know that?"

"Thanks." She still wasn't willing to ask why he'd stopped by. John, it seemed, had no such compunction.

"What brings you over, Chad?"

He set the uneaten portion of his muffin on the napkin. "We got a hit on those prints we lifted after your break-in. They belong to a couple of ex-cons who did time in Huntsville State Pen. They were paroled last month."

"What are their names?"

Teresa thought John's question was odd until she remembered that he'd spent time in the Huntsville State Pen. Then she felt horrified to think the kind of men who'd vandalized her house were the kind of men he'd been incarcerated with.

Chad reached into his shirt pocket to extract two small photos. He laid them on the table so the two could see them and pointed to each in turn. "Benito Ortega and Silas Dolcy." He looked at John. "You know them?"

John shook his head. "No, but it was a big place, and I did everything I could to keep a low profile, do my time, and get out," he admitted.

"What makes a couple of ex-cons come all the way to Las Palomas and decide to vandalize my house? I would have thought they'd go for one of the big cities," Teresa said.

"I don't think it was random," Chad continued. "Benito Ortega is Juan Ortega's great nephew. I don't know if you know, but Juan Ortega is the prisoner who shared a jail cell with Donny for a short time."

"So, they were here looking for the diamond," John concluded.

Chad nodded. "That'd be my guess."

Teresa gave a huff of exasperation. "Well, it's not here. She got up from the table and walked over to the kitchen counter where she'd put the marble and note, still in the leather pouch. She carried it over to Chad and handed it to him. "Go on," she said after he took it. "Open it."

He opened the pouch and looked inside. A moment later, he dumped the contents into his hand. He stared a moment at the marble and then read the note.

"That's proof that Bobby and Sarah took the diamond with them when they went to Mexico," John said. "There's no diamond hidden in this house."

"Maybe I should post something online to that effect," Teresa mused aloud.

"I doubt it would do any good." Chad sighed. "Listen, there's no reason to believe Ortega and Dolcy are still in town, but all the same, be careful and keep your eyes open."

"We will," John assured him.

"Any news on the remains?" Teresa finally asked, unable to wait any longer.

"We don't know much, but the M.E. confirmed the remains are female and the preliminary cause of death is blunt force trauma to the head. Neela is still looking through boxes of old X-rays to see if she has a set for your mother. Back then, the practice didn't load X-ray images onto the computer like they do today."

John put his hand over hers on the table. "There was a fifty-fifty chance the remains would be female. It still doesn't mean they belong to your mother."

But there's still a chance they do. "Did you find only one set of remains?" Her father's disappearance was just as much a mystery.

He nodded but looked like he hadn't wanted to answer, and she knew why. She'd watched enough Forensic Files on TV to know that if her father hadn't been killed when her mother was, then he became the chief suspect in her mother's death.

A breath escaped her. She knew as much now as she had before Chad came over.

"Thanks for coming over." She got up from the table and went to the pantry to grab a couple of gallon-sized baggies. She filled them with muffins and then held them out to Chad.

"I baked extra. Why don't you take these back to the station and share them?"

"I'm tempted to keep them all for myself," he admitted, standing to take the bags from her. "But I suppose, to help spread interest in your new venture, I'll share them with the others."

John also rose from the table, and the three of them headed to the front door.

"I'll let you know as soon as we know something more about those remains. In the meantime, remember what I said about staying alert. Ortega and Dolcy might not be the only dangerous people after the diamond."

"Thanks for the heads up," John told him. "We'll keep our eyes open."

Thanking them again for the muffins, Chad left.

John closed the door and turned to her. "Are you okay?"

She offered him a small smile, appreciating his concern. "I guess. I mean, I don't really know how to feel about the remains. And as far as the two guys who broke in are concerned, they're probably long gone. No one's come snooping around for a few days now, so maybe all the interest in this house has finally died down."

"Maybe," he replied doubtfully. "Just in case, we should remain vigilant."

"Makes sense."

He gestured to the kitchen. "If you think the muffins have cooled enough, we can run them into town and deliver them. And maybe while we're there, we can grab lunch."

She thought about it. She was tired after baking all morning and depressed after finding a marble buried in the floorboards instead of the Stanford diamond. "Maybe we could pick up something and bring it back here to eat? After we eat, we can tackle the utility room."

He smiled. "I like that idea even better. If you'll bag the muffins, I'll put stuff away upstairs. Then we can run into town."

By mid-afternoon, the utility room finally had fresh drywall. Teresa carried two glasses of iced tea onto the front porch and handed one to John, who leaned against the railing, shirt damp from the afternoon's work. Wiping a streak of joint compound from her arm, she was grateful for the hint of breeze that softened the heat.

"Feels good to have that part done," he said, taking a swallow.

"Done until we sand and paint tomorrow," Teresa teased, settling beside him.

They stood in easy silence, cicadas buzzing from the oak trees along the road and the scent of sawdust and paint hanging in the air.

The moment stretched, quiet and close, until the low hum of an engine carried across the afternoon stillness.

A patrol car slowed on the paved road, tires crunching as it pulled against the curb. Dust swirled faintly in its wake.

They both turned as Chad climbed out, hat tucked under his arm, his face more somber than usual.

"Afternoon," he greeted them, coming toward the porch.

"Don't tell me you're back for more muffins," Teresa teased him.

"No, unfortunately." He stopped at the bottom of the steps. "There's no good way to say this. We found Bubba. Dead."

The words hit hard. Teresa's stomach clenched. "What? When?"

"This morning, after I left here. Out past Miller's Bluff. His truck was half off the road. His body was twenty yards into the mesquite. From the looks of it, he died last night."

John's jaw tightened. "Accident?"

He shook his head. "Not from the looks of it."

Teresa gasped. Bubba had been unpleasant, but who'd want to kill him?

"How?" John asked.

Unease flickered in Chad's eyes. "That's the strange thing ... looks like an animal got him from the tears and scratches, but there weren't any tracks. No blood trail. Just drag marks, like he'd been hauled there."

Teresa's voice dropped. "Like from a wolf?"

"No, there aren't any wolves in Texas."

"Maybe coyotes, or wild dogs?" John suggested.

Chad hesitated, then lowered his tone. "I don't know. Some of the nearby residents said they heard howling last night, but not like any coyote they've ever heard. Between us ..." He exhaled, shaking his head. "Bubba ran with rough company. And, from what we've learned, he had some gambling debts he couldn't pay. Wouldn't shock me if the people he owed money to got tired of waiting." He sighed. "But he worked for you—"

"Chad!" she interrupted. "Really? You think I killed Bubba? I was mad at him, sure, for setting fire to my house and all the damage he did, which now I'm wondering if he wasn't looking for the diamond in order to pay off his debts. Sure, I was mad at him, enough to rip him apart—figuratively, not literally. I wanted him to pay for the damage he caused. He can't do that if he's dead."

"No, I don't seriously consider you to be a suspect, but still," Chad continued, voice steady. "I have to ask. Where were you both last night?"

"We were here," John replied, tone even. "Together. All night."

Chad nodded, like that checked out. "I believe you. Right now, I have zero leads, so I need to eliminate as many people as I can."

He replaced his hat. "Lock your doors tonight. And if you hear anything—anything—you call 9-1-1." Then he walked back to his patrol car.

It disappeared down the paved road, leaving only the faint shimmer of heat above the asphalt. Teresa stood frozen on the porch, glass of tea slick in her hand.

John broke the silence first. "You okay?"

She shook her head. "Bubba may have been lazy, but he didn't deserve that."

John set his drink down on the railing, eyes narrowing toward the tree line. "You heard what Chad said—Bubba had enemies. More than a few."

"Yeah, but torn up?" Teresa asked softly. "Dragged like that? What kind of person does that?"

He didn't answer right away. His jaw worked, muscles ticking. Finally, he said, "Chad didn't seem sure it was a person."

The cicadas had gone quiet, and Teresa felt the hairs on her arms rise, though the air was still warm. She forced a shaky laugh. "A lot of people go out to Miller's Bluff to smoke and drink. Bubba liked to do both, plus he was over-weight. Maybe he died of a heart attack while he was out there? And then coyotes or buzzards found his body and did what coyotes and buzzards do. That makes more sense than a wild animal attack."

"Maybe." John's tone carried no conviction.

They stood a moment longer, listening to the empty afternoon.

At last, Teresa exhaled. "We should get back to work. That dining room isn't going to paint itself."

John nodded and followed her inside. After he closed the front door, he threw the deadbolt. With all the strange things going on in this town, leaving the front door unlocked, even when they were home, no longer made sense to him.

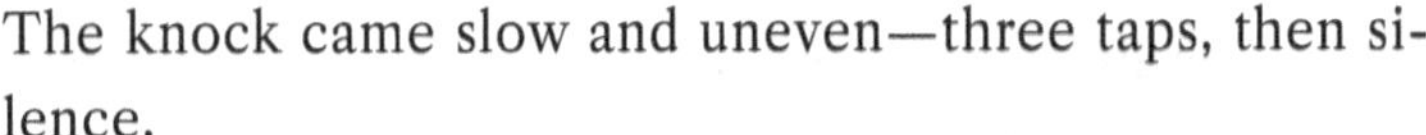

The knock came slow and uneven—three taps, then silence.

John and Teresa had only just returned from town after making copies of the ledgers and blueprints, followed by dinner and a quick trip to Katherine's Kozy Korner for a cup of specialty coffee. The fresh smell of drying paint and coffee lingered in the air. At the sound, John looked up from the blueprint copies spread across the kitchen table. "You expecting anyone?"

Teresa shook her head, setting her coffee down as she moved toward the door.

She flipped on the porch light and peered through the peephole. Confused, and a little surprised, she opened the door.

Felipe Velasquez stood on the porch, leaning heavier than before on a cane. His body appeared thinner, one eye was swollen and his clothes hung loose. Bruises covered his forearms, the dark purple of recent injuries and the mottled green and yellow of older ones. His mouth drew taut, as though even a smile might tear the skin.

"Felipe," Teresa said, concern rising. "Are you okay?"

He waved a hand, dismissing the question. "I've been worse." His tone carried the weight of a man who had lived through things no one should have to. "I came to collect the ledgers and blueprints, if you're finished with them."

"Come in," she urged quickly. "We've got your things ready."

Felipe stepped inside slowly, stiff in his movements. John rose from his chair, nodding respectfully. "Evening, Felipe."

"Evening," Felipe murmured. His gaze flicked over the blueprint copies before settling on the cardboard boxes sitting on the counter.

Teresa brought them forward. "Would you like to sit for a bit? I can offer you coffee, tea, or water?"

"Yes, thank you. That would be nice, but nothing to drink, thanks."

"Of course." She gestured to the kitchen table. "I haven't fully furnished the house yet, so I'm afraid we'll have to sit here at the table."

John stepped forward, ready to help the older man should he need it, but contrary to his appearance, he moved about easily. Taking a seat, he leaned back in his chair and rested the cane against the table.

"Were the ledgers helpful?" he asked.

"Yes, they were. Well," she qualified, "they confirmed that Donny Rangel stayed here back in the 1940s. As for helping us locate the missing diamond—" She shrugged. "Turns out, it's not hidden here."

"Diamond?" Felipe sounded confused.

"Yes, the one that's supposedly hidden here? It seems that's all anyone's been talking about lately."

He gave her a sad smile. "I guess I've been preoccupied." He fell silent, and for a long moment, no one spoke.

When the silence started turning awkward, she said the first thing to come to mind. "Did you hear about Bubba?"

Felipe froze, fingers gripping the edge of the table. "I heard."

"It's awful," she went on, arms folding as if bracing herself. "Chad said it looked like an animal tore him up—but there weren't any tracks. How does that even make sense?"

"It doesn't, unless ..."

John leaned forward, studying him. "Unless ...?

Felipe seemed reluctant to meet their gaze. "There are old stories. Whispers from before Las Palomas had pavement and neon signs. Things people said when someone vanished—or was found torn apart."

Teresa frowned. "What kind of stories?"

Felipe's jaw tightened for a moment and Teresa wasn't sure he'd answer.

"Stories about *El Cadejo*."

The name meant nothing to her. She glanced over to see John shrug. Apparently, the name was unknown to him as well.

"Who or what is *El Cadejo*?" she asked.

Felipe exhaled as if speaking the name had cost him. "They say *El Cadejo* is a dog, or a wolf. Maybe both; maybe neither. *El Cadejo* doesn't exist in this world."

Teresa studied him. "Are you saying *El Cadejo* is a ghost wolf?" Saying it out loud made it sound silly.

"Not wolf—wolves. There are two. One white, one black. *Cadejo Blanco* protects lost souls, the innocent. *Cadejo Negro* ..." His gaze drifted toward the kitchen window, where night pressed heavy against the glass. "... it doesn't need a reason to attack. It waits in the dark for innocent blood to spill. Sometimes it follows evil. Sometimes it IS the evil."

John arched a brow. "So, what are you saying? A black ghost wolf killed Bubba?"

Felipe's eyes lifted then, looking clearer than before. He gave a mirthless chuckle. "Don't listen to me. I'm just a silly old man, getting on in years. I don't even know what I'm saying half the time." Teresa opened her mouth to argue, but he didn't give her the chance. "I should be going."

He stood, using the cane to steady himself, before moving over to the counter where his boxes sat. "Thank you for keeping these safe," he said. "And for humoring an old man with his stories."

John stepped closer. "I'll carry those to your truck for you."

Felipe nodded. "Thank you."

"Mr. Valesquez, are you sure you're alright?" Teresa asked as she walked with him to the front door.

Felipe gave a faint, lopsided smile. "I'm always alright ... until I'm not."

He and John went out the front door and, after bidding the older man goodbye, Teresa went to stand by the front window. John joined her a moment later and they watched Felipe drive away. They continued watching in silence until long after the shadows swallowed him.

Only then did John speak. "What the hell was that all about?"

Teresa didn't answer. Her mind was still on the bruises. The scratches. And the shadow in Felipe's eyes when he'd said, *I'm always alright ... until I'm not.*

CHAPTER THIRTY-TWO

Teresa turned to John, her voice subdued. "I need air."

"Yeah," he agreed. "Let's take the coffee out back."

They carried their to-go cups onto the patio, the evening air cooler now, but heavy with silence after Felipe's strange warnings. John dropped into one of the lawn chairs with a sigh, stretching his long legs. Teresa settled beside him, curling her hands around the warm cardboard cup.

For a while, neither spoke. The cicadas had quieted for the night, leaving only the faint rustle of branches. John tipped his head back for a swallow, eyes on the darkening sky.

"Hell of a day," he muttered. "I don't know which is more disturbing, Chad's warnings, Bubba's death, or Felipe's crazy talk."

Teresa managed a faint smile. She had grabbed the leather pouch off the table when she'd grabbed her coffee. Setting her coffee down, she dumped the marble into her hand. "At least we solved the diamond mystery."

"True."

She brushed her thumb across its glassy surface. "Do you think Donny knew Bobby found the diamond?"

John reached over, taking the marble from her. He studied it carefully. "No," he finally said. "If Donny opened the pouch and realized the diamond was gone? He'd have gone ballistic. He wouldn't have saved either the marble or Bobby's note. And he sure wouldn't have bragged that the diamond was safely hidden."

Teresa nodded slowly. "So, Bobby and Sarah run off with the diamond. Donny wakes up one morning, discovers they're gone, but he's not too worried because he thinks he still has it?"

"Right. But then he gets arrested before he learns Bobby swapped it out. The cops can't pin the theft on him because they can't find the stone."

"I wonder what happened to them," Teresa mused. "Bobby and Sarah." She liked the idea of Bobby and Sarah running away together, selling the diamond, and building a life. Happily, ever after.

She was lifting her cup to take another sip when it jerked from her hand as if slapped away. It hit the patio, and coffee splattered at her feet.

"Damn it!"

"Bummer," John said, rising. He slipped the marble into pocket as he leaned over to get her cup. "I'll go brew you another cup if you promise not to drop it."

"I didn't drop that one," she protested, frustration slipping into her tone.

"What do you mean?" He sounded skeptical.

She shrugged, though the back of her neck prickled. "It's like someone slapped it out of my hand."

John's gaze met hers. "Uncle Bill?"

"Maybe."

At that moment, his own cup flew out of his hand. It hit the patio, coffee spilling everywhere. Then, even though there was no breeze blowing, the cup slowly rolled across the patio, coming to a stop a short distance away.

"What the—" John broke off, his expression shifting, something sparking behind his eyes. "Huh. Maybe ... wait here while I run inside and grab those blueprints."

She didn't argue. He returned a moment later and flipped through the pages until he found what he wanted.

"Can you hold that side?" Once she did as requested, he used his free hand to point to a spot on the page. "There," he murmured, tracing the lines. "This shows the back patio under construction. They expanded it in '45, right after the rooms were renovated."

Teresa leaned closer. "So?"

He lifted his head, studying the backyard, then looked down at the page. Slowly, his mouth curved. "Earlier, when I was checking the floorboards upstairs ... my pry bar slid across the floor until it pointed straight out that same window."

Her pulse quickened. "The one that looks out over the patio?"

"Exactly." He tapped the blueprint, then turned to look at where his coffee cup rested on the concrete. "What if part of the story is true? That Donny's fiancée and brother fell in love. From all accounts, Donny wasn't a nice guy. I doubt he'd be all that understanding. If Bobby and Sarah planned to run away together. If Donny caught them, he might have been mad enough to kill them. If the concrete for the patio had just been poured, hiding the bodies would have been easy. Look how tall the patio is? It's hard to climb on top without taking the steps. If it was wet, all Donny would have to do is push them to the bottom and smooth over the surface. By morning, the concrete is dry on top, and Donny explains away the missing couple by saying they ran away together."

Teresa stared at the place where the cardboard cup rested, unease settling deep in her bones. "No one ever heard from them again," she reasoned. "And it's hard to believe a diamond as famous as the Stanford diamond would just disappear, especially if they took it with them, intending to sell it and live off the money." She took a tentative step toward the cup. "You think Bobby and Sarah are buried under the patio?"

"And maybe the diamond with them," he added grimly.

A silence stretched between them before Teresa drew in a steady breath. "I think there's a sledgehammer in the garage."

"I'll get it." He handed her the blueprints and then headed for the garage.

While she waited, she carried the blueprints back inside and set them on the table. She was still holding the leather pouch and took it with her, on the chance they found ... she refused to let herself think about what they might find under the concrete and hurried back outside, flipping on the back porch light as she went.

When John returned, sledgehammer in hand, they both paused, staring at the concrete.

"If I'm wrong, I'll pay to fix the patio," he said quietly.

"I'm just as eager to know as you are," she replied. "Besides—I've been thinking of putting in a pool, anyway."

His mouth twitched. "In that case—step back."

The hammer came down with a crack, then again and again, until sweat darkened John's shirt. Teresa started moving the broken chunks of concrete to one side. Then, just as she was thinking they'd been wrong, a chunk of concrete gave way, and beneath it, something pale glinted in the back porch light.

She dropped to her knees. "Oh, my God. John—look."

He crouched beside her, pulling out his phone to shine the flashlight. White bones gleamed through the rubble.

"Looks like a skeleton," he said quietly. "I think we found them."

Teresa studied the fragments of clothing clinging to the remains. "I think it's Bobby. That belt—it's too masculine for a woman."

John leaned down to brush the concrete dust aside. Something caught the light. He pulled it free, crusted but unmistakable.

Teresa's breath hitched as he held it up. "The Stanford diamond."

"Bobby had it on him the whole time," John said, his voice grim. "And Donny never knew."

Teresa's pulse thudded in her ears. "What now?"

Hearing a footfall nearby, she turned toward the sound.

A slow clap broke the silence, followed by a mocking voice.

"Now," the man drawled, "you give the diamond to us."

Two figures emerged from the shadows at the edge of the patio, stepping into the spill of light from the house. Silas Dolcy stood grinning, his brown teeth barely visible in the dim light. Beside him was Benito Ortega, his eyes blinking in a rapid staccato rhythm. Their posture was casual, but their expressions were as hard as the cold metal of the guns they held.

Teresa's heart slammed against her ribs. She and John rose together, his body instinctively shifting to shield her as she clutched the small leather pouch in both hands. The air felt heavy, suffocating.

Ortega's grin was cold. "Be smart now. Hand it over nice and easy." He raised his pistol until it lined up squarely with John's chest. "No one's got to get hurt."

Dolcy's laugh was low and ugly. "Though I wouldn't mind a little sport if you make us work for it."

Teresa's throat went dry. "We—we didn't find anything," she stammered.

Dolcy's grin widened as he closed the distance between them. "Then you won't mind me checking that little pouch, sweetheart."

Before she could react, he lunged forward and ripped the pouch from her hands. He loosened the drawstring, looked inside—and his face twisted with rage. "It's empty!"

Ortega's eyes narrowed on John. "Where's the diamond?"

He didn't move. "That's all we found."

Dolcy's temper snapped. He crossed the space in two strides, grabbed Teresa by the hair, and yanked her head back until she gasped in pain. "You lying son of a—tell me where it is, or she bleeds."

Tears springing to her eyes as she silently pleaded with John for help.

His jaw visibly tightened as his face grew pale, but his voice sounded steady when he spoke. "Let her go."

"After you hand over the diamond," Juarez barked.

For a long, breathless second, no one moved. The only sound was Teresa's ragged breathing and the faint rustle of leaves in the wind. Finally, John reached slowly into his pocket, drew out the diamond, and held it up so they could see its dark shape.

Teresa felt Dolcy's grip on her hair loosen slightly as Ortega took the pouch from Dolcy and held it open. "Drop it in."

John hesitated, then did as he was told. The small *thud* of stone against leather sounded final.

Ortega closed the pouch and gave a satisfied grunt. "Smart man."

Teresa exhaled shakily—then screamed as Ortega's gun whipped out and cracked across John's temple. The blow landed with a sickening thud.

"John!" She tried to reach him, but Dolcy's grip on her hair held her in place. She watched in fear and horror as John collapsed, blood streaking down his temple.

Then Dolcy was shoving her forward, toward the house. "Move," he growled.

She wanted to know what was happening behind her but couldn't turn her head to see. Dolcy guided her through the kitchen, jerking her to a when they reached the front room. As they stood there, Ortega joined them, dragging John's body by one arm. Then he dropped John's arm, leaving his body on the floor, his head lolling, blood streaking his temple. Dolcy shoved Teresa to the floor beside John and then stood guard over them with his gun, while Ortega disappeared outside. He returned a moment later with a can of gasoline. He upended it, sloshing the liquid across the floorboards. The stench filled the air, sharp and suffocating.

They were going to burn down her house!

It was ludicrous to be upset over the loss of the house when their lives were at stake, but the thought of all the hard work she and John had done going up in flames made her chest ache.

Ortega struck a match, and a tiny flame hissed to life. "Goodbye," he said simply, then blinked twice, and let the match fall.

The fire caught instantly, racing across the floor. Heat licked upward, devouring furniture, climbing walls.

Teresa's thoughts raced. If they would just leave, maybe she could drag John outside and put out the fire before the house was completely destroyed.

Dolcy stepped forward, his shadow long and flickering in the glow of the flames. He crouched low, gun in hand, and gave her a smile that didn't reach his eyes.

"We can't have you calling the police, now, can we?" His voice was almost gentle. "Sweet dreams."

The last thing she saw as the butt of his gun swung down was his large smile and mouthful of rotten teeth. Then white light exploded behind her eyes and everything went black.

John surfaced to consciousness like he was clawing his way out of dark water. His skull throbbed, a pounding ache that felt like nails driven behind his eyes. A shrill ringing filled his ears, impossible to tell if it was coming from inside his head or from outside.

"Wake up."

The voice was urgent, close—impossibly close.

A face bent over him. Not Teresa's.

A woman's face. Pale, familiar, luminous in the haze.

For one wild, disoriented second, John thought his mind had finally cracked, then recognition slammed into him like another blow to the skull.

Marie.

Her lips moved, her voice cutting through the roar of flames with fierce clarity, "Save her."

John jolted, forcing his battered body to move. The motion sent knives of pain through his head, but he shoved it down, every nerve shrieking as he rolled onto his side. Smoke scalded his throat with every breath. He coughed, staggered, and then remembered—Teresa.

Terror clawed his chest. What if she was already—

No. He couldn't think it.

With smoke choking him and heat pressing in against him, he moved the short distance to her side. She lay limp on the rug, pale against the glow of firelight. His hand shook as he pressed trembling fingers to her neck. For an endless moment, nothing—then, a faint flutter under his touch. A pulse. Alive.

Relief ripped through him so hard it left him dizzy.

But the fire was closing in. He had to get them out. Now.

Gritting his teeth, John hauled himself to his feet. His vision swam, the walls buckling in and out of focus, but he bent and hooked his arms around Teresa. She was dead weight in his grip, her body slack. Summoning every ounce of strength, he hoisted her onto his shoulders in a fireman's carry. His knees nearly buckled under her weight, but he forced them straight, staggering forward.

The front door loomed ahead, flames crawling the frame. He reached for the knob—red-hot, searing his palm—but he ignored the pain and wrenched it open. The door groaned wide and a blast of night air hit him, cool and clean compared to the hell inside.

He stumbled down the porch steps, each one threatening to take them both to the ground. Somehow, he kept moving, his legs wooden, lungs on fire. He didn't stop until they reached the middle of the yard, far enough to be relatively safe from the fire.

Then his body gave out. He dropped to his knees, easing Teresa from his shoulders to the ground.

The scream of sirens swelled, this time real and close. Red lights strobed against the smoke as fire engines screeched to a halt. Firefighters leaped into action, shouting orders, hauling hoses, charging toward the blaze.

Teresa stirred with a ragged cough, smoke-rough and painful. Her eyes blinked open, dazed and shining with tears. For a second she looked only at him, confusion warring with relief. Then, her gaze slid past him to the house engulfed in flames.

Her lips parted. A broken sound escaped her, halfway between a sob and a gasp. "My house ..."

John's chest tightened. He ignored the throb in his skull and eased down beside her, wrapping his arms around her trembling frame. She collapsed against him, crying as the fire devoured everything she'd tried to rebuild.

He held her tighter, as if he could shield her not just from the flames but from the ruin of all she'd lost.

And above the roar of water and fire, John swore he heard a whisper—soft, almost tender.

"You did well."

Marie's voice.

Then it was gone.

Teresa clung to John, sobbing into his smoke-stained shirt. He said nothing, just held her tighter, one broad hand steady at her back, until at last the tears slowed to hiccuping breaths. She wiped her face with the back of her hand, forcing herself to breathe.

She wasn't alone. Not anymore. That thought steadied her enough to sit upright. Wrapped in the acrid stink of smoke, she leaned into John and watched her house burn. Flames chewed through the roofline, devouring shingles like paper, while sparks hissed into the night sky. Her chest tightened with each crack of splitting timber, each shuddering groan of collapsing beams. This wasn't just a building going up in flames. This was her childhood, her grandmother's legacy, every dream she'd dared to build here—all of it being reduced to ash before her eyes.

She wanted to scream, but all that came out was a coughing fit that wracked her ribs and left her gasping. Tears blurred her vision again—part smoke, part grief—and she blinked rapidly to clear them.

Red and white strobes slashed across the yard as firefighters directed torrents of water at her house. It occurred to her they were trying to contain the fire because it was too late to put it out.

Just then, paramedics hurried toward them, voices brisk, practiced. One kneeled beside her, looping a blanket around her shoulders. Another checked on John.

Reluctantly, she let them guide her and John into the back of the ambulance. The world inside was sterile and bright, a jarring contrast to the chaos outside. A medic examined the gash on John's temple, then her own. "You're both lucky. No stitches. Just some bruising, maybe mild concussions. I'll clean and dress that burned hand," he said to John. "And oxygen for you both."

A moment later, the cool plastic of the oxygen mask pressed against her face, and blessedly clean air filled her lungs. Slowly, her heart stopped hammering so hard.

When the paramedic stepped away, John turned his head toward her. His eyes were bloodshot but steady. "How you doing?" He paused. "Yeah. Dumb question."

Her throat closed, but she forced the words out. "I'd be a lot worse if you hadn't come to—if you hadn't saved us."

His gaze softened. "Your mother saved us. She ... woke me up. I swear it was her."

For a heartbeat, Teresa forgot to breathe. "Mom? She came to you?"

He nodded, the conviction in his voice undeniable.

Disappointment stabbed her, sharp and unexpected. Why him? Why not her? She'd been the one searching for her mother her whole life, yearning for one more word, one more moment. Instead, John had seen her. Twice, now.

Her chest ached, but she didn't have time to sink into self-pity.

"Teresa!"

Chad rushed up, eyes wide with alarm. He looked first at her, then at John, as if checking to make sure both still had all their limbs. "Are you okay? Jesus, when I realized where the fire was—" He broke off, dragging a hand over his jaw. "I thought I was going to lose you both."

Her throat tightened again, but she nodded. "We're alive."

Chad blew out a breath, relief etched across his face. Then his tone shifted toward practical. "These old houses ... faulty wiring's a hazard waiting to happen."

John's head came up, sharp. "It wasn't wiring."

Chad blinked, eyes narrowing. "No?"

Teresa leaned forward, voice raw but steady. "Ortega and Dolcy came back. They"—her voice wavered, but she pressed on—"they knocked us out and set the fire."

For a moment, Chad just stared. "Jesus. Why?"

"We found the diamond," Teresa said. When Chad simply stared at her, she clarified, "the Stanford diamond."

"You're telling me this is about that damn diamond?"

John let out a rough laugh, half cough, half disbelief. "Yeah. Apparently the legend's true."

Chad shook his head. "Unbelievable. You feel up to telling me exactly what happened?" When they nodded, he fished a notepad from his pocket, flipping it open as his expression hardened into a no-nonsense mask. "Start at the beginning."

Together, she and John laid it out: the men's return, the threats, the fight in the yard, the fire. John's burned hand. Their escape. Chad scribbled, jaw tight, only glancing up once when Teresa faltered.

"Damn," he muttered at last. "You're lucky to be alive."

"Don't I know it," John rasped.

A new voice cut in, brisk as ever. "Alive, but shaken. They need something stronger than oxygen."

Mrs. Petrie appeared at the door of the ambulance, apron still dusted with flour, a battered thermos in one hand and two paper cups in the other. She poured a splash of amber liquid into each and handed one to Teresa, the other to John.

"Drink," she ordered.

Teresa obeyed, then coughed as bourbon burned a trail down her raw throat. John, after only a moment's hesitation, followed suit.

Chad tucked his notepad away. "I'll put out a BOLO on those two. In the meantime, you need a place to stay. I'll call Ruby Mae, see if she's got a room. If not, my place is open."

"Nonsense." Mrs. Petrie's voice cracked like a whip. She planted her hands on her hips, glaring at both men. "They're staying with me. End of discussion."

John gave a weary half-smile. "Guess that settles it."

"Thank you," Teresa said, pulling the blanket tighter around her shoulders, gaze drifting back to the smoking ruin of her house. Her chest ached with the thought of everything she'd lost.

And then the sharper pain cut through. "They got the diamond. They could have just left." She couldn't help being bitter. "They didn't have to burn down my house."

John blinked, as if remembering something for the first time. "Oh. I almost forgot."

He reached into his pocket, fingers fumbling for a moment before he pulled out a dusty stone. He held it out to Chad.

"What's this?" Chad asked, taking it and turning it over.

Teresa's jaw dropped. "The diamond? But I saw you give it to them!"

"You saw me drop the marble into the pouch," John corrected, a ghost of a smile on his lips. "Bobby gave me the idea."

"So Ortega and Dolcy got—"

"A slightly dusty marble," John finished for her.

Chad let out a low whistle. "I'll be damned." He took the diamond carefully, holding it up to the light. "I'll lock this up until the courts figure out where it belongs. For now, it's safer out of circulation."

Teresa sagged, relief flooding her so suddenly that if she hadn't already been sitting, she might have fallen. Not everything was lost.

As Mrs. Petrie's bourbon began soothing her frayed nerves, Teresa held her paper cup out to the older woman, a silent request for another splash. With a smile, Mrs. Petrie refilled both their cups and then poured a splash into the thermos cup for herself. Then the three went to sit on Mrs. Petrie's front porch.

Hours later, when the police and EMTs finally pulled away and the fire crews packed up their hoses, the night grew quieter, though the air still smelled of smoke and ruin. Mrs. Petrie rose from her rocking chair.

"Come along," she said briskly, starting for the front door. "There's a bed for each of you, or the bed in the front room is big enough for both of you, if that's the way things are. It's none of my business, but I don't want any arguments. You're staying with me, and that's that."

Too tired to protest, Teresa rose to follow, John walking close beside her. All she wanted was to close her eyes and forget about everything—for just one night. Tomorrow, she'd figure out the future.

CHAPTER THIRTY-THREE

THE DAY AFTER THE fire passed in a blur but by the next day, Teresa was dealing with her stress the only way she knew how—by baking like she was trying to outrun her thoughts. Mrs. Petrie's muffin tins stretched across counters. There were blueberry, lemon, and cinnamon-sugar muffin orders to fill and hands to keep busy. Flour dusted the air like fog, and the aroma of baked goods made the old house smell comforting.

John was outside in the garage, tinkering with the late Mr. Petrie's woodworking equipment. Mrs. Petrie hovered in the kitchen nearby, more grandmother now than neighbor—refilling coffee, swapping trays, vetoing Teresa's "I'm fine" with a look that said, nice try. At some point she remarked, almost offhandly, that the fire inspector had "been and gone"—something about spotting a tag on the ruined doorframe. Teresa hadn't seen him; she'd been elbow-deep in batter, grateful not to think.

A knock cut through the hum of the mixer, and Mrs. Petrie headed toward the front hall.

Teresa wiped her hands, smearing pale streaks of flour down her borrowed sweat pants, and arrived just as Mrs. Petrie opened the door. Chief Samantha Hunter stood on the porch in uniform—back on duty, eyes clear, seeming a shade older in ways that didn't come from years.

"Hey, Sam," Teresa said. "Come on in. You're back to work, then?"

"I am." Sam stepped inside, lifting her nose to smell the air. "It smells good in here."

"Stress baking," Teresa admitted. "Want a muffin?"

"Always."

They went back to the kitchen and Mrs. Petrie poured them all fresh coffee while Teresa took out a plate. She handed it to Sam and then waved her hand over the assortment of muffins, quickly identifying each flavor. "Help yourself."

Once Sam had selected a muffin, they all sat at the kitchen table. Teresa and Mrs. Petrie politely sipped their coffee, giving Sam time to eat her muffin.

"The rumors around town are right," she said finally, swallowing her last bite. "These muffins are tasty."

"Thanks," Teresa said, pleased to know people were talking favorably about her baking.

"The reason I came by," Sam explained. "I have a few quick updates. The fire inspector's preliminary report says the accelerant patterns match arson. No surprise there. Also, Ortega and Dolcy were apprehended near the Mexican border. They're being transported back here, and we'll hold them, no bail. District Attorney's moving fast, so they'll be back in prison soon." She paused. "Also, we found your mother's dental records, and they are a match for the remains. I'm sorry."

Teresa leaned back in her chair, her knuckles white where they gripped the edge of the table. She had expected it, but expectation didn't blunt the shock. "So, she really is dead." Tears stung her eyes. "She didn't abandon me."

"No," Sam said gently. "She didn't. She was killed. And now we know for certain."

Relief and grief twisted together inside Teresa. "And my father? What happened to him?"

Sam's jaw set. "That's the part we don't know yet. But we've started the search for him. There's no guarantee we'll find him, of course. Especially if he's living in another country. I'll let you know if we find anything."

Teresa nodded. "Thank you."

An awkward silence settled until Sam cleared her throat. "There was something else I wanted."

Teresa tilted her head. "What's that?"

"Would you walk with me over to the patio? Where you found Bobby and Sarah's bodies." Sam kept her tone neutral, giving no hint of her actual intent.

Teresa hesitated but then nodded. "All right."

They went outside and stepped off the porch together, crunching across the brittle lawn toward the blackened skeleton of the house.

The side door to the Petrie garage banged open, and John came out wiping sawdust from his hands. "Where are you two headed?"

"Sam wants to see the patio," Teresa answered. "Where we found Bobby and Sarah."

John studied them for a moment, then tossed his rag back inside the garage. "Then I'm coming with you."

Instead of entering Teresa's house, they circled around to the backyard. The fire had left the walls charred and sagging, but the patio was still visible—scorched concrete, cracked in places, yellow police tape strung between trees.

John gestured to the scarred slab. "This is where the bodies were found."

Sam nodded but wasn't looking at the concrete. Her gaze was sweeping the yard, searching for something only she might see.

Teresa frowned. "Sam? What are you really doing?"

Sam let out a slow breath. "I wasn't going to say anything until I was sure, but ... after I was shot, I coded on the way to the hospital—more than once. Since then, I can see and hear ghosts." She said it plainly, no drama. "I wanted to come here to see if Bobby and Sarah's spirits are still bound to this place. Maybe they'll tell us what really happened."

Teresa's eyes widened. "I didn't know you had that ability."

"It's new," Sam admitted. "Apparently near-death experiences can open a door. It's not just me. Gina Castillo Wolfe nearly drowned weeks ago. When they revived her, she woke up being able to see ghosts."

John shifted, expression unreadable. "That makes sense."

Both women looked at him.

"In prison, I was attacked once. Bad. They said I flatlined, but they brought me back. I didn't think much about it then, but ..." His voice trailed off. "Maybe that's why Marie appeared to me when she never appeared to Teresa."

Teresa's throat tightened. "And why you saw her when the house was on fire." She looked back at Sam, shaken. "So that's the rule, isn't it? The closer you come to death, the thinner the veil?"

Sam gave a quiet nod. "That's what it seems."

She turned back to the patio, ducked under the tape, and stepped onto the broken concrete. Closing her eyes, she stilled herself. The air shifted, pressure dropping heavy in her chest. Her eyes flew open—and there they were. A young man and woman, pale but distinct, their outlines shimmering in the heavy air.

"Bobby? Sarah?" she whispered.

Sarah inclined her head. "You can see us?"

"Yes. And I can hear you."

Bobby's gaze flicked past her. "And so can he."

Sam turned, startled, and saw John staring fixedly at the figures.

John's jaw tightened. "Yeah. I see you now."

Teresa, standing just beyond the tape, scanned the patio with wide eyes. "I don't. I don't see anything. Just shadows." She hugged herself. "It's enough to know they're here."

Sam drew in a steadying breath, then asked the question that had been burning in her chest. "Can you tell me what happened? How you died?"

"Donny killed us," Bobby said flatly. "I don't know how he found out that Sarah and I were running away together, but he did, and he was furious. That night, Sarah and I agreed to meet back here. Sarah arrived first, Donny showed up and shot her. Then, when I came down to join Sarah, he shot me. He buried us in the wet concrete, and we've been bound here ever since."

Sam's gut clenched. She relayed the words carefully to Teresa.

"Please ask them about my mother. And Uncle Bill," Teresa begged.

Sam turned back to Sarah and Bobby.

"Her uncle was never here," Sarah replied kindly. "He passed over shortly after his accident years ago."

Sam shared the news with Teresa.

"So, all the noises, the moving objects—that was Bobby and Sarah?" Teresa asked, staring at a place to Sam's left even though the ghosts were standing to her right.

Sarah smiled faintly. "Yes. We didn't mean to hide from her, It's just—after what happened—we weren't... whole. Everything was fog and noise. We knew we were dead, but couldn't understand why we hadn't moved on. The longer we were here, the stronger we became and we eventually learned how to move objects. By then, everyone believed we were Uncle Bill and it didn't seem important to correct the misunderstanding. We've watched generations of Teresa's family grow up in that house. When her grandparents passed, we were there to ease their transition and stay with them until they moved on. We watched Teresa grow up, and we welcomed her when she moved back home. We tried to warn her about Bubba and protect her, especially when talk of the diamond started up again."

Sam's chest tightened. She turned slightly toward Teresa and relayed what she'd been told.

Out of the corner of her eye, Sam caught John's frown.

"Why couldn't I see you before? Back when you were ... Uncle Bill?" he asked, his gaze never leaving the ghosts.

This time, Bobby answered. "Because there was no need to show ourselves." He hung his head. "Not until it was almost too late. We summoned Marie when those men set the house on fire. You and she have a connection and we hoped she'd be able to wake you. You didn't see us because we had to focus all of our energy on keeping the fire from reaching you and Teresa."

"Thank you," John told them, then shared the response with Teresa.

"You summoned my mother?" Teresa whispered suddenly. "Is she still here?"

The ghosts exchanged a glance before Bobby answered gently. "No. Her spirit is bound to another place and the pull of it was too strong for her to remain here once she saw you both were safe."

Sam repeated the words softly and watched Teresa swipe away the moisture gathering in her eyes.

Just then, the sun seemed to brighten, creating a light so intense, Sam had to squint against it.

"It's time for us to move on," Bobby said, breaking into Sam's thoughts. "Now that the truth about us is known and the diamond has been found. You'll return it to its rightful owner?"

"I will," Sam promised as Bobby reached out for Sarah's hand, and they stepped closer to the light.

"John, take care of our Teresa. We wish you both luck and happiness," Sarah said. Then they stepped into the light and disappeared. A moment later, the intense light faded, leaving Sam, John, and Teresa standing alone.

Sam took a moment to process what had just happened, then turned to Teresa and John. "They're gone, and I don't think they'll be back. They're at peace now, and they wish you and John luck and happiness."

Teresa nodded but remained silent. John stepped closer to her and put his arm around her shoulder. "I might know where we can find your mother. We need to go back to where we found her remains."

Teresa's expression turned hopeful. "Can we go out there now?"

"Of course," he replied.

"I'd like to go along, if you don't mind," Sam said. When they both nodded, she led the way around the side of the house.

"I'll drive," John said, gesturing for them to climb into Teresa's truck.

As they drove away from the house, Sam reflected on what she'd just experienced. Despite all her training to deal calmly with unexpected situations, she was freaking out just a little. The ability to see and talk to ghosts was monumental. To have that ability while living in a haunted town? Mind-blowing.

There was no manual or rulebook for this. She'd have to figure it out as she went. In the meantime, she had a decades-old mystery hanging over her head. The house had yielded its secrets. Now the road would have to give up the rest.

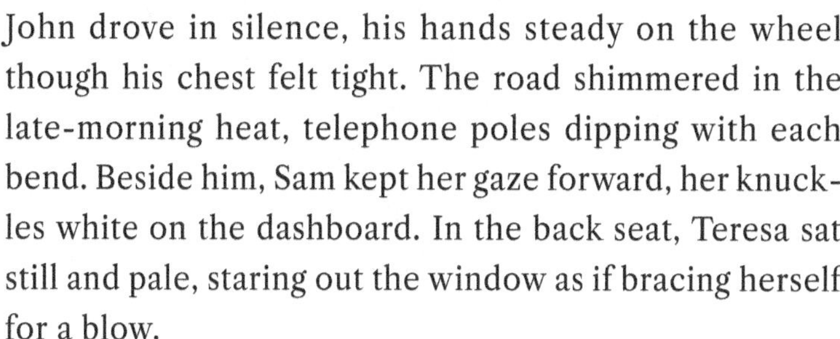

John drove in silence, his hands steady on the wheel though his chest felt tight. The road shimmered in the late-morning heat, telephone poles dipping with each bend. Beside him, Sam kept her gaze forward, her knuckles white on the dashboard. In the back seat, Teresa sat still and pale, staring out the window as if bracing herself for a blow.

John knew the spot they were heading to. He remembered the night he picked up Marie's ghost—though back then, he hadn't even known what she was. Just a woman in white on the side of the road, her voice soft and sorrowful. Now, after the fire and the veil-thin moments he couldn't deny, he understood. He could see her.

He slowed as the river bend came into view, pulled onto the gravel shoulder and parked. His eyes swept the area, the road, the sun-bleached grass. Then he saw her.

She was standing near the ragged stretch of earth where the police had marked the site, her outline sharp against the glare of heat. White top, white slacks. Teresa's face reflected in older features.

John's breath caught.

"She's here," he said, his voice low.

Teresa's head snapped up. "My mom?"

He swallowed. "Yeah. She's right there."

Sam nodded. "I see her."

As soon as they exited the car, he felt the heat pressing down hard. The four seasons in that part of Texas were three months each of hot temps, hotter temps, scorching hot temps and hot temps accompanied by rain.

They were at the tail-end of a scorching hot season, and this stretch of ground looked like any other stretch of roadside—sun-bleached gravel, burned grass, and the slow shimmer of heat off the asphalt.

They neared the site where the remains were found, and where Marie waited for them next to a stake to which a strip of police tape was tied.

John and Sam exchanged glances, then Sam spoke. "Marie. We need to know what happened to you and your husband. Why did you both disappear and leave Teresa behind?"

Marie's eyes locked on hers, then she nodded. "My daughter deserves to know the truth."

She began pacing along the fence line, steps leaving no impression in the dirt. "It started before Roger Thacker and I married. Daniel Petrie and I grew up living next door to each other. For most of my life, he was my best friend, but then in high school, he became more. We fell in love and were so happy together. I knew he was planning to propose, and I would have said yes. But he died in that accident, and shortly after, I learned I was pregnant."

Marie's voice carried on, heavy with memory. "I was scared. I didn't know what the Petries or my parents would do when they found out. Back in those days, pregnancy outside of marriage was still frowned upon. Then I met Roger Thacker. He was charming, had a decent job and wanted a family. We started dating and when I told him I was pregnant, he assumed the baby was his and proposed right away. I thought it was salvation."

Sam's throat tightened as she repeated it all, watching Teresa's tears gather.

"Everything was fine until we couldn't get pregnant a second time. When the doctors told Roger he was sterile, he realized Teresa wasn't his biological daughter. He started staying out all night. Drinking. That's when the hitting started—" She faltered.

Sam pushed gently. "What happened? Why did you and Roger disappear?"

Marie's voice broke. "We'd been arguing a lot, and he was drinking more than ever. I told him I'd finally had enough. I was divorcing him and taking Teresa. I came home from work and packed bags for me and Teresa and carried them to my car. We were going to my parents. Teresa had gone to bed early, but when I tried to wake her to leave, I couldn't wake up. That's when I learned Roger had fed her early and put drugs in her food to make her sleep." She shook her head. "I was furious. When I threatened to call the police, he ripped the phone from the wall. Locked the doors. Said we had to talk. I screamed. Threw things. I think I hit him. I hope I did. The next I knew, I was here—on this road—and I couldn't reach my little girl."

John relayed it all to Teresa, sounding steady even as the words scraped something raw inside him. Then turning back to Marie, he asked, "Why me? Why did you show yourself to me?"

Her gaze softened, her voice carrying across the charged air. "Because I sensed you could see me. The veil was thinner for you, John. I don't know what you've lived through, but I felt it—something in you brushed against the other side once, left a mark. That's why you saw me when others only drove by."

Her expression shifted, turning tender. "And because I saw something else in you. Strength. Kindness. The makings of a protector, a friend ... a man my daughter could lean on. Someone more like my Daniel—and nothing like Roger."

His throat went tight, but he gave a nod and turned slightly, repeating it all for Teresa.

Teresa's hand flew to her mouth, her eyes shining. "Momma ..."

Marie halted, her gaze brimming with regret. "Tell her I'm sorry. Tell her I love her. Always."

John drew in a breath. "She says she's sorry. And she loves you."

Teresa lifted her chin through her tears. "I love you, too, Momma."

Relief lit Marie's face. She reached out, her hand trembling, just shy of her daughter's cheek. For a heartbeat, John thought Teresa almost leaned into it.

"Thank you," Marie whispered.

And as it had before on the back patio, the sun grew brighter until an intense light appeared nearby. Marie seemed momentarily surprised by it, but then she smiled and stepped toward it.

When the light faded, Marie was gone.

The air snapped back, as still and hot as before, the roadside once again just burned grass and gravel.

John stood there a long moment, his jaw locked. Then he turned to Teresa. She collapsed against him, sobbing, and he wrapped his arms around her, holding her as tight as he could, as if to shield her from every ghost, every hurt.

Sam looked away, giving them space. To anyone else, this was just a stretch of roadside. But John knew better. This was where a woman's life had ended, where her spirit had waited, and where, finally, a daughter's questions had been answered.

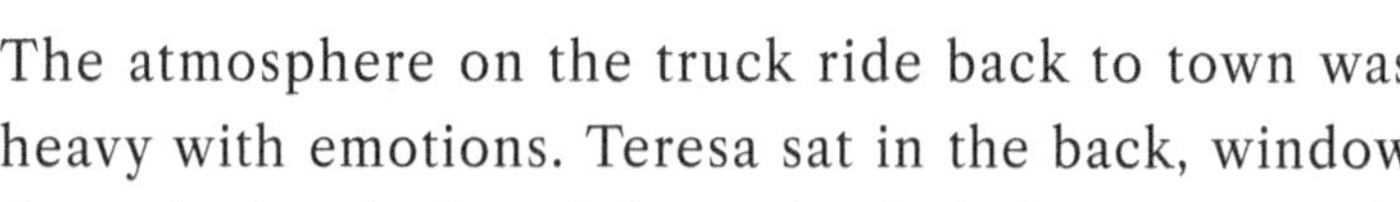

The atmosphere on the truck ride back to town was heavy with emotions. Teresa sat in the back, window down, letting the hot air batter her hair, hoping it would blow the ghosts out of her head.

John drove with one hand, the other tapping a slow, restless rhythm on the wheel.

"Teresa," Sam finally said from the front passenger seat, turning slightly. "I'm going to keep looking for Roger Thacker. I'm not saying he killed your mother, but he's definitely a person of interest."

Teresa watched the rows of power lines flick past, neat and endless. "Okay."

"I can't make any promises, but I'll try my best."

Teresa tried to imagine what she would say to Roger if she ever saw him again. For years, she'd carried a slow-burning ache, a wish for an explanation of why her parents had left her. Now, the truth might be far uglier than she first imagined.

She glanced at John and knew she was about to lose him, too. He'd only agreed to stay long enough to help her with the house. Now, the house was gone. There was no reason for him to stick around.

She had lost her parents. Lost her house. Lost Uncle Bill. And she was about to lose John.

Loneliness gripped her like an iron vice, her heart plummeting into a pit of self-pity that threatened to swallow her whole until the truck rolled to a stop in Mrs. Petrie's driveway. The old woman stood on the porch, haloed in the late-afternoon light, smiling as if they'd been out for ice cream instead of resurrecting the past.

Teresa and John climbed out of the truck in near-silence. They said goodbye to Sam who, after giving the older woman a quick wave, returned to her truck and drove off, leaving Teresa and John alone to talk to Mrs. Petrie.

Mrs. Petrie's eyes narrowed as they reached her. "My dears, you look like you've been wrung out and left to wither on the line." Her tone was gentle but laced with worry.

Teresa's throat felt raw. She swallowed hard. "We ... we need to talk to you. Inside." Her voice cracked on that final word; her pulse thundered in her ears.

Mrs. Petrie lifted one skeptical brow. "Well, that doesn't sound ominous at all. Come on in, then." She steered them through the door into the familiar warmth of her kitchen and sat them at the scarred wooden table.

Teresa pressed her palms flat against the grain, grounding herself. Her fingers trembled as she met Mrs. Petrie's sharp gaze. "There's something you need to know." Mrs. Petrie went still, her grip on the edge of her apron tightening until the fibers creaked. A shaky breath escaped Teresa. "I don't even know where to begin."

"Start at the beginning," came Mrs. Petrie's gentle command.

Teresa glanced at John. He offered a quick, steadying nod.

So Teresa told her the whole story, starting with John giving Marie's ghost a ride, the brittle bones they unearthed outside of town, then the bones they'd found in the patio's concrete and her mother's spirit reaching out to John while the house burned around them. Each confession landed like a stone on the table. When she fell silent, Mrs. Petrie sat motionless, her mouth parted, eyes clouded as though clearing dust from a pane.

"I know it sounds impossible," Teresa whispered, "but it's all true."

Mrs. Petrie swallowed. "I believe you."

Teresa's breath hitched. "You do?"

A tremulous smile cracked the old woman's face. "Child, I've lived in Las Palomas all my life. Your grandmother and I used to play ball with Uncle Bill's ghost when we were kids." She shook her head, as if clearing a fog. "When someone you can't see tosses you a ball, it becomes easier to believe in ghosts. So, yes, I believe you. I'm just trying to take it all in."

"There's more." When Mrs. Petrie raised an eyebrow, she pressed on. "That wasn't Uncle Bill's ghost. It was the ghosts of Sarah Novak and Bobby Rangel, whose remains we found buried in the patio concrete. Sam confirmed it." Seeing her confusion, Teresa quickly explained about Sam's near-death experience leaving her with the ability to see ghosts.

"Is that what has you so upset?" Mrs. Petrie asked. "Learning that Uncle Bill wasn't Uncle Bill?"

"No. It was learning that the remains found on the side of the road belonged to my mother. We went there hoping to see her again. And she was there."

Mrs. Petrie reached out, her fingers soft and trembling against Teresa's. "Oh, sweetheart."

Tears stung Teresa's eyes. "It was ... comforting, actually. She couldn't tell us how she died, but she told us something else—about her and your son. About me. My mother was pregnant with Daniel's child when he died." She paused. "You're my paternal grandmother."

The words rang through the room like a church bell at midnight.

Mrs. Petrie's hand flew to her mouth. "Daniel ..." Her voice quavered and tears spilled freely, gleaming on her cheeks. She stared at Teresa as though seeing her for the first time. "All these years, I thought he was lost forever. But you—" Her voice cracked on grief, then surged with fierce joy, "You're his daughter. My granddaughter."

Teresa let herself cry then—years of grief, loss, and longing breaking free. She leaned across the table, and Mrs. Petrie pulled her into her arms, apron and all, rocking her as though she were still that eleven-year-old girl who'd lost everything.

John slipped quietly away, leaving them to this moment.

When they finally pulled apart, Mrs. Petrie cupped Teresa's face, her thumb brushing away tears. "You're not alone anymore, child. Never again. You've got me." Her voice was soft but unwavering.

Teresa closed her eyes, letting the truth sink into every fractured shard of her heart. She wasn't just the girl left behind. She was someone's granddaughter. She had family. And for the first time in years, she felt whole.

CHAPTER THIRTY-FOUR

IT HAD BEEN ALMOST a week since the fire and Teresa stood at the front window watching the line of clouds drifting over Mrs. Petrie's house. She tried to guess which one would burn off first. It was a pointless game, but so was everything else she'd tried this morning. Summers in Texas were a kind of purgatory, with an unrelenting heat that was inescapable. This late August day was no exception; the Texas sun was working overtime, and the moist heat clutched at her like a kid who didn't want to let go.

She pressed her forehead to the living room window and watched John out in the yard, moving with an efficiency that looked effortless from a distance. Up close, she knew every muscle ached, every motion calculated to avoid the battered places on his body left by the fire and the men who'd nearly killed them both. He hefted a walnut bench onto his shoulder, carried it to the battered Ford idling in the drive, and laid it in the bed with a kind of reverence. The man buying it—someone from two towns over, she thought, though she hadn't bothered to ask—counted out bills and stuffed them into John's hand. John grinned, the rare kind that dimpled his cheek and reached his eyes.

He lingered at the tailgate, talking over the roar of the truck's engine, nodding and gesturing in that way he did when he actually liked someone. Teresa squinted, tried to lip-read, but all she caught was the last line. "Take care of her." She was pretty sure he meant the bench, and not the woman watching from inside the truck.

She straightened up and retreated into the kitchen before he could catch her watching him. The clock over the stove said 11:41, and Mrs. Petrie was already prepping lunch, as if the world needed more sandwiches and not a single minute of stillness. The old woman clucked over her battered Corelle plates, smearing mayonnaise onto bread with a shaky but determined hand.

"Chicken salad or egg?" she asked, not looking up.

"Egg," Teresa said, though she hated egg salad. She just wanted to prove she still had agency over something.

Mrs. Petrie's eyes flicked to her, sharp like a bird of prey. "You're worried about that boy."

"Mrs. Petrie, he's not a boy," Teresa shot back, but it was hollow.

Mrs. Petrie snorted. "Well, you're worried. Don't bother lying to me. And I told you to call me 'Grandma.'"

She nodded, acknowledging the request, but didn't answer, afraid that if she did, all of her worries and concerns would spew forth. And what good would that do? Since the night of the fire, she and John had lived in a holding pattern—eating, sleeping, rebuilding. Sometimes she caught him sketching blueprints for her ruined house on scraps of paper; other times he vanished into Mrs. Petrie's garage for hours, coming out reeking of sawdust and sweat. But they never talked about what came next; they never talked about the job waiting for him in El Paso and how the month he'd promised her was nearly over. She'd wanted to ask him about it, wanted to ask him to stay, but every time she opened her mouth the words turned to grit on her tongue.

She sat at the kitchen table and stared at the yellowing lace curtain, the way it filtered light into fractals across the Formica. She could feel Mrs. Petrie's gaze, could sense the words building up like a dam in the old woman's throat.

Before they could break through, John came in through the front door, carrying the smell of dust and warm metal with him. He wiped his face with the hem of his shirt—showing a slice of his belly and the fresh bandages on his ribs—then ducked over to the sink to wash his hands.

"Sold the bench," he said, voice careful, almost apologetic. "The guy wants three more by Christmas."

Mrs. Petrie clapped her hands, delighted. "I knew that bench would go quick," she said. "You did such fine work on it."

John looked at Teresa, a flash of something vulnerable in his eyes. "I made it for you, really," he said, as if it was a small thing. "For the porch. I started it right after I fixed Mrs. Petrie's rocker." That was before the house burned down, the words implied but not spoken. "I can make another."

Teresa wasn't sure how to respond, so she just picked at the frayed edge of the tablecloth and nodded.

Mrs. Petrie cut the silence by shoving two sandwiches in front of them and ordering, "Eat. You both look like you're about to faint."

They ate in parallel, not quite facing each other. Teresa's mind ticked over everything she wanted to say. *I know you're leaving; please don't go; I need you.* But the silence was safer, and John seemed to appreciate it, because he ate without comment, just the soft scrape of bread and the steady movement of his jaw.

When the sandwiches were gone, Mrs. Petrie started stacking plates. "I'm going to make a pie for after lunch. You two go sit outside. Fresh air will do you good."

John glanced at Teresa, eyebrows up. "How about it?"

She almost said no, but he was waiting, and there were only so many days left before he'd be gone. Not that he'd said anything about leaving, but she knew it was coming. His absence would be a different kind of ghost than she was used to.

She followed him out the door, and they sat together on the old porch swing, the one Mrs. Petrie had covered in a crocheted Afghan.

They swung in silence for a while, the only sounds being the creak of the swing's chain and the drone of flies. Teresa studied the cars on the street, counting the blue ones, then the red, anything to keep from looking at him.

John's voice was soft when he finally broke the silence. "We need to talk," he said, and she almost laughed at the cliché.

"About the pie?" she joked, but it came out sounding brittle.

He smiled, but it faded quickly. "No. About us. About what happens next."

She cut him off, staring at the horizon. "You have a job waiting in El Paso."

He blinked, surprised, then nodded. "Yeah, that's true."

"You should take it." She wrapped her arms about her waist, as if she could hold herself together that way. "With no house to renovate, I can't afford to keep paying you."

"Teresa—" He paused, then finally said, "I don't want to leave you, but I also don't want to hold you back. If you want me here, I'll stay, and not because you're paying me. But if you don't want me here, I'll go."

There it was, right on the table. All she had to do was say it. *Stay. Please, for the love of God, stay.* Instead, she said nothing, though her head was filled with her own screams. *Tell him how you feel. Tell him you love him.*

The silence stretched on, becoming awkward. John leaned forward, elbows on his knees, and sighed. "You don't have to answer now. Just—think about it, okay?"

She nodded, though her head, like her heart, felt ten pounds heavier.

He stood then. "I'll be in the garage. Need to clear my head."

She watched him go, and when he was gone, she let herself fold forward, head between her knees, and breathed until the world steadied.

She thought about calling after him, about running down the steps and throwing her arms around him, begging him to stay. But she was so tired of needing things, so tired of being the weak one. She waited instead, counting the cracks in the porch boards until her vision blurred with tears.

The sound of a truck pulling to a stop in front of the house caused her to look up. Sam exited the truck, looking official in her uniform. She caught sight of Teresa, smiled and waved, her stride purposeful as she strode up the front walk.

Teresa straightened, wiped the moisture from her eyes, and tried to look composed. "Hey, Sam," she called, voice steadier than she felt.

Sam nodded. "Mind if I join you?" She didn't wait for a reply, just mounted the steps and settled on the far end of the swing.

They rocked together, a careful distance between them.

"Got some news," Sam said. "Wanted to tell you first."

Teresa braced herself. She didn't think she could take more bad news, but it was out of her hands now.

As if reading her mind, Sam looked at her with something almost like sympathy. "It's good news, mostly." She looked around. "Is John here? He'll want to hear this, too."

Teresa hesitated, then stood. "I'll get him." She went down the porch steps, rounded the house to the garage. John was sorting through a toolbox when she stepped inside. He looked up, eyebrows raised.

"Sam's here," she said, breathless. "She wants to talk to both of us."

He wiped his hands and followed her back around the house. When they got to the porch, Sam was staring out at the street, her posture loose but her eyes sharp.

Teresa returned to her place on the swing while John leaned against the porch banister. They looked at Sam expectantly.

"I'll get right to it," she said. "The diamond? The Stanford family put up a reward for its return. A courier arrived this morning." She reached into her uniform shirt, produced two legal envelopes, and handed them over like she was dealing blackjack. "They wanted you to have these, along with their thanks."

John stared at his, blinking as if afraid it would vanish. Teresa took hers, felt the weight—heavier than she'd expected—and thought of her unpaid bills and no revenue stream. Any amount of money now was welcome.

She opened the envelope and pulled out the check.

Across from her, John did the same.

Teresa read the amount. *Fifty thousand dollars!* It was more money than she'd expected, and she felt some of her financial stress ease. Then she heard John's gasp and looked up to see his shocked expression.

"Is this right?" he asked.

Sam smiled and nodded. "That diamond was worth a fortune. The owners thought five hundred thousand each was a small price to pay for its return."

Five hundred thousand? Teresa took another look at her check. Counted the number of zeros trailing after the five. She'd misread the amount. Her check was also for five hundred thousand dollars.

Oh, my God!

"In other news," Sam continued as if she handed out five hundred thousand dollar checks every day, "the fire chief's report is completed. Arson—obviously. The insurance company's already got the preliminary details—I called your agent myself, Teresa. They'll have an adjuster out tomorrow. I'll send them the official report once I have it in hand."

Teresa nodded, fingers still tight around the envelope. "Thank you. For everything."

Sam waved it off. "That's my job. Though ..." She hesitated, her usual confidence faltering. "I do have some harder news."

Teresa braced, already weary from shock. "What now?"

Sam exhaled. "Felipe Valesquez was found dead this morning. His housekeeper came by and found him in his study. Looked like he'd taken a bad fall, but ..." She paused, choosing her words. "The coroner says his injuries don't match a fall. Too many scratches. Bruises. Broken ribs. It looked like ... like something tore him up." She paused. "Whatever happened, he didn't go easily. That counts for something."

Teresa's breath caught, the memory of Felipe's battered face flashing before her—the cane, the bruises, the way he'd waved off her concern. She swallowed hard, grief and guilt tangling in her chest. Should she have done something?

Perhaps sensing her distress, John came over and brushed a hand along her back, offering silent support.

Sam let the silence stretch a moment longer, then gently steered them back. "I've got one last thing. We tracked down Roger Thacker. He's in San Antonio. Changed his name, but it's him."

Teresa felt the world contract around her, the edges of the porch closing in. She'd thought he was gone forever, maybe even dead. A memory to keep her awake on sleepless nights. The thought of him living, breathing, existing in the same state, living only a couple hours away, made her stomach twist.

Sam continued. "The San Antonio police did some investigating. According to their information, he's on disability, some kind of respiratory thing, and stays in most days, but he's still mentally sharp. They're going to pick him up for questioning, but I thought you might want a chance to talk to him first, so I called in a favor."

Too stunned to know how to reply, Teresa looked at John. His jaw was clenched, the first sign of anger she had seen from him since the fire. "When?"

Sam shrugged. "Sooner the better. But if you'd rather I handle it—"

"No," Teresa said, louder than she meant to. "I want to talk to him. I need to know what happened."

Sam nodded, a quick, almost military acknowledgment. "We'll need to leave soon. Pack enough for an overnight stay and we can be on our way."

Teresa glanced at John.

"I'm going with you," he told her, saving her from having to ask. She smiled and nodded gratefully. He turned to Sam. "Do I have time for a quick shower?"

She nodded and he hurried inside.

"You might as well come inside to wait," Teresa suggested. "It's hot out here."

She left Sam sitting in the front room with Mrs. Petrie—Grandma—and hurried to the room she'd been sharing with John.

Most of what she owned had been reduced to ash or reeked of smoke, so "packing" meant little more than gathering the change of clothes and toothbrush they'd purchased after the fire. Even so, the weight of it pressed down on her until she felt hollowed out.

Zipping closed her duffel bag, her thoughts snagged on Felipe, on the last time she'd seen him leaning on that cane, his face mapped with bruises. He'd looked so frail. Who had killed him—and why?

A gentle cough sounded at the door, interrupting her thoughts. John stood there, hair still damp from his shower, his gaze, softer than usual, searched hers.

"You holding up?"

She tried for a smile and missed. "I'm not sure. It's a lot."

He crossed the room and crouched in front of her, so she had no choice but to meet his gaze. "You don't have to go through it alone. I'm right here."

This wasn't the first time he'd said that and hearing it yet again, something loosened in her chest—just enough for her to nod. "Thanks."

He reached out, brushed her hand with his, a fleeting warmth before standing again. "We'll get through this."

She zipped the duffel, feeling more in control. They carried their bags into the family room, where Sam sat waiting with Mrs. Petrie. Sam rose immediately, crisp and businesslike, but Mrs. Petrie didn't move from her chair. She reached for Teresa's hand, giving it a squeeze that was equal parts comfort and claim.

"You be careful," she said, her voice firm but threaded with worry. "And you come back. Both of you. I'll have pie waiting."

"Thanks, Grandma," Teresa said softly. The word still felt new on her tongue, fragile and precious.

John took both duffels and headed for the door. "We'll be back."

Out on the porch, the afternoon sun pressed down in a haze. Sam headed for her truck, keys already in hand. Teresa started after her, but John stopped short, turning toward his own car parked at the curb.

"I'll follow behind you," he said.

Teresa blinked. "You're not riding with us?"

Before she could say more, Sam touched her elbow. "Might be more comfortable riding with him," she suggested gently, her tone free of judgment.

Teresa hesitated, glancing from one to the other, then nodded. "All right."

Glancing back at the house as they drove away, she caught the blur of Mrs. Petrie's white hair glimmering at the window. She lifted a dish towel and waved it like a flag until they disappeared down the street.

CHAPTER THIRTY-FIVE

THE DRIVE TO SAN Antonio stretched out like every other long Texas road trip—scrubland rolling by, truck stops with sun-faded signage, and the occasional hawk circling overhead. It should have felt momentous, the last leg of a lifelong pursuit, but it didn't. It was just another stretch of highway.

Teresa spent most of the drive staring out the window, counting telephone poles and praying for a sign—any sign—that she wasn't making a huge mistake. John drove one-handed, the other hand drumming the steering wheel in a syncopated tattoo, as if he could tap his way through the silence.

Halfway there, she finally spoke. "Why did you want to drive?"

He shrugged, but it was the kind of shrug that said everything. "I've ridden in the back seat of a police vehicle. Don't plan on doing that again. And ..." He flicked her a quick glance before returning his gaze to the road. "Figured it might be good to have another car, just in case ..."

She wanted to ask for clarification, but she was afraid he'd tell her he was leaving from San Antonio to drive to El Paso, leaving her to return to Las Palomas with Sam ... alone.

Reaching over, she turned on the radio, and they drove the rest of the way listening to music.

When they reached the city, Sam led them through a sprawl of traffic and underpasses until they stopped in front of a squat apartment building, its beige paint peeling in ragged curls.

John turned off the car. "You ready?"

No. "I guess."

They got out and met Sam on the sidewalk. "His apartment's on the ground floor, first unit to the left."

Together, they walked down the sidewalk, past the cracked paint and the sunburnt shrubs, stopping in front of a battered metal door with a faded '1A' sticker peeling at the corner.

Teresa raised her hand to knock, but paused, her knuckles inches from the metal.

John nodded, once. "You've got this."

She nodded back, drew in a breath, and rapped sharply on the door.

Inside, something shifted—a cough, then the scrape of feet against old linoleum. A voice called out, raspy but unmistakable.

"It's open."

Teresa glanced at John, then pushed the door inward.

Roger Thacker sat slumped in a battered recliner by the window, a tangled coil of oxygen tubing looping at his feet. Pill bottles lay toppled on a TV tray, their labels worn away. The apartment reeked of stale air and neglect—a mausoleum of unwashed dishes and dust. Sunlight oozed through the filthy windowpanes, pooling in yellowed puddles on cracked linoleum. Only the slow swing of a ceiling fan stirred the heavy air.

For a moment, Teresa saw only her father—old, frail, silver hair matted at the temples, eyes clouded with illness. Then he lifted his head, and, for an instant, fear cracked through his expression. His lips parted, and he rasped, "Marie?"

The word was both plea and accusation, carrying fifteen years of dread.

Teresa froze. Hearing her mother's name in his ruined voice sent a shiver down her spine. But she straightened, keeping her own voice steady. "No, Dad. It's me. Teresa."

Confusion flickered, then recognition crept across his features. "Teresa," he echoed, softer this time, as though testing the name after too many years. A strained smile tugged at his mouth. "My girl. You came back for me."

He said it as if it were obvious—that she had returned to take care of him, forgive him, fold him into her life as if nothing had happened.

Teresa shook her head, cutting through the moment like glass. "I'm not here for that. I'm here to find out what happened to my mother."

Something shifted behind his eyes—panic first, then calculation. His shoulders stiffened as he leaned back, clutching the armrests. "She didn't love either of us, so she ran away," he said quickly, as if the story had been rehearsed a hundred times. "With another man. I was hurt, confused.

Drinking too much. How was I supposed to raise a daughter alone? I thought I'd leave until I got better. Then I'd come back for you."

The lies landed with a weight that threatened to break her. For years, she'd wanted to believe some version of them. Now she knew better.

"We found Mom's remains." Her voice cracked, but she forced the words out. "On the side of the road leading into Las Palomas. Right where you left her."

It was a gamble, but as soon as the words left her mouth, she saw it—the flicker of guilt, fear, resignation. He didn't even try to mask it. Emotions flitted across his face—denial, anger, despair. And then, like a man deflating, he sagged deeper into the chair, eyes glassy, the fight draining out of him. "You don't understand," he rasped. "I never meant for it to happen. I just ... I lost control."

Teresa's pulse hammered in her ears. She forced herself to stay steady, though every instinct screamed to bolt. "Then explain it. All of it. No more stories. No more excuses. Just the truth."

His chest rising and falling with the slow rasp of his breath, he closed his eyes for a long moment. When he opened them again, there was a flicker of defiance. "You think you know what it was like? Marie was ready to walk out—said she'd take you with her. I couldn't let that happen."

"Why not?" Teresa snapped.

"I loved her!" he barked, the word jagged and raw, his thin frame trembling with it. Then calmer, "I thought if I could get her to stay, eventually she'd learn to love me again."

Teresa's hands tightened into fists. "What did you do?"

"The truth," Sam cut in, her voice sounding cold and professional.

Something in Roger cracked. His shoulders sagged, and the air wheezed out of him in a rattle. He looked at Teresa again, but this time the manipulation was gone. What was left was a man who'd been running so long he no longer had anywhere left to go. He closed his eyes, fought to steady his breath. Minutes passed.

At last, he exhaled a ragged breath. "When we first married, we were happy. We had you, a home ... I thought it was perfect. Then I learned you weren't my blood." His lips quivered. "Your mother ... she'd been with another man before me. She never told me."

"Daniel Petrie," Teresa said, flat and cold. "It was before she ever met you."

He blinked as though he'd never heard the name. "Doesn't matter," he rasped. "The truth... it destroyed me. I started drinking." His hand trembled. "That morning, she told me she wanted a divorce. I begged—" he broke off, retching slightly. "I thought if we could talk uninterrupted, I could make her see reason." He paused to catch his breath. "I fed you early and put something in your food to make you sleep. I didn't want you to hear us arguing."

Tears stung Teresa's eyes. "You drugged me."

His shoulders sagged. "I know. I was afraid to give you too much, so I might've underdone it. When I went back later to check on you ... you sat up for a second, looked right at me. Scared the hell out of me. I thought maybe you were dreaming, but ..." He let the sentence trail off, shame thick in his voice. "I'm sorry, Teresa. I never should've done it."

It was too little, too late. Teresa had no intention of forgiving him. "Go on."

"I'd been drinking—hell, I was always drinking back then. She came home from work and wondered why you were already in bed. I made up some excuse and suggested we let you sleep. We ate dinner and, afterwards, I thought I could talk her down, make her see reason, but she wouldn't listen. She packed your things, but when she couldn't wake you, I told her what I'd done. She was so angry that she threw things. And I ... I shoved her. Too hard." His voice shook. "She slipped. Hit her head on the counter. I thought she'd get back up, but she didn't." He pressed a hand to his mouth. "She was just ... gone."

Teresa shook her head, horrified. John's hand found hers, grounding her, steady as stone. "Why didn't you call 9-1-1?"

He stared at his shaking fingers. "It was too late, and I ... I panicked. I knew if I called the police, I'd go to jail. And you—who would look after you if that happened?" He shook his head, tears leaking down his cheeks. "So, I ... I put her in the trunk of my car and cleaned the house until morning."

Teresa's stomach churned, the smell of bleach and the sound of the vacuum from her nightmares slamming into her with sudden clarity. She mentally reviewed the notes she'd made of her nightmares in the notebook. She had remembered more than she'd known.

Roger went on, voice thin. "When you woke up, I told you she'd been up all night cleaning because we had company coming over and that your mother was still asleep. You believed me. After I dropped you at school, I drove out of town and buried her by the road."

John leaned forward, voice edged with steel. "But you didn't stay. You left Teresa to grow up without either of you."

Roger closed his eyes. "A car passed while I was burying her. I panicked again. If I went back, I'd be caught. I knew your grandparents would raise you until I figured things out. I never planned to stay gone." He gave a bitter laugh that dissolved into a cough. "But one day bled into another. Days became years. I gave up the bottle that night, but I picked up cigarettes instead. Last year, I was diagnosed with cancer. That's why I came back. To die here. To face it."

Teresa stared at him, a thousand accusations rising and falling unsaid. At last, she whispered, "You could have turned yourself in."

"I could have," he admitted, eyes wet. "But I didn't. And that's on me. But I will now."

Sam rose, all business. "Roger Thacker, you are under arrest for the murder of Marie Thacker." She recited his rights, her tone steady, practiced.

Roger listened without protest. "I understand," he said, voice worn thin. "No need for cuffs. I have stage 4 lung cancer. I'm not running anywhere. Hell, I can barely walk."

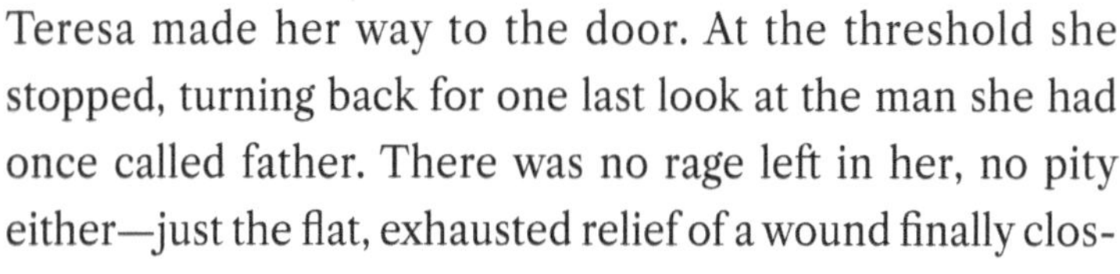

Teresa made her way to the door. At the threshold she stopped, turning back for one last look at the man she had once called father. There was no rage left in her, no pity either—just the flat, exhausted relief of a wound finally closing.

"Goodbye, Dad," she said softly.

Roger lifted his head, looking every bit his years—frail, shrunken, beaten by life. "Goodbye, baby girl."

She stepped out, with John close by her side.

The sunlight hit her like a slap, hot and unrelenting after the dim tomb of the apartment. Teresa staggered forward, lungs aching for air, until she reached the edge of the parking lot where a San Antonio police cruiser sat waiting.

Folding at the waist, she braced her palms on her knees and drew in a ragged breath.

John bent beside her, his hand moving in slow, steady circles between her shoulders. "You did it," he murmured.

She swallowed hard, but some part of her recognized he was right. She had.

For a long moment, they stood together in silence, watching as Sam brought Roger out in custody. The old man shuffled, leaning hard on his walker. The SAPD officers helped him into the back of their squad car. A door slammed. Then the cruiser pulled away.

Sam crossed over to them, her expression somewhere between professional restraint and human concern. "You two okay?"

John answered for them. "We will be. We just need a minute."

Sam gave a single nod, then glanced toward the road where the cruiser had disappeared. "I'm going to follow them to the station, finish the paperwork. After that, I'll meet you back at the hotel."

For Teresa, the world outside the car windows peeled by in a blur of sun-scorched strip malls, forklifts, and chain-link fences sagging under the weight of bougainvillea.

Beside her, John stared out the windshield, hands fixed at ten and two, as he drove them to the hotel. Every so often, she saw him glance over at her, like he was waiting for her to implode or start screaming.

"You want to talk about it?" he finally asked, voice low.

She thought about it. The urge to rehash every detail was strong, but so was the exhaustion pressing down on her shoulders. "He didn't even try to deny it. All those years, I thought there had to be some explanation. Some twist. But there wasn't. He just lost control and killed her. I don't think he even feels bad."

"Would you feel better if he did?"

She thought about it. "Yes, actually, I would. He should suffer for what he did."

"You don't think he's suffered?"

She shot him a look. "You sound like you're defending him."

He shook his head. "No. There's no defending what he did. He made a bad decision and his actions had consequences."

Suddenly this conversation was sounding familiar. Hadn't John done the same thing? That's why he'd gone to prison. A horrible accident with tragic consequences.

"You paid for what you did," she said. "My father ran away from what he did. He hasn't paid for his crime."

"Hasn't he?"

She thought back to how Roger Thacker had looked. Frail and haggard. Hooked up to an oxygen tank and gasping for every breath.

"I guess you're right. It's like he might have escaped human justice, but not divine justice."

"And now he's going to jail, to face human justice and pay for his crime."

He was right, and with the realization came a lessening of the injustice she felt. John always knew the right thing to say and do, which made the prospect of his leaving that much harder to deal with.

She didn't know if she'd been a victim all of her life or it just felt that way given recent events, but she was damn tired of waiting to see if things worked out for her. Her entire world had been falling apart around her when she was trying to renovate the house, and she'd never been happier. Never been more fulfilled. Not because of what she'd been doing, but because she'd been doing it with John.

And she thought John had been happy, too. What if, like her, he was too afraid of rejection to tell her how he truly felt?

"Don't go." The words were out before she could stop them.

"What?"

It was too late to pull them back. She needed to push forward and be honest about how she felt. If he rejected her, it would hurt—badly—but at least if he left, it wouldn't be because he didn't know how she felt.

She took a deep breath. "I don't want you to go to El Paso. I want you to stay in Las Palomas. With me." He glanced sharply over at her, a question clearly written in his expression. She knew she had to do a better job of explaining. Make sure he understood how she felt. "I don't want you to work for me. Maybe we could be partners? If you're interested." She sighed. "No, I'm saying this all wrong. I know I told you I was okay with a short-term relationship, but I lied. I don't want to say goodbye." Now, the really hard part. "I'm in love with you. I didn't plan it. It just happened, but now that it has, I want it all. Marriage, a home, maybe even kids, someday. I want that with you." She stopped then, thinking, hoping, he would respond, but he remained silent. "I'm sorry to dump it on you like that. I won't pressure you or try to guilt-trip you into staying, but I couldn't let you leave for El Paso without telling you how I felt."

His silence sparked of rejection, bringing hot, quick tears to her eyes. She quickly turned her head to stare out the passenger side window to hide them.

"Hey, CJ, man. How you doing?" At the sound of John's voice, Teresa turned back to see him talking on his cell phone. "I know," he continued. "I meant to call earlier, but I've been busy. Listen, I'm sorry to keep you waiting, but my situation has changed. I no longer need the job you're holding for me. I really appreciate you thinking of me, though." A pause and then he gave a soft chuckle. "Yeah, I'd say so. A much better deal. And that's not all. You're not going to believe this, but I'm getting married. Yeah, I know. Who would have thought it possible?" He glanced over at her and smiled. "Her name's Teresa and she's the prettiest thing you ever saw, not to mention smart and funny. And the best damn cook I've ever known. I'll be lucky I don't put on a hundred pounds." He paused to listen. "Yeah, man. I love her with all my heart." Another pause, then John disconnected the call after promising to stay in touch.

Setting his cell phone on the console between their seats, he reached over to take her hand in his. He lifted it to his lips and pressed a kiss to the back of it—an old, intimate gesture that felt like sealing a promise. "I love you, Teresa. I've been sitting here, racking my brain for a way to tell you. Afraid you'd tell me to take a hike. Especially after talking to Roger."

The tears were freely running down her face now. "You thought the similarities were too close," she deduced. "What you did compared to what he did? That every time I looked at you, I would be reminded of what happened to my mother?"

"Yeah. Something like that."

"I can't promise I won't remember my mother some-times," she said, voice small. "But those memories won't be about him. They'll be about what my mother gave me. She brought you here."

John's fingers curled around hers. "We'll figure out the house. The town. All of it. Together."

They sat with the echo of that for a long beat, letting possibility settle in like dust. Finally, she asked, softer than she expected, "Can we stay with Mrs. Petrie ... I mean,

Grandma ... a while longer? It's ... nice. To have someone who actually calls me family."

He smiled, the kind that reached his eyes and softened whatever scars were left. "We'll stay as long as she'll have us. I have one request though."

"What?"

"Before we leave San Antonio, I want to stop at a jeweler," he said, a boyish grin tugging at him. "I can't promise the Stanford, but I'd like to buy you a ring—make this official."

She wiped her face with the heel of her hand and thought about broken houses and burned kitchens and the way this moment felt both ordinary and life-changing.

"It'll remind us we fell in love searching for a diamond," she said, and laughter bubbled out of her again—soft, incredulous, whole.

He squeezed her hand. "And if it reminds you of anything else, let it be that sometimes the things you're hunting for have a way of finding you back."

They rode on, the city lights softening into the growing dark, and for the first time since the house burned, Teresa felt like something in her had been rebuilt.

Chapter Thirty-Six

Teresa missed the smell of real food. She missed the sunrise spilling across the Rio Maldito, missed the clatter of Mrs. Petrie's kitchen, even missed the way John sang off-key when he thought she wasn't listening. She did not, however, miss San Antonio, with its endless highways and plastic grass, its warehouse tracts, and grocery stores big enough to lose a child in.

Driving John's car, because she'd left her truck in Las Palomas for John to use, she let her tired eyes drift for a second. In the rearview, the last of the city faded behind her; ahead, Las Palomas shimmered in the haze, a mirage of home. The sky arched blue and cloudless, promising nothing and demanding nothing, and for once she liked it that way.

Three weeks. It should not have taken three weeks to box up a dead man's life and throw away the key, but Roger Thacker, even in death, was nothing if not a headache. There were banks that had never heard of him, creditors who claimed to have, a half-dozen boxes of legal documents in a lawyer's conference room downtown. There was the apartment, too—a mausoleum of expired inhalers and microwave dinners, the walls yellowed with old smoke. The whole place smelled like surrender and death.

As Roger's last legal next-of-kin, she'd gone in thinking it would be a quick job—clear the clutter, sign some forms, maybe salvage a photo or two. Instead, it ate a month of her life. She spent nights in a cheap hotel room, eating take-out on a plastic tray table, staring at the unfamiliar ceiling and counting the days until she could go home.

But home had changed. She had changed. She was no longer haunted by the ghosts of her past or the ones that lived in the walls of the old Meyers house. Now she drove home because she had someone waiting for her, which was as strange and alien a feeling as any she'd known.

Her mother's funeral had been small. She remembered the exact number of chairs (seven), the wilted lilies by the headstone, the taste of rain on her tongue as she watched the pastor shuffle through his notes. She'd arranged for the grave to be dug next to her grandparents'. Afterward, they ate sandwiches on the hood of John's car and tried to pretend it was just another Tuesday.

There was no wake. No speeches. Just a quiet, stubborn refusal to let death have the last word.

Roger's confession at the arraignment was almost an afterthought. He told the judge everything in a raspy monotone that reminded her of Sunday sermons. "I did it," he said, and that was that. He was sentenced to life, but his lungs had other plans, and he only lasted two weeks in the prison hospital before expiring. "Expired" was the word the nurse used when she called, like he was nothing more than a gallon of milk past its "sell-by" date.

When Roger's will had been read, Teresa learned that everything he owned—a car, a modest savings account, the battered family Bible and a hoarder's amount of crap—had been left to her. It felt like a sick joke, as if in the end he wanted to prove she still belonged to him. In reality, there wasn't much to inherit. She donated the Bible to a little church in the neighborhood, sold the car to a dealership that specialized in "fixer-uppers," and let the landlord keep the security deposit, just to get rid of the place faster.

It had taken weeks, though, to sort through the crap. In the end, most of it was thrown or given away. There was one box, though, that she'd kept. A small, battered cardboard thing, sealed with duct tape and Roger's shaky handwriting, "For Teresa, when she's ready." She'd put it in the trunk of John's car without looking inside it. Every time she thought about opening it, her stomach did a slow somersault.

She hadn't been the only one settling family matters these past few weeks. At her urging, John had finally called his parents. The conversation, according to John, had gone better than expected—gentle, emotional in places, with more warmth than he'd dared hope for. He'd told his parents that he was doing well, starting his own business, and that he and Teresa were getting married. John said his mother had cried, his father had cleared his throat a dozen times, and by the end of the call they'd agreed to come for a visit, maybe as early as next month. To Teresa, it felt like a step toward healing what had once seemed broken beyond repair. It made her happy for John.

She checked the clock on the dash. Another hour and she'd be home, if she kept to the speed limit. She pressed the gas anyway, watching the world blur by in streaks of green and gold. Every so often she'd catch herself scanning the roadside, half-expecting to see her mother's ghost at one of the crossroads, arms folded, waiting to be picked up.

Instead, it was always just telephone poles and the dry whisper of cotton fields accompanied by the smell of sunbaked dirt.

The closer she got to Las Palomas, the more her body ached for stillness. She missed sharing her bed with John, missed the cool stone of Grandma's old house, missed the kitchen that always smelled of muffins and hope. She missed John—who, for all his rough edges and awkward pauses, made her feel safer than anyone ever had.

And she missed Mrs. Petrie, the grandmother she never knew she had. They were still living with her. In part, out of necessity, but also because the kindhearted woman insisted, and there was something about her insistence that made it impossible to refuse, especially when she played the "we're family" card.

They had fallen into a rhythm in those weeks before Roger—she could no longer think of him as "father"—had died. In the mornings, John would make coffee and Grandma would cook breakfast, her hands always moving, always making. Teresa would then start baking muffins to deliver in town. Sometimes she would find John and Grandma bent over the kitchen table, heads together, arguing over furniture design.

"Every respectable bedroom has a proper four-poster bed," Grandma would argue.

"Every respectable carpenter saves his lumber for something useful," John would counter. In those moments, it almost felt like a real family—albeit a strange, cobbled-together one.

Her house, formerly the Meyers B&B, sat scorched and battered, until the blueprints could be completed. The insurance company, after some gentle prodding from Chief Hunter, paid out enough to cover most of the renovations.

The highway narrowed and she passed the Las Palomas city limits sign—pop. 294, though she doubted anyone had counted in years—and felt her heart give a small, joyful leap.

She was almost home.

She pulled into Mrs. Petrie's driveway just after sunset, her car caked in dust and bug carcasses. The porch light was already on, casting a yellow pool over the steps. The front door opened before she even set the parking brake.

John stood there, his shirt untucked and his face split in a grin that looked almost as tired as hers. Her grandmother hovered behind him, arms crossed and apron dusted with flour.

Teresa killed the engine and got out. From the trunk, she withdrew her duffel bag and the box from her father.

As soon as she reached the front porch, the door opened. Smiling, John took the box and duffel from her, set them gently inside next to the front door, and then kissed her with an intensity that nearly made her toes curl.

She was home, and nothing had felt more right in her life.

Dinner tasted like nostalgia and hope. Her grandmother had pulled out all the stops—fried chicken crisped to perfection, a stack of buttermilk biscuits wrapped in a towel to keep warm, mashed potatoes whipped and buttered, and a bowl of corn so fresh it must have come from someone's backyard garden. There was even a lemon meringue pie cooling on the countertop.

After dinner, Grandma shooed them into the living room while she cleared the table. "Go on, you two," she said, stacking plates with the kind of precision that spoke of decades of practice. "I want to finish these dishes."

John led the way, the old floorboards creaking beneath his boots. He paused at the threshold of the living room, then turned to her with a strange, nervous energy in his posture—like a man standing on the edge of something he couldn't name but had desperately missed.

"Hey," he said, his voice pitched low, almost reverent. "Glad you're home."

She blinked, caught off guard by the tenderness in his tone. "Me, too," she said softly. "I missed this."

She meant it. Every word. And the look in his eyes told her he'd missed it, too—missed her. For a fleeting moment, she braced herself, afraid he might say something to upend the fragile peace between them. But he only smiled and sank onto the old sofa, sprawling like he was finally where he belonged.

Teresa joined him, careful at first to leave a polite three inches of space. He closed the gap without hesitation. Their elbows touched. A spark leaped between them, quiet but undeniable.

She'd forgotten how much a simple touch could say. Or maybe she'd never fully understood until now.

They sat in companionable silence, the hush broken only by the soft clatter of dishes in the kitchen. John's presence grounded her—or maybe it undid her. Either way, she felt more herself with him than anyone she had dated.

He nudged her knee with his. "You never said what was in the box."

It took her a second to realize he meant the one she'd carried in from the car. Just thinking about it made her stomach tighten.

"I haven't looked yet," she admitted. "It's probably just old photos. Paperwork. Maybe an old flask of whiskey he never finished."

"You want help going through it?" he asked, his hand brushing her wrist—cool against her skin, but somehow setting her pulse racing.

She hesitated, not sure what she wanted, but she knew what she didn't want. She didn't want to be alone with whatever ghost her father had left behind.

"Yeah," she said finally. "Later though." She leaned her head against his shoulder. "Just ... not tonight."

He nodded, and the silence between them grew warm and deep, wrapping around them like a quilt. Then, slowly, he turned toward her, his arm slipping around her back, the other hand lifting to her cheek, his thumb brushing a path to her jaw.

Then he kissed her.

It wasn't rushed. It wasn't tentative. It was a homecoming.

A kiss that spoke of lonely nights and quiet longings. Of words left unspoken and hearts that had waited too long. His mouth was warm, sure, and aching with promise. She answered him with everything she had—every hope, every ache, every breath she'd held since they last parted.

When the kiss finally ended, they rested against each other, foreheads touching, hearts thudding in unison.

"Have you shown her?" Grandma asked, walking into the room as she dried her hands with a dish towel.

"Not yet," John said.

Teresa looked from one to the other, eyebrows arched. "Shown me what?"

He stood and removed a worn manilla folder from the corner bookcase, and carried it back into the kitchen. She followed after him, stopping at the table where he'd laid the folder. She recognized his handwriting on the top cover—neat block letters, every T crossed with the discipline of a reformed perfectionist.

"What is this?" she asked.

John took a breath, then opened the folder and laid out the first sheet. "These are plans for the B&B, with some modifications. I worked with someone in town to make them."

He spread out the blueprints—real, honest-to-God blueprints, with measurements and annotations and little sketches of what could be. "I figured, if we rebuilt, we could add a larger kitchen, maybe a bigger pantry. Better fire suppression, obviously. Add a second bathroom to the second floor. We could swap out the old furnace for a modern one. I even budgeted for solar panels, if you wanted to go green."

He rifled through the pages, showing her each variation—one with a garden path, another with a wraparound porch. In every version, there was a room labeled "Teresa's Office," and in every version, the kitchen was twice as big as the old one.

She was floored. Not just by the work, but by the implication that someone had cared enough to dream for her, to spend hours sketching out a future she'd barely let herself want.

"These are ... amazing," she managed, running her fingers over the crisp blue lines.

John's ears went red. "You don't have to pick any of them. I just thought—"

"No, I love them," she interrupted, letting her excitement bubble up through the exhaustion. "I never thought about doing it like this. I mean, I always wanted to make the place better, but this—" she gestured to the plans, the breadth of his vision, "—this is something else."

He grinned, all bashful pride. "I've got more in the garage. Different elevations, different color schemes. Mrs. Petrie likes the one with the rose trellis, but I'm partial to the stonework."

She laughed, the sound light and clean in her chest. "I always wanted a secret garden. You're making me believe it could happen."

He shrugged, but the look he gave her was tentative. "I did have one other idea I wanted to show you."

He withdrew another set of papers and laid them out. These were different— hand-drawn images marked with careful pencil lines, and labeled "Meyers-Morris Bakery & Wood Shoppe" in John's blocky script.

He fanned the pages out like a deck of cards, then stood back, hands in his pockets, suddenly uncertain.

"I know you're on the fence about the B&B," he said, not quite meeting her gaze. "And honestly, I'd help you run it if that's what you want. But I started thinking—maybe we could do something different. Something that fits both of us."

He gestured at the first drawing of a big Victorian house, porched and turreted, but with a glass-fronted bakery on the main floor. Through the picture windows, she could see small tables with chairs, a rack of muffins and a long counter with an espresso machine. Behind the bakery, instead of guest rooms, was an open-plan workshop—benches, lathes, a sawdust-scented haven for anyone who preferred splinters to spreadsheets.

"I thought we could run it together. You'd have your bakery—sell your muffins, maybe even get into wedding cakes if you wanted—and I'd build custom furniture in the back. Sell it, maybe teach classes. That way, we both do what we're good at."

He flipped to a floor plan, tracing the rooms with his finger. "There's an industrial kitchen, like you always wanted. And I made sure the whole place is ADA-compliant, so we don't have to worry about lawsuits."

He grinned at his own joke, but the nerves were obvious. "If you hate it, just say so. We can burn the blueprints and never speak of it again."

Teresa stared at the sketches, at the way John had rendered her dreams in sharp graphite, down to the row of window boxes bursting with petunias. He'd even included a little "Kids' Corner" near the front, complete with a play table and a crate of wooden toys.

"It's perfect," she said, and was surprised to find herself on the edge of tears. "I never thought ... I mean, it never occurred to me to do something like this."

He shrugged, sheepishly. "Guess I just wanted a place I could call home. For real, this time."

They stood there, the words hanging in the air like scent of freshly baked muffins, and Teresa felt the slow, unfamiliar swell of possibility. The bakery/woodshop was a wild idea—probably doomed, maybe even foolish—but it was also exactly the kind of life she wanted, busy, messy, full of people and laughter and the smell of muffins baking in the oven.

She ran her hand over the drawings, imagining the chaos and noise, the clatter of mixing bowls and the hum of a bandsaw in the back. She saw herself there—flour-dusted, tired, but happy—and beside her, always, was John.

"I love it," she said, then cleared her throat. "I want to do it."

John let out a breath, shoulders dropping, and grinned. "You mean it?"

"Yeah. I do." She laughed, and the sound was bright and unguarded.

"Good, because I've made a few repairs to the house, but I wanted to hold off doing more until I knew what direction you wanted to go. The good news is that we won't have to do the renovation work ourselves. The reward money should pay for most of it."

It sounded perfect to Teresa, but she had one nagging thought. "Where are we going to live?"

"Over the bakery, if that's what we want to do. Another option would be to stay here," his lips twitched into a smile as he looked over at Mrs. Petrie. "With you." He withdrew another set of plans and laid them out. "And maybe, eventually, we build an addition, should we need the extra rooms."

Mrs. Petrie didn't miss a beat. "I love it. And if I'm going to be a great-grandmother, I get first dibs on babysitting."

"Deal," John said, extending his hand across the table. Mrs. Petrie shook it, then surprised him with a kiss on the cheek.

Teresa watched the exchange, something warm and complicated bubbling up in her chest. For the first time, she saw the house not as a refuge, but as a starting line—a place where life could finally get big, messy, and real. She could hardly wait to start.

The End.

Author's Note: I hope you enjoyed The Locket and the Lie. *Look for* Shadow of El Cadejo, *the fourth book in my* Texas After Dark *series (coming in 2026) and find out what really happened to Bubba and Felipe.*

9 781961 835153